Dancing with Statues

CAROLINE DOHERTY

DE NOVOA

Dancing With Statues

Caroline Doherty de Novoa

First published by Papen Press, 2013

ISBN: -13: 978-1481827447 ISBN-10: 1481827448

To our mothers, Elizabeth and Clara Lucia,
and to their mothers before them.

"The only truth is music."

Jack Kerouac

CHAPTER ONE

It is a moment that will stay with her forever—the menacing black and white figures marching across the screen, the monotone voice describing the rise of the Third Reich, Sister Claire's plump figure appearing in the yellow light of the doorway, the whisper of her name.

"Dear, I've come to take you home," Sister Claire says in the hallway.

"Take me home?"

"There's been an accident."

Laura feels the blood in her veins freeze. "An accident?"

Sister Claire tucks a stray hair back under her habit. "Don't worry. It's nothing."

"Who had an accident?"

"I don't know."

"What do you mean, you don't know?"

"I was just told to come get you and take you home. I wasn't given any details, I'm sorry." Sister Claire can't look her in the eye, she's clearly lying.

"I don't understand."

"It's just better if you go home now, rather than staying here all afternoon worrying." Her words sound rehearsed and mechanical. "Just go get your bag, I'll drive you home."

Laura feels nausea right down to her capillaries. She tells herself not to worry, that it'll be something like her mother has tripped and broken a leg and that she shouldn't overreact. She should just get a grip on her imagination and do what she's told.

Laura sees herself from the outside; a gangly fifteen year old, skinny inside her oversized school jumper, gathering her bag from the darkened classroom, placing the seatbelt around her in Sister Claire's car, thanking her for the lift when they pull up at home.

The sight of the two police officers, a man and a woman, hovering in the corner, hats in hands, is the first thing she sees when she walks into the living room. Her stomach lurches and she casts around for something familiar. Her eyes find her father, shrunken into a chair. She looks from him to the male police officer to the female police officer and back again. No one is able to meet her gaze.

"Where's my mother?" she whispers.

The policeman and woman exchange a glance. The woman steps forward and says, "I'm so sorry. She's passed away."

'She's passed away.' Those words are burnt onto Laura's brain forevermore—they create a huge crevice, which marks the divide between her life before and what comes afterwards.

Somehow the hours pass—her aunt arrives from England and her uncle from Dublin, and a coffin installed in her parents' room that they say holds her mother. Apparently her face is so twisted and misshapen that it's barely recognizable, so the coffin remains shut. The weed killer destroyed her from the inside out, collapsing her organs one by one. So people pay their respects to the wooden box, as Laura keeps a vigil next to it, watching the candlelight flicker off its mahogany sheen.

She has been to funerals and wakes before, and they have always followed the same pattern, part sombre/part celebratory. The Irish are professional mourners. Laughing in the face of death, they hold three-day parties that are talked about for years to come.

When her grandmother died, her little semi was packed within two hours of her taking her last breath. It was like they were attempting to break a world record for the amount of people that could be stuffed into a house. Chairs borrowed from the local school were lined up along the walls in every room of the house. It made a comical sight: all the adults sitting in the colourful miniature plastic chairs, sipping tea and chatting and laughing—and through all this her grandmother had lain like a queen in her coffin in the bedroom, listening with a restful smile as her family and friends spun tales about her life.

But her mother's wake is different; even the Irish cannot wave a joyful goodbye to someone who has chosen to end their life early.

She listens to her mother's friends, led by Carole, her mother's best friend, as they try to remember her in her fun-loving times—but these conversations peter out almost as soon as they are started, weighed down by the only image people could have of her now, alone in the woods late at night, draining down a bottle of weed killer, writhing in agony, scratching at the ground.

Laura corners her father coming out of the toilet. "Why didn't you tell me she hadn't come home all night?"

"Love, I didn't want to worry you."

"You lied to me, when I asked you why she'd not come down for breakfast, you told me she'd been out late with Carole and was sleeping in late."

"I know. I thought she was still over at Carole's house—I promise."

"Carole hasn't even seen her in a week." Laura stares into his eyes, feeling her own bulge with the weight of the tears she's battling to contain.

"I didn't know, I honestly didn't," he reaches for her arm and she flinches.

An arm reaches for her shoulder from behind. She turns round—it is a woman in her fifties—another stranger who must've known her mother in the distant past. She looks just like the type who "loves a good wake"—here to join in the grieving for a brief moment before leaving, no doubt muttering about "that poor family" and feeling better about her own lot in life by comparison.

"You poor child," the woman sniffs, "if there's anything we can do, anything at all ..." the woman pulls her close; the smell of her heavy perfume is suffocating. Her father, like a coward, steals past them and back into the wake room. He'll have to give her an answer sometime. Through the crack in the doorway, she can see him standing by the coffin, shoulders hunched, hands trembling.

On the morning of the funeral, the undertaker asks if any of the family would like them to raise the coffin lid to say one last goodbye before it is nailed down. Her aunt says yes; she doesn't seem to truly believe her baby sister has gone. But Laura simply shakes her head. She can't bear the thought of seeing her mother, cold like a statue inside the coffin. Her uncle ushers her out of the room just as the undertakers are lifting the lid—the sound of her aunt howling a deep carnal wail reverberates through the house. Like a victim of an earthquake, Laura seeks shelter in the doorway to her bedroom, gripping on to it for support. Tears like lava pour down her face.

During the procession to the church, Laura walks in front, just behind the hearse—her aunt on one side holds her tight and on the other her father walks, head down, arms by his side. They can't look at each other. The mass is long and meaningless, and when it is over she has to follow the hearse again, this time up the hill to the graveyard. Suddenly, far, far too soon, she is watching them lower her mother's coffin into the ground to the low murmur of the rosary.

Laura breaks free of her aunt's grip and staggers to the edge of the graveyard. The town below looks the same. Life hasn't stopped, cars and lorries scuttle along the bridge over the river, smoke billows from the chimneys and the sky is still blue. It wouldn't have surprised her if it had been purple—it feels like all the universal truths no longer apply.

For shouldn't it be universally true that mothers want to watch their children grow into adults, if only to know if the pain of childbirth had been worth it? In those final moments, did her mother wonder how her only daughter would turn out? And if she did, why didn't she stop?

CHAPTER TWO

Laura stared out through the glass panel at the top of the door to the main school building opposite, which was framed by a dirty, white sky. The only sound in the room was the rain on the metal roof. She watched the water gush from the gutters, flow down the pathway and get swept away into the drains. All the power of the rainfall captured and concentrated, hurtling towards nothing.

The doors of the main building suddenly flung open and a gaggle of girls screeched out. They should have been a solid block of grey in their school uniforms, but they looked like an artist's palette floating towards her through the blurred window, with pink and green and purple and red files held up above their heads in a pointless attempt to keep themselves dry.

Laura felt the temporary classroom shake as the girls pounded up the steps. She straightened her back and reached down to open the door, forcing a smile onto her face. It was showtime. Every teacher is an actor as soon as the audience arrives.

"Okay, come in, get settled. Find a spot."

The girls filed in and the air that had been so still before was suddenly alive with movement as the girls shook water from their hair, scraped the chairs back and threw their soaking files on the desks in front of them.

"I'm filling in for Sister Claire today. She's got a dinner with the bishop tonight, so she's taken the afternoon off. She asked me to go over your homework with you. Melanie, remind me what it was again."

"Short story, Miss."

"Okay, and what was it on?"

"People come into your life for a reason."

Laura fought the urge to roll her eyes in disgust. She could already imagine the over-sentimental ramblings that exercise had produced in a bunch of sixteen-year-old girls. They were all so hopeful and naïve. Had it really been only ten years since she was their age, sitting in those very seats imagining her future self?

"Okay, well I suppose you should all take turns reading them out. Kathy, let's start with you." Kathy was the science fiction/fantasy geek of the group. In Laura's literature class, Kathy found a way to compare every book to "The Lord of the Rings" trilogy. Laura silently willed her to have produced something original. With her wavy brown hair and eyebrows like two caterpillars resting just over the top of her heavyset glasses, Kathy didn't seem concerned by the same things the other girls were. She imagined Kathy was already planning where she'd travel to when teletransportation became a reality.

Kathy opened her file and hung her head low.

"I heard a thud outside and pull ... "

Laura couldn't hear the rest of the sentence, which Kathy had directed at her own lap.

"A little louder, dear."

Kathy looked up, biting her lip. Laura smiled and nodded for her to continue.

"I heard a thud outside and pulled back the curtain to see a bright light nearly blinding me, someone, or something had arrived unexpectedly—and I just knew my life was about to change ..."

7

Laura sat back on her chair and fixed the top of Kathy's head with her most encouraging look, so if Kathy glanced up again she'd get the impression she was listening intently. As Kathy continued reading, in her quiet, monotonous tone about an alien visitor coming to earth, Laura let her mind wander. Unsurprisingly, Sister Claire hadn't bothered to leave a full lesson plan. She supposed she'd just get them to read out their work in turn and say something generic at the end of each. She'd have to set them homework, too, something better than this drivel. Maybe she should get them to write about the opposite. Instead of thinking about people coming into their lives, maybe it was time the girls thought about what it was like when someone leaves. For that was the truth of life; it just gets smaller and smaller. They had to realize that. They had to come to terms with the fact that no enigmatic stranger was magically going to appear to change their lives, especially if they stayed in this town.

CHAPTER THREE

The man spoke in a string of garbled R's. At the end of each sentence, his tone inflected up as if he were asking a series of questions, without waiting for the answers. When he was done, he looked at Miguel expectantly.

"Eh, sorry. Would you mind repeating that for me?"

"Down thur, through those doors. Turn right. Cross the ro-ad. Its yur third bus stop on yur right. Alright?"

"Yes. Okay." He had managed to capture most of it the second time.

"And ye want the Londonderry via Omagh. Not Dungiven. Omagh. Should be one along on the hourrr."

"Thank you." Miguel dragged his luggage in the direction he'd been shown. Emerging from the automatic doors, he felt the chilly, damp air push through his coat and penetrate deep into his bones. He turned right, crossed the road, and walked to the third bus stop. He looked at his watch. 5:45 pm. Fifteen freezing minutes until the next bus.

Night was already approaching, colouring the clouds, like a paintbrush covered in black paint dropped into a jam jar of milky blue water. A watercolour sky. It seemed appropriate, given how much it rained here.

People emerged from the terminal and jumped into warm cars waiting with loved ones. No one else turned right to the bus stop. After ten minutes, he began to worry that he was in the wrong place, but finally, just before six, he was joined by a group of young women followed by a family with three children and then an older couple. Listening to them, he could only catch odd words and phrases emerging from the background melody of their conversation. He'd thought his English was better than this. If he couldn't understand them, he'd be useless as a chronicler of their history.

Miguel reminded himself to be patient. Their accent would just take some getting used to. In all his twenty-eight years, he'd left Colombia only once and then for only a few hours to cross the border into Brazil and Peru when he'd been visiting the border area deep in the Amazon. Today, he was pleased to have added Spain and England to the list, even though really he had just passed through them on the way to his new home. He supposed it could now go on the list too—but the country he'd just landed in was still a matter of debate. Many years of conflict had not settled that question.

Finally the bus arrived. Miguel hurled his heavy luggage into the hold and stretched out his fingers. His hands were stiff and swollen from the cold. He made a mental note to buy some gloves tomorrow. He climbed into the bus and found himself a seat by the window. Hot air blew out of the vent at his feet and he moved closer, already feeling his body relax a little as it thawed—he'd been travelling for about twenty-four hours and his muscles ached. As the bus pulled away, his head bobbed with sleep—he blinked, forcing his eyes wide open—he wanted to stay awake and watch the country pass by outside his window After all he'd read, he wanted to see what Northern Ireland was really like.

Going through each small town, he tried to guess if they were "catholic" or "protestant." It often wasn't hard, the identity of each community was usually still recognisable in the painted pavements and the flags jutting out from small rows of terraced houses set back from the road. The pavements must have gleamed brightly just a few years ago, but now the paint looked faded and chipped and the flags appeared old and tired. Maybe no one had the fury left to keep the paint fresh but equally no one was ready to wash it off and fold away the flags. Not whilst the sons and daughters of those who had fought and died for what those flags represented still lived there.

In between the towns, the views of the quiet rolling countryside were spectacular—a full palette of green, still visible in the retreating evening light, interrupted with the occasional white farmhouse off in the distance. He thought it was remarkably similar to the countryside just outside of Bogotá.

Eventually Miguel saw the name of his new hometown illuminated on a road sign as the bus slowed at a roundabout—they were nearly there. Outside, the dark countryside gave way again to rows of identical houses, illuminated with streetlights, signalling the start of the town. A few shops and pubs appeared along the roadside, which narrowed and sloped down into a small town square where the bus stopped.

"Hi fella, this is your stop," the driver called back to him. He had arrived.

Miguel watched the bus pull away, a retreating oasis of warmth and light abandoning him in a cold and lonely place. He was expecting Mr. Quigley to meet him —they'd estimated that all going well, he should have been arriving at seven; it was now half past.

There were three taxis parked in a row at the other side of the square, waiting hopefully for some business, but otherwise the place was deserted. The town looked better than he'd expected—he recalled what he'd read about it on the Internet: "There are signs that people live in this town, but little sign of life." It was a quote from a 1970s documentary when the town was the most bombed place in Europe since World War Two. In the 1980s, that grim superlative was replaced with another one, equally as depressing: the unemployment black spot of Great Britain. But it didn't look so bad. It wasn't pretty and yes, the buildings all looked like they had been thrown up without any thought for architectural grandeur, but a few of them had been painted with charming reds or greens and the signage over the shops and pubs had all been done with quaint nostalgic lettering. He started to wonder if he'd got off at the right stop.

Finally, a car pulled up next to him and a slight man in his fifties jumped out. He was wearing jeans and a tweed jacket, and his nearly bald head was completely uncovered, leaving the wind free to play with his final few wisps of grey hair.

Rushing round the car, the man called loudly, "Discúlpame, Discúlpame," enunciating every syllable. "Yo soy Harry Quigley. Es un placer conocerte." He spoke with an odd accent, using the "th" sound of Spanish from Spain mixed with an Irish lilt. He also used the second person familiar verb tense, which no one in Colombia would use when they first met someone.

"Hello. It is very nice to meet you, too."

"¿Como estás? ¿Qué tal el viaje?" Mr. Quigley asked.

"It was good. Long. Eh, if you don't mind, I'd like to speak in English."

"Oh." Mr. Quigley looked disappointed.

Miguel immediately regretted what he'd said—he hoped he didn't seem rude.

"You know, I must to get used to listening to the accent," he silently cursed his own slip in grammar; he knew better than that.

"Yes, of course. I'm sure you've not had much exposure to it. And well, being a linguist, I respect the

English language—but some of the people you'll come across here completely butcher it."

"I did have to ask the man at the information desk at the airport to repeat himself three times before I understood where was the bus stop." There he went again, messing up the sentence structure.

"Well, I'm sure you'll soon pick it up, and we can speak Spanish on Fridays when you're up at the school helping me with my conversation classes. It's worked out well that the Tribunal only sits four days a week."

"It'll make a nice break. I imagine the work at the Tribunal and the work with Survivors' Stories will be fairly intense."

Survivors' Stories was a charity, led by Mr. Quigley, for people in the local area who had been victims of the troubles. They were sending Miguel to the Hudson Tribunal four days a week to act as a victim liaison, but the plan was for him to help out with some of their other work too in his spare time, including interviewing victims to help chronicle their experiences for the historical record.

"Mmm ... we haven't really got as far as we wanted to with Survivors' Stories. It'll be good to have an extra pair of hands, or an extra pair of ears, more like! Anyway, let's get you in out of this cold." Mr. Quigley grabbed Miguel's suitcase and put it into the boot of the car.

Miguel folded himself into the front seat of the little car with his rucksack on his knees.

"It's just five minutes drive to the flat. My sister bought it as a wee investment years ago and has always rented it out. You'll have to excuse the potted plants. The last tenant left them all sitting in the bath when she moved out, and we haven't had time to move them yet."

"That's okay." Miguel hoped he sounded much more confident than he felt—this was the first time in his life that he'd have to take care of himself, never mind another living thing (or several of them, by the sounds of things).

"And I'm so sorry for having left you waiting like that," Mr. Quigley said. "I was here from ten to seven and then about ten minutes ago my birdbrain wife rings and says she's at her yoga class and thinks she's left the iron on, so I had to rush back up to the house to check it."

"And was it on?"

"No. The bloody thing was in the hall cupboard where it always is!" Mr. Quigley's eyes became wide with exasperation. His face was rubbery, the kind of face that could be contorted into all sorts of over-the-top expressions. Miguel smiled. He remembered his boss at the Reconciliation Commission telling him that Mr. Quigley dressed quite outrageously when they met in Spain as students—the outrageous clothes had gone, but he still had the flamboyant air.

"Carlos Andres sends his regards," Miguel said.

"Is he well? It's been years since I've seen him. But it's easier to stay in touch now than it was years ago. It's so good that he was able to give you six months off to come and work with us. When the board of trustees heard that Survivors' Stories was going to be able to send a lawyer to the Tribunal to help deal with the victims, we decided it had to be someone fresh, someone who wouldn't already have their own ideas about what happened that day. So it became obvious quite quickly that it shouldn't be anyone local. But we also needed someone who would appreciate the sensitivities of the conflict. And then I hit on the idea of contacting Carlos Andres, I'd always kept an eye on his work at Colombia's Reconciliation Commission. He speaks very highly of you: 'one of their rising stars,' he said."

Miguel never knew how to respond to comments like that. Was the correct response to say thank you? Or was he supposed to protest? But that just seemed fake when he considered the compliment to have been validly made.

Mr. Quigley pulled the car over in front of a Chinese takeout. "Here we are." They got out and Mr. Quigley opened the boot. Miguel reached for his luggage but Mr. Quigley batted his hand away.

"Let me. I'm not as old as I look, you know! You've been travelling all day, and you've got that big rucksack, too."

Miguel followed Mr. Quigley down a small passageway by the Chinese place to the back of the building, which opened up into a tiny yard, lit only by the glow of the restaurant kitchen, dominated by three large black bins and a wooden staircase. Miguel looked up; there was a blue door on the first floor at the top of the stairs.

"It's nice that it's got its own private entrance," Mr. Quigley said, yanking Miguel's suitcase up the stairs as Miguel followed him up, wishing now that he'd insisted on carrying it himself.

"Voila," Mr. Quigley flung open the front door and flicked on a light.

The small hallway was completely bare except for the dark blue carpet on the floor, the paper lampshade hanging from the ceiling and a couple of coat hangers on the wall. Even so, it was hardly big enough for Mr. Quigley, Miguel and his luggage. Each wall was effectively nothing more than a closed door, the one they'd just come in and three others. Starting on the right, Mr. Quigley moved around opening them and turning on the lights in each room.

"Kitchen, bathroom, and finally—well, bedroom, living room—basically everything else."

Miguel popped his head into the first two rooms. The kitchen and bathroom were almost as small as the hallway, and the bathroom did look like a greenhouse, with about ten plants of all different sizes lined up in the bath. He followed Mr Quigley through the third door, which opened up into a large room with big windows looking out onto the street. The room had the same blue carpet as the hallway, and in the corner diagonally from the door, by the windows, there was a small brown sofa. On the wall opposite the sofa there was a wardrobe, a basic desk and a bookshelf all lined up next to each other. In the corner to the right of the door was a double bed with a blue-and-white-striped mattress on top. Piled up in the middle of the bed were a duvet, some pillows and some sheets. It was very basic, nothing like his home in Colombia.

"We've left you some plates and things in the kitchen, so I think you won't need to buy anything. Your trunk arrives on Monday, so I'm sure it'll feel a bit more homely when you have your things. You'll be at the Tribunal, but I'll get the wife to come and wait here for it to arrive, if that's okay."

"That'd be great."

"Now, do ye fancy a wee pint or would you rather rest?"

Miguel didn't fully understand the question.

"There's a nice pub just up round the corner."

Of course—he meant beer. Here they drank it by the pint. He knew that from the Irish bars in Bogotá.

"Thank you. That sounds good, but I think if I have one drink now, you might have to carry me back from the pub. It wouldn't be a very good first impression for the neighbours."

"Righto. Well, I'll leave you to get settled in, then." Mr. Quigley handed Miguel the keys. "Oh, and before I forget, I've left a bicycle for you down by the back fence there in the yard." Mr. Quigley pulled another key from his pocket. "Here. This is for the lock."

"Thank you. That's very kind of you."

"I bought it about five years ago, with grand plans of taking up cycling, but in truth, I think I've only used it about four times. Since then, it's been lying in our utility room, which doesn't make me very popular with the wife. So anyway, it's yours whilst you're here if you want it— help give my head peace for a few months."

Miguel had never owned a bicycle in Bogotá. It was far too dangerous, with so many erratic drivers.

"Thank you. Really, thank you for everything. For the bike, for arranging the flat, and for having me over to work with you on Survivors' Stories. It is such an important job that you're doing, and I'm really pleased to be a part of it."

"Right. Well, I'll leave you to rest, then."

Miguel followed Mr. Quigley out to the front door and watched him disappear into the night.

Turning back into the stark hallway, Miguel suddenly realised that he was completely alone, in a stranger's flat, in a town that seemed one million times smaller and quieter than home, and he started to wonder if six months of this had been such a great idea after all.

CHAPTER FOUR

Miguel flinched, banging his head on the wall behind him. Where the hell was he? He blinked—the room, flooded with sunshine, was white and cold and bereft of any reference points, but then he saw his rucksack and suitcase lying at the foot of the bed unopened, yesterday's jeans and jacket flung over them. He felt around the floor for his watch.

"Puta," he muttered. It was just after midday—his first full day in Northern Ireland, and he'd slept through half of it.

In the bathroom, he looked at himself in the mirror. He wasn't exactly going to blend in out there. It had nothing to do with what he planned to wear—he was sure jeans, trainers and a sweater were fairly standard attire everywhere—but he couldn't hide his Latin features and his skin, which, while it wasn't especially dark for a Colombian, was still a few shades darker than anyone he'd seen yesterday. And that was before he even spoke. No matter how good his English was, there was no denying he had an accent, and it certainly didn't sound anything like a local. The fact that it was such a small town made it worse.

The scrutiny of ten eyes is always greater than ten thousand. He looked out the window to the garden below—perhaps he'd take the bicycle. Whizzing past people on a bike he couldn't draw as much attention, and, even if he did, he'd be gone before he could feel the force of the inevitable glares.

Coming out of the passageway, by the Chinese, he saw a car park across the road and beyond it there was a narrow river path. It looked like the river ran parallel to the street Mr. Quigley had driven him down the night before. He figured if he followed the path he should eventually find himself near the square in the town centre. He got on the bike and cycled across the road, wobbling slightly as he tried to steady himself and adjust the gears. It had been so long since he'd ridden a bike, what was that English expression, "It's like riding a bike, you never forget"? He hoped that was right.

He made his way along the river path. It had grass along one side that sloped down to the water and along the other side was a row of thin, white, two-storey terraced houses. Every ten or so houses there was a break to allow for a footpath. Up ahead, a huge mural on the side of an end of terrace house came into view. He cycled towards it and stopped next to it to take a closer look. It was the smiling face of a young man with wavy black hair, about twenty feet tall, painted in various shades of grey. Across the top it read: "Bobby Sands – RIP."

Miguel knew the name. He had studied the Hunger Strikes in university in a conflict resolution class—back then, it was just a case study for him, a way for his professor to illustrate some textbook theory. That was nearly nine years ago now. He'd never imagined when he was sitting in the lecture hall, when the peace process was just in its infancy, that one day he'd be here playing a part in cementing that peace.

Two young children kicked a ball against the mural and a couple of mothers had stopped for a gossip next to it, rolling their pushchairs back and forth in unison to keep their babies quiet as they chatted. They all appeared oblivious to the dead eyes staring out at them from the artwork above.

Suddenly something flew out of the long sparkling grass beside him and grazed the front of the bike. Miguel looked up, his heart beating fast from the shock.

It was just a bird. It looked like a pheasant, but he couldn't be sure, as it had already flown high into the sky. The young mothers looked over and giggled. Miguel started pedalling again, smiling to himself as he raced along the path, the gentle breeze flowing over him. He'd been so nervous about coming out of the flat, but the only fright he'd had was from a stupid bird. He needed to relax. He took in a long, deep breath—even though autumn would soon make way for winter, Ireland seemed acutely alive. Miguel felt he could simply reach up and pull the life down from the air around him.

At the end of the houses he turned right and, as he had expected, he found the main square just around the corner. It was so different to the scene that had greeted him the night before. Pensioners bustled up and down the street, dragging tartan canvas bags on wheels behind them. Everywhere there were small groups of people stopped in animated conversation—groups of teenagers hung around in shop doorways, the younger kids by the supermarket, the older ones outside the music and DVD shop. It looked like they took life at their own pace, unlike in Bogotá where Miguel sometimes felt rushed along by a momentum outside of himself.

Miguel cycled over to a small sandwich shop he'd noticed in the square last night. He got off the bike and leant it against the shop wall. He looked in the basket and cursed under his breath—he'd forgotten to bring the chain to lock it up. He was really hungry and didn't want to have to cycle back to the flat just to get the lock, but he couldn't risk Mr. Quigley's bike getting stolen on the first day he took it out. He looked around trying to figure out what to do.

Across the road there was a young woman—probably in her mid twenties—sitting on the bench by the bus stop reading a book. She didn't look like the type who'd run off as soon as his back was turned.

"Excuse me. I'm very sorry to bother you," he called as he crossed the street to join her.

The girl looked up at him from large grey-blue eyes—she was startlingly pale, with thick black hair framing her face. Miguel was so used to the Latina look of dark eyes, hair and skin that for the first few seconds her contrasting features struck him as exotic—almost otherworldly.

"Eh, is it okay if I leave my bike here for a few minutes whilst I get a sandwich?"

"I don't think so; I think any one of those boys over there would be away with it in a flash if you just leave it there unattended."

"You're right, but it won't be unattended if you watch it for me, will it?"

"And what makes you think I won't run off with it myself?"

Miguel hadn't planned on having to persuade her to help him. He could tell her that she looked far too angelic and beautiful to be a thief—but he doubted a cheesy line like that would work. He read the title of the book lying on her lap.

"Well now, I see you are reading Brian Friel's 'Philadelphia, Here I Come'—any girl who is a fan of Brian Friel must be trustworthy."

"You think so? And what do you know about Brian Friel then?"

"Well, let me think. He wrote 'Philadelphia Here I Come,' a classic novel about people helping each other out in times of need."

"Actually, it's a play, and no one helps anyone in this; the opposite, in fact."

Well she'd sure told him. What was wrong that he couldn't even get a smile from her?

"They've adapted it into a play, have they? So are you an actress, then? Are you that famous actress they have been telling me about?"

"No, no famous actresses from here. You must have the wrong town."

"Well what do you do?"

"Not that it's any of your business, but if you must know, I'm a teacher."

Finally a way in. "Really, where do you teach?"

"Why are you so interested?"

She was unbelievably prickly, but he persevered. "Well I might be one of your colleagues. I'm starting at the Girls Convent School next Friday as a Spanish language assistant."

"Oh, of course, it's you."

"Yes, it's me!" So she'd heard about him.

"You're the Colombian, right? They mentioned you in our staff meeting last week."

Finally she was smiling.

"Hopefully it was me, I'd hate to think there's another Colombian in town stealing my job. So you'll watch my bike then? Anything for a colleague, right?"

"Well I'd love to, but my bus is due any minute now."

"No problem. I'll only be a moment." He set the bike against the bench in front of her and ran back across the road towards the shop. She called after him in protest, but he didn't turn around. He'd be very quick ordering his sandwich, he wanted to get back to this girl. This was the first time he'd had a chance to really interact with anyone here—apart from Mr. Quigley, of course—and now that he'd broken through and raised a smile from her, he wanted to talk to her, to ask her about the school, to learn more about the town.

Ordering a simple ham and cheese sandwich was a frustratingly long exercise—there were too many questions to answer: What kind of bread did he want, did he want butter or margarine, and did he want it toasted? The whole time he kept an eye on her through the shop window. She was sitting upright with one hand gripping the bike, careful not to let it run away all by itself—there was something comical, almost childlike in the serious way she watched over it.

As he was paying for the sandwich, a bus pulled in from around the corner, so he rushed out, leaving his change behind. She immediately stood up and hurried past him to get on the bus.

"Gracias—by the way, what's your name?"

"Laura," she said, just as the bus doors closed and she was gone.

CHAPTER FIVE

Laura walked to the back of the bus and watched the Colombian wave her off. He was slim, with broad shoulders and a mass of dark curly hair. She tried to recall what Mr. Quigley had said his name was when he mentioned him at the staff meeting but she couldn't remember. Her first reaction when she heard the news had been to wonder why anyone would want to come so far to such a ragged little spot on the edge of nowhere. She almost felt sorry for this poor stranger; she was sure this town was not what he'd been expecting. The town had an inappropriately beautiful name for its current incarnation. History had christened it with a haunting Gaelic name that evoked a now-lost natural beauty, which had been replaced with cheap housing estates and a myriad of bars. If the town was being discovered by settlers today, it would be called Disappointment or, better yet, Nothing. "Welcome to Nothing," the sign would read, "Population 20,000 and falling." *Colombia*, she thought, *what a distance to travel to arrive at Nothing.*

Laura got off the bus just outside the chip shop along the Main Road.

"Two fish suppers?" Marie asked as she stepped into the shop. Laura wasn't surprised that Marie knew her order before she was even through the door; she stopped by nearly every Friday evening.

The scene at home was also painfully familiar. There was steam coming from the kettle, two tea bags had been thrown into the pot, and there were two cups sitting on the kitchen table. He always expected her back at this time. As usual, there was a dash of milk inside each cup—he was trying to be helpful, she thought, as she threw the milk from one cup into the sink. After all this time stuck living together, he still hadn't noticed that she preferred to put the milk in afterwards.

"Daddy, dinner's ready." She unrolled the two white packages containing their fish and chips.

Her father appeared at the doorway between the kitchen and the living room. "Thanks, love. I was just waiting for the kettle to boil."

"Don't worry. I'll do it. Here, take this. Go on in and sit down. I'll be in in a minute."

Laura took up her usual place alone on the sofa. Her father sat in his armchair right in front of the TV. She picked out the crumbled pieces of fried fish from the pile of thick-cut chips lying on the white paper on her lap. Friday night's fish supper used to be a treat when she was a little girl; now it was just an excuse to get out of making dinner for one night.

When they were both finished eating, her father scrunched up his vinegar-sodden paper and picked up his teacup. "Here, give me those," he said motioning to the papers on Laura's knee. "You made dinner, so the least I can do is clean the dishes."

Laura handed him the papers and forced a smile—he made the same joke almost every Friday. As he shuffled off into the kitchen she stared at the TV, not watching it, and tried to remember the last Friday night that had been any different than this. It must have been the last weekend in August when Catherine, her old friend from school, was home from London. That was almost two months ago now. Hopefully it wouldn't be long until Catherine was back for another visit—even if they had almost argued the last time Catherine was home.

Catherine had got drunk and given Laura a lecture about how she needed to get out and enjoy herself more. As if she needed someone to tell her that—she could probably count on one hand the number of evenings she'd been out since August, and she suspected that a night out watching the local amateur dramatics society's production of "The Third Policeman" with Sister Claire and her sixth-formers was not what Catherine had had in mind when she said, "You have to start living, Laura, not just breathing in and out twenty-eight thousand times a day."

Laura wondered what self-help book Catherine had copied that from. Although it had got her thinking—sometimes she felt like she was just gasping, gulping down air when she could, when no one was looking—never free to breathe it all out. Twenty-eight thousand sounded like a luxurious amount of breaths, far too big a number for her small life.

"Right, well, that's the dishes sorted," her father said, returning to the room. "Was there anything you wanted to watch?"

"No, you watch what you want. I'm just going to lie here and read." She picked up a book from her handbag on the floor and got comfortable on the sofa. She could just go to her bedroom, but her father was alone all day, so the least she could do was read in the living room and provide him with some form of company for a few hours as he stared dolefully at the television, sporadically muttering something without expecting a response.

At half ten her father announced that he was going to bed. He always went to bed fairly early. She supposed after sitting all day doing nothing he needed his rest. At the door to the living room, he hesitated.

"I know you probably know what date tomorrow is."

"Yes. Of course." It was a silly question, she was hardly going to forget her mother's birthday.

"Well I phoned down to interflora and ordered some flowers for the grave. Just a wee arrangement. If you don't mind picking them up in the morning."

"Sure, no problem." She wondered what he'd do if she just said no—that he should go do it himself. Every birthday and Christmas, Cemetery Sunday and on her anniversary he remembered to call the florist for an arrangement, and he always relied on Laura to deliver it. He hadn't been to the graveyard himself since the funeral; he hadn't been anywhere since that day. She wanted to ask him why it was still so important to him that the grave was properly adorned throughout the year. What point was he trying to make with all the flowers? What message could he want to send to the world that he had retreated from? She didn't ask, though, she just told him yes, tomorrow she'd go visit the grave.

CHAPTER SIX

It was quite a walk to get to the graveyard, which sat high up on a hill at the edge of town. The town was built deep inside a valley with the graveyard on one side, farmland on the other and a river running through the centre. Cars could only make it halfway up the hill and the remainder had to be done on foot.

Miguel stood at the edge of the graveyard taking in the view and wondered why they had put the graveyard in such an inconvenient location. Was it to give the dead a clear vantage point over all the goings-on in the town, so they could happily gossip for eternity? Was it so the living could demonstrate one last act of love for the dead by carrying their stone-filled coffins up the steep path? Or was it, like his favourite explanation, to give hope to the living, so that in their darkest hour of grief they could lift their eyes from the graves and see a zigzag of green tapestry and the bustling town nestled in the middle and remind themselves that the world is beautiful and life still goes on?

Miguel looked through the viewfinder to the moody panorama before him. The sun still glinted off the green hills in the countryside at the edge of his picture, but a huddle of dark clouds had now come into view. Perhaps if he used a different lens he could get a better balance of light. In the past couple of days he had already started recording images of his new home using the slim digital camera he carried everywhere in his back pocket, but today he had the whole kit with him: Nikon camera, four different lenses, and his mini-tripod.

He was just adjusting the lens when he heard footsteps behind him. He glanced round—it was the pretty teacher that he'd met yesterday. She must be coming over to say hello, he thought. In the two hours that he'd been in the graveyard he'd noticed that even there, amongst the dead, the Irish, always cheerful, liked to chat with one another.

Miguel arranged his face into a smile, ready to say hello when their eyes met, but as she got closer her eyes remained downcast. It was like she was purposefully trying to avoid meeting his gaze. She had an old jam jar in one hand and a bunch of flowers in the other. She wasn't making her way over to chat with him after all. She obviously just needed to get fresh water for the flowers from the nearby tap.

He smiled and tried to catch her eye as she passed him on the path. She looked up just long enough for him to nod a hello as he moved out of her way, but then she averted her gaze once more.

Didn't she remember him? She must have recognised him. The only Colombian in town couldn't be that hard to forget. He hadn't made that bad an impression yesterday, had he? Maybe she was wary because he was a foreigner, or maybe she had some negative impression of Colombians. I'll change that, he thought.

He pretended to look through the viewfinder again and adjust the settings of his camera, but all the while he watched her out of the corner of his eye. He could see she was struggling to open the tap, which had become stiff. Even though she was tall, she was delicate, with tiny white wrists peeking out from her dark green coat.

"Can I help you with that?" he asked, reaching for the tap just as she pulled her hand away. With a bit of effort he managed to dislodge it and get the water flowing.

"Thanks." She hunkered down again to clean out the old jam jar in the freezing cold water, her hands turning blue as she worked.

He wanted to speak to her, but he wasn't as adept as the locals at making small talk in the company of the dead. Grappling for something to say, the weather seemed like a safe place to start. "It looks now like it will be making winter for the rest of the day, what a shame after the lovely summer it started to make this morning."

"I'm sorry, what was that?" She said, looking up at him. He was struck by how dark her eyes were—a mixture of grey and blue he'd never come across before.

"Looks like it will be making winter for the rest of the day"

"You know, here we say it *is* winter or it *is* summer, we don't make the seasons." She closed the tap and stood up.

Miguel knew exactly what he was saying. "Really? How dull! In my country there are no seasons, instead the weather remakes the seasons each day and then remakes them again the next."

"No seasons? How can there be no seasons?"

"Well for example in my city the weather is very mild, with average monthly temperatures throughout the year remaining almost constant, but averages are such liars, don't you think?"

"I suppose—I'm an English literature teacher, so I've never trusted numbers."

"Exactly! The average monthly temperature hardly moves, but in any given day, any time of the year, it can be eighteen degrees in the day, dropping half that, to about nine degrees at night." Internally, Miguel rolled his eyes at himself, disappointed by how dull his attempt at conversation was.

"Okay, so maybe you do make seasons," she conceded.

He followed her gaze out across the midday sky, which was now almost black. "Thinking of it, maybe we make seasons daily here, too."

"Told you," he smiled at her, glad he'd made some progress and gotten her to chat with him, even if it was only about the weather, the smallest of small talk.

"Well, if you'll excuse me. It's been nice talking to you. I have to get on." She motioned to the flowers in her hand and turned away from him.

"Okay. Nice talking to you, too," he said, but she was already striding up the path away from him.

One more glance at the horizon was enough to convince him that he wasn't going to get any good shots today, not with the rapidly decreasing light, so he folded down his tripod, carefully wiped his lenses and packed them with his camera into his bag.

He was on his way out of the graveyard when he spotted her, hunkered down by a grave, arranging the flowers in the jam jar so they leaned up against the headstone. She inspected her arrangement and started to clear the twigs and decaying leaves from the grave, seemingly engrossed in her work. He automatically slowed down, and almost stopped, loitering nearby, watching her as she wiped down the black marble headstone with a cloth, resting her hand momentarily over the gold lettering of the name. He could just make out the words:

"*Diane Kennedy*
Beloved Mother of Laura and Wife of Peter
May she Rest in Peace"

He suddenly caught himself. What was he doing staring at this poor girl as she tended to her mother's grave? He moved to walk away, but just as he did so she turned and caught his eye—embarrassed by his voyeurism he felt the need to say something, to start a conversation and close the distance between them, so that they would no longer be the watched and the watching.

"I'm going now. I came to get a picture of the town, but there's not enough light. I'll come back another day."

"The light's always pretty bad from up here. The sky is usually dark and miserable, especially this time of year."

"Be careful you don't get caught in the rain. You'll get sick, or what is the phrase I have heard people say? You will catch your something of cold? Your fill of cold is it?"

"Death."

"Sorry?"

"You will catch your death of cold. That's what we say here."

"That's not very optimistic. I just meant you might get sick for a few days." He saw her face soften into a smile.

"Either way, you're right. I'm going to head home soon, too." She lifted the small plastic bag of dead leaves and weeds she had picked from the grave and the trowel she used to clear them and for a second time today he watched her walk away from him.

Miguel paused for a minute, feeling awkward. The conversation was over but they were both heading in the same direction, and there was only one path leading down from the graveyard back into town. He thought about waiting and letting her get a head start, but he really wanted to talk more to this girl.

"Wait," he called. She stopped and turned, so he hurried to catch up.

"Maybe I can walk with you? I'm on my way to Mr. Quigley's for lunch."

"Oh, umm. Of course."

He fell into step next to her. She continued walking, staring straight ahead—the painful silence between them seemed to freeze his thoughts. The crunch of the gravel beneath their feet was frustratingly loud, taunting his silence. *Just say something*, he thought, *this is easy for you—you always know what to say. You'd know exactly what to say if you were in Colombia; well, it's just the same here, she's just another girl*, he told himself, but his still tongue felt dumb. To his relief, she spoke first.

"So how are you settling in?"

"Good. Great. Mr. Quigley has been very kind you know, helping me with the apartment, inviting me to the pub. We went to the Greyhound Pub last night. You know it?"

"Yes, it's a small town, so I kind of know all the pubs."

"You do, do you?" He felt like he could tease her about this last comment more, but he was not sure, he was still not completely relaxed around her. He didn't want to attempt a joke that might fall flat.

"You know what I mean," her pale cheeks flushed a light pink. "Speaking of Mr. Quigley. Do you see that big grave over there?"

They were now at the exit, and she pointed to the first gravesite on the left next to the gate. It had a large double grave with a shiny marble surround and huge headstone, standing much higher than the average. When they got closer he read the gold lettering:

"Martin Quigley. Beloved Father and Husband. Inspiration to Many Young Minds. 1950 to   . Padre Pio Pray For Him.

Sarah Quigley. Beloved Mother and Wife. 1948 to   . Padre Pio Pray For Her."

"Is that?"

"Mr. and Mrs Quigley. Space is getting tight up here, so they bought themselves a family plot a year or so ago, and then they must have decided as they already have the plot they might as well erect a headstone they like. 'Can't enjoy it when you're dead,' Mr. Quigley says. Although I never figured out what there is to enjoy about a gravestone."

Miguel had never heard anything like this before. "You Irish are very strange."

"It's not all of us! Believe me, this is odd even by our standards."

"So now, when they do finally die, all they have to do is fill in the year?"

"That's right. He thinks it's a great idea. I bet you if you mention you were at the graveyard, he'll tell you all about it. He even has some photos of it on his phone; if you pretend you didn't see it he'll be wanting to show you—although he might be a bit disappointed if he thinks you were here and you missed it. As you can see, it was designed to be bigger and shinier than the rest."

"He is quite a character, isn't he?"

"That's one way of putting it. You should see him in the Christmas Pantomime. I've never seen a more convincing Dame."

"I'm sorry, you are going to have to help me out here. Dame? What is 'Dame'?" Miguel thought of the Spanish *dama*, meaning woman. Even if Mr. Quigley was a bit flamboyant, Miguel couldn't imagine a high school teacher wandering around dressed as a woman. It'd never happen in Bogotá, so he couldn't see it in a small town like this.

"Oh, it's like a woman, a lady."

"So Mr. Quigley is a *woman* once a year on Christmas?"

"No. Only for the Panto!"

Miguel didn't think this was much of an explanation.

"Panto?"

"Pantomime," she said, although it was still no clearer to him what she was talking about.

"What is this Pantomime thing? Is it like Halloween but at Christmas?"

"No. It's in the theatre, like a kind of play. How can I explain? Hang on a sec." She suddenly stopped and started to look in her bag. "Damn, I've left my phone at the graveside. If someone sees it, they'll be thinking my mother is one of those crazy people who want to have a phone handy by their grave, just in case they come back and need to make a call."

"There are people here who do that?"

"Well, you said yourself we Irish are a strange lot."

"Let me run back for you."

"No, it's fine, really. You go on, though. I don't want you to be late for your lunch."

Miguel no longer felt like going to the lunch. He'd much rather spend the afternoon just like this—walking with this strange, charming girl.

"Well hopefully I'll see you again. You need to teach me what this Panto is."

"Of course. I'll see you when you start up at the school. Enjoy your lunch."

"Thanks."

"Bye," she said, turning to climb the path to the graveyard again.

He sauntered away slowly, looking behind him every thirty seconds, hoping she would catch up with him again, but she was nowhere to be seen.

On the walk through town to Mr. Quigley's house, Miguel's thoughts were filled with her—he recognised in her the particular loneliness that comes from growing up without a mother. He hoped sometime he'd be able to tell her that he understood—unfortunately, it was one thing they had in common. Although he had no idea then just how different the circumstances surrounding their mothers' deaths had been.

CHAPTER SEVEN

Miguel was glad when the streets started to become familiar. The blood pushing through the small vessels in his eyes felt like boiling water and his scalp tingled. Just another five minutes and they'd be pulling into the square. A short walk and he'd be home. Well, not home, but at least back through the front door that was opened by the key in his pocket, to the place where he slept and where his clothes hung in the closet. That was at least some comfort after the hell he'd seen today.

He remembered what Richard, his boss at the Tribunal, had said to him that morning. "You have to familiarize yourself with all the evidence. That's your only job this week—get to know these files inside out. You need to know this stuff, and it'll help desensitize you before you meet the victims and their families. You'll be no good to them if you can't detach yourself from it all."

"Yes, of course. I'll go through it all in detail." Miguel was eager to get stuck in and prove himself on his first day.

"Just to warn you. Some of it's pretty harrowing stuff."

"That's fine. I think I know what to expect."

Miguel sat at his desk and opened the first file. It

contained the coroner's photos of the dead, taken in the makeshift morgue set up in the community centre. There was the body of a woman, probably in her sixties, who looked quite well-dressed despite the film of thick dust covering her clothes. She lay on a foldout table, her sensible shoes still laced up on her feet. Miguel moved quickly to the next photo. It was of her head, alone on another table. The accompanying notes said she'd been decapitated by a large piece of shrapnel.

Miguel took a deep breath and turned over the next photo, which was of a random collection of body parts arranged on a white sheet to best resemble the person they had once belonged to. "Joe Bloggs" was scrawled on the back. It was so divorced from anything he had ever experienced that it felt like he was looking at stills from a movie and not at something that was once an actual person, with family and friends and a life.

Miguel picked up the next photo in his hands. It was of a small baby, swaddled like any sleeping infant in a thick white towel, one half of its face at complete rest, the other half missing. On the back of the photo it read "Clarissa Scannel—approximately six months old—found hanging from a tree near the blast." She'd obviously been thrown from her mother's arms by the force of the explosion.

Clarissa Scannel would have been ten years old by now. Miguel would no doubt be meeting her mother and father in the next few weeks when the Tribunal started hearing evidence from the victims. His job was to get them ready for that, to explain the process and any legalese, to make them as comfortable as possible. It suddenly dawned on him that the gruesome picture he held in his hand wasn't fiction —it was real, and he was overcome with a torrent of emotions that made him sweat ice and flipped his stomach on its side. He jumped up and ran towards the toilets, his hands covering his mouth trying to keep the vomit in. He made it into the toilets just in time before the contents of his stomach came flying out and into the bowl.

He flushed the toilet and stumbled out of the cubicle.

He dipped his face down close to the tap and scooped some water into his mouth with his hands. His teeth felt rancid and the back of his throat was raw. He threw more water over his face and patted it down with a paper towel. It was no use, he still looked shaken. And now he'd have to go back out there to the open plan office he shared with the other young lawyers and interns—he was sure he'd knocked a pile of papers off one of their desks in his rush to get past. He'd have to apologise for that. He took a deep breath and swung open the door to the toilets and out again to the office area.

One of the girls gave him an understanding smile as he walked past. A wave of shame swept over Miguel when he saw Stephen, who sat at the adjoining desk, sorting through his scattered papers.

"I'm sorry about that. Can I help you at all?"

"No, don't worry about it. I can do it myself. I thought Mr. 'I've got a Ph.D. in this shit' could handle himself a bit better."

"It's just a master's degree, looking at truth commissions around the world." It was probably best just to stay matter-of-fact and not get drawn into an argument with a co-worker on his first day.

"Well it hasn't prepared you very well for the real world, has it?"

And the Irish are supposed to be known for their friendliness, Miguel thought. The girl at the desk in front turned round.

"Oh, shut up Stephen and leave him alone, would ye."

Miguel smiled at her and took his seat again.

"Don't worry about him, he's always grumpy on a Monday morning. Too much of the sauce at the weekend, probably."

Stephen glared at her and went back to his papers.

"Thanks," Miguel said. He wished he could remember her name, although even if he could, he would have no hope of pronouncing it. It was an Irish name, as Irish as her wavy long red hair and her white freckled skin, with lots of vowels broken by the letter "F."

"So tell me about the truth commissions you studied. What did you think of them?" She wasn't at all pretty, but she had a wide smile and seemed friendly.

"I don't know, they have their pros and cons. They often have as their objective the reconstruction of the truth," he'd said this phrase a hundred times before.

"Reconstruction? What, like the truth is an object shattered across the country during the conflict that you can just piece together?"

"Something like that."

"I'm not sure I buy it. Don't they create a new truth? A new version of history that only becomes true if it's seen as legitimate?" This was obviously a pet subject of hers. What she was saying was a widely held view, he knew that from his master's, he just didn't agree with it.

"But it's not a version of the truth. It's just the truth. Something specific; something singular and defined. That's why it has 'the' in front of it."

"Going to teach us all English now, are you?" Stephen sneered and Miguel immediately regretted what he'd just said.

"Interesting point," the girl with the funny name went on, thankfully ignoring Stephen's snide comment. "But what about judicial truth, which has to stand up to the strict test of proof? Or emotional truth, that feeling which comes from deep inside when you just know something is right? For example, we're not looking for judicial truth here. The Tribunal is not looking to prosecute anyone, we're just looking to create a version of the truth that everyone can live with. We've all heard the rumours: that the security forces knew about the bomb but didn't evacuate because they wanted to protect their source, that the ambulance service wasn't prepared because they thought the troubles were more or less over; that the terrorists deliberately gave the wrong target in the warning so people were ushered towards the bomb instead of away from it. In all the confusion, the victims' families just want an agreed, legitimate … cohesive version of events. They just want some answers."

Her reference to the victims' families reminded him that his work was no longer merely theoretical. At the Reconciliation Commission in Colombia he had advised on policy, and back then, labels were all important to him. But really, it was just a question of vocabulary—finding the right word to describe what they were doing here— and whether it was reconstructing or creating—what did that matter to Clarissa Scannel's parents? Miguel decided it was probably best to just change the subject before they got into another deep discussion on semantics.

"What part are you working on?" he asked her.

"Witnesses. The police took a load of statements that day. And a lot of them have agreed to give evidence. So I'm liaising with them and also seeing if there are any other witnesses we might need. I'm trying to track down a Mrs O'Donnell. Apparently, she was the closest survivor to the blast—looks like she saw someone she knew blown up, but we're not sure who. Here, have a read yourself."

She threw a sheet of paper onto Miguel's desk. It was a copy of the policeman's handwritten notes. It started with a verbatim quote from the witness: "*I waved at him across the road and then something behind him, I think it was a car, exploded with the most incredible noise. At the moment of the blast it was like my other senses shut down and I only heard the noise. When my other senses came back to me, and I don't know how long that took, I was on the floor, and everything was grey and dusty and I started to feel warm rain on my skin. It took me a moment to realise it was blood. There was blood in my hair. There was blood splattered on my face, but none of it was mine. I called out to him. I had just seen him a second ago, right in front of me, but he was no longer there. There are just parts of him now. I never wanted this. This is not why I came here today.*"

The image of Joe Bloggs, the selection of body parts, flashed through Miguel's mind. Beneath this quote the policeman had scribbled, "*Miraculously appears to have only minor cuts. Must be suffering from shock. Passed her over to paramedics.*"

"So what happened to her?"

"We don't know. After she gave her statement, she just walked away through the rubble and the sirens and the smoke and was never heard of again. When the police went back to get a more formal statement from her, they realised that in all the confusion the officer hadn't recorded her contact details correctly—they've never tracked her down. I spoke to the officer recently just to see if he could remember anything. But it's so long ago, and I think he was probably shell-shocked himself. He couldn't remember the colour of her hair; he wasn't even sure of her age. He thought probably middle-aged. But you know what he did remember? Her eyes. He was quite specific. He said they were blue, a dark grey-blue, like the flint from the Irish shore."

Even though Miguel had no idea what flint looked like, the description struck a chord. Just then Richard walked back into the room and the girl whispered, "I'll let you get on with your work," and turned away from Miguel, leaving him to face the papers and photos on his desk once more.

He couldn't risk another incident like earlier, so he put the photos to one side and pulled out the Coroner's report instead. The language was dry and academic, just what he needed. In clinical terms, the Coroner explained in detail what was meant by where the bodies were found, revealing the secrets betrayed by the way that the life shattered out of them, flinging limbs and organs in all directions, splattering blood down shop windowfronts.

Miguel spent the rest of the day reading reports, immersing himself deeper and deeper into the detail. He had lunch and afternoon coffee in the little café next to the office with the rest of the lawyers and interns. They called it a greasy spoon—an odd and not particularly appetising way of describing the place they ate in on a daily basis. Most of them were really interested in Colombia, and he was happy to tell them about all the wonderful things his country has to offer: the eternally beautiful city of Cartagena, the exquisite beaches of Park Tayrona along the Caribbean coast, the truly awe-inspiring Amazon rainforest—only Stephen asked the stereotypical questions about drug dealers and the FARC.

In the afternoon when Miguel got back to his desk from the toilet, he found an article printed from *Time* magazine's website called "A Day in the Life of Medellin—The Drug Lord's Playground."

"Not as fabulous as you make out, then," Stephen said.

Miguel scanned the article—the conflict-ravaged, corrupt and violent city it described was nothing like the "City of Eternal Springtime," as they called it in Colombia, that Miguel knew from visits.

"Well I suppose if I went to *Time* magazine's offices and did a report from the toilets, there'd only be shit to write about, too," Miguel responded—that should shut him up, he thought.

After such a first day, Miguel was glad to get back to the peace and quiet of his flat. Flicking on the lights, he saw the familiar silver trunk waiting for him in the middle of the main room—the rest of his belongings had arrived. He had packed the trunk over a month ago now. Funny he had to fill it with all the things he couldn't live without and then put them on a ship, out of his reach, for nearly six weeks.

His record player was the thing he'd missed the most in recent weeks. He'd brought an mp3 player, too, with thousands of songs on it, but he much preferred vinyl. It had taken him almost a full week to select just twenty records from his entire collection to bring. How was he supposed to know what music he would need with him in Ireland? For it was a question of need, not want—some songs are absolutely vital for certain situations, and how could he predict all the situations he might face here?

He heard rapping on the front door.

"Helloooo," Mrs. Quigley walked into the flat with a casserole dish in hand, filling the room with a meaty aroma. "I brought some shepherd's pie. I'll put this in the oven for you. It won't take long to heat up." She squeezed past Miguel and into the kitchen. Mr. Quigley followed her in, smiling and obviously eager to hear all about Miguel's first day.

"So how was it?"

"Good, they're a nice team. I just spent most of the day reading in."

"Right, what did they have you reading?"

"You know, just coroner's reports, that sort of thing."

"Interesting stuff?"

"Yes." He could see Mr. Quigley was waiting for more detail, but Miguel didn't want to throw himself back into the darkness he'd seen earlier—there'd be time for that tomorrow, and the next, and almost every day for the next six months. He was exhausted just thinking about it.

Mrs. Quigley came back into the hallway. She had wild curly grey hair that shone like silver and was the same height as her husband though probably twice as heavy. But she carried it well, filling her clothes with a strong sense of her own presence.

"I've set the timer so it should be ready in ten minutes."

"That's very kind of you. And thank you for waiting for my trunk today." Miguel knew the polite thing to do would be to invite them to sit down, maybe offer them some coffee, but he wasn't sure when he'd get rid of them. They were a childless couple and he got the impression that Mrs. Quigley already looked on him like a foster child—a twenty-eight-year-old foster child.

"You wouldn't believe the excitement at the school about you." Mr. Quigley said. "I think some of the girls have seen you cycling about the town and well, the way they're chatting you'd think we had a pop star coming to teach them. Just to warn you, I've already found a blackboard with "We Heart Miguel" scrawled across it, so god knows what mischief they've lined up to embarrass you when you start."

"Well, I'm sure being the object of some teenage crushes won't be so bad. It must be better than how they treat you, darling," Mrs. Quigley said. To Miguel she said, "They call him the old woman."

"They do not!" Mr. Quigley looked horrified.

"Oh you know they do, love."

"And what about the staff? I hope they don't think my joining the faculty is going to be disruptive," Miguel said. What he really wanted was to ask whether a certain English teacher had mentioned him.

"Of course not. They're all keen to meet you."

"Actually, I've met, is it Laura? The English teacher?" He knew full well what her name was. He'd spent a lot of time over the last two days thinking about her, but he didn't want Mr. Quigley knowing that.

"Really? Where?"

It probably wasn't a good idea to mention how he'd handed custody of Mr. Quigley's bike to a complete stranger, so he skipped over their first meeting. "In the graveyard of all places. Yesterday before lunch at your house."

"She must've been up visiting her mother's grave. That was a terrible tragedy. We were all still shaken about the bomb, I mean it was only two days after, and even if it wasn't in our town everyone knew somebody that'd been affected, and then they phoned us at the school with the news that Diane had killed herself—we had to take Laura out of class and send her home. We just said there had been an accident, what else could we say?"

Miguel pictured Laura young and alone in the back of a car on the way to hear the worst news any teenager could get. No wonder she seemed so wary. Moments like that can shape a whole life. Miguel tried to think of an appropriate way of asking for more information, but Mrs. Quigley jumped in first.

"Martin Quigley. For God's sake, I think this poor boy has heard enough about death for one day."

"I was just saying …"

"You were just gossiping. No wonder they call you the old woman! Now, we'll leave this poor boy in peace to eat his dinner. C'mon, Martin."

"Yes dear." Mr. Quigley rolled his eyes and followed his wife out the front door.

After dinner, Miguel opened the trunk. He'd packed it with thick woollen jumpers and winter clothes, together with a few prized possessions: a handful of books, his small record player and selection of records, photos of him with his father and grandmother, the Colombian football team t-shirt that Natalia had bought him when they were seventeen, and finally the letter from his mother that his grandmother had given him when he was fifteen. He opened the letter carefully and reread his favourite line from the letter: "*Live life passionately to the end.*" He tried to remember that each day, but it wasn't easy, especially on a day like today.

CHAPTER EIGHT

Miguel and his family spend months at the hospital, at least to a five-year-old it feels like months; maybe in reality it is only a few weeks. When he is tired he sleeps on the plastic chairs in the visitor's room with a cushion brought from his grandmother's sofa. The chairs are the same pale, lifeless green as the doctors' uniforms.

His grandmother's two maids make huge vats of food that they bring to the hospital to feed the family who gather there each day. Even his uncles come from their offices to eat with the rest of the family at lunchtime. Assembled in the visitors' room, they look like any typical extended family out for a picnic, his uncles telling jokes and going back for seconds, the teenage cousins fiddling with their gadgets and the women gossiping. He notices other families staring at them, but no one else in his family seems to notice or care. The maids make everyone's favourite food: hearty stews, beans, thick soups; all dishes typical of the region where his grandmother grew up. She oversaw the training of both of the maids to make sure they knew the recipes of her mother and her grandmother to the exact half teaspoonful measure of salt or spice. She never got round to teaching these recipes to her only daughter, who now lay dying a few doors away.

The illness has transformed his mother. She has lost her thick dark hair and now wears colourful scarves to brighten up her appearance. Otherwise, with the exception of her emerald eyes, she is devoid of colour. Her eyes are starting to fall deeper into her face, encircled with skin so dark it looks like charcoal next to her white cheeks. But otherwise her eyes do not change. They still shine out from within the black circles as beautiful as always. When he becomes frightened by all the physical changes, when he feels he does not recognise his mother in the woman lying pale and lost in the huge hospital bed, then he focuses on her eyes, and there she is again in front of him, the mother who reads him bedtime stories, the mother who took him to his first day at school and waved him off on his first weekend away with the boy scouts.

The cancer has robbed her of her all physical strength. She used to be able to swing him high over her head. He loved soaring above her in a fit of giggles, so safe and free, but now she barely has the energy to read a newspaper. His father turns the pages for her and folds them to make it easier for her to hold. She dispenses with each page quickly. She says she only has the energy to read the headlines and look at the photos. She does not have enough time left to bother with the detail. His father jokes that she only ever looked at the pictures, anyway. He loves the smile that his father's jokes bring to her face. It gives her energy from an unknown source, bringing back the colour and the light, if only momentarily. He wishes he could have the same power to bring someone back to life with a simple joke.

Though one joke frightens him. He is playing in the corner of the room and his parents do not realise that he is listening.

"I'm afraid that I'll get eaten by worms. You know of all the crazy things, that's what gives me nightmares. I'm such a fool," his mother says.

"Well, don't worry about that," he hears his father say, "we'll just burn you instead. Problem solved." And there is that smile again. This time she even manages a laugh, a spontaneous laugh and a playful slap for her husband—done before her body remembers that it does not have the energy for such mirth.

Miguel is confused. He doesn't understand why she is afraid of worms. The hospital is clean; there is no soil anywhere. He checks the potted plants, but they are plastic, held into their pots by foam. He follows his uncle outside when he goes to smoke a cigarette.

"You won't burn her, will you?" he asks. "You'll be careful with your lighter."

As his mother gets weaker, the family spends more and more time in prayer. His grandmother leads the rosary three times a day at six-hour intervals in the visitors' room. Miguel copies everyone else and lowers his head as his grandmother races through the first half of the prayer, not stopping for breath. Then he hums the second half with the crowd. He doesn't know the words, although he isn't sure if anyone knows the words or if they are all just humming along hoping not to get caught out. In the beginning, his father gets annoyed with all the praying and storms out.

"This is what they do at funerals. My wife is not dead. She is down the hall and can hear you."

His father's lack of faith is a constant source of conflict with his maternal grandmother, but eventually as the weeks pass, he starts to join them for prayers. The women on their knees, with straight backs and eyes out in front of them, look like they are conversing with God as equals, but his father looks like a beggar, crumpled and desperate, with no other option than to bow down and beseech the kindness of a greater power. He hopes his father can make a pact with God and they can keep his mother here on earth.

Playing quietly in the corner of his mother's room as she sleeps, eating and praying with the family in the visitor's room, telling jokes to the nurses, making friends with the other children that visit, all becomes routine, normal.

One day his aunt comes with his two cousins to pick him up after school. She hugs him tightly as she says hello. Her face looks different. Her eyes are heavier, swollen, she is not wearing any makeup. She tells him that they are not going to the hospital for lunch, that she is taking him and his cousins to the mall for hamburgers and to play in the arcade. Miguel asks when he will see his mother.

"Later, darling, you will see mama later. She wants you to be out having some fun." But they don't go to the hospital that evening. Instead, his aunt takes him home with his cousins for a sleepover. She lets them stay up late watching videos and orders pizza for dinner. His uncle comes home very late, after Miguel and his cousins are in bed. The door is slightly open and he can see his aunt and uncle embrace, his aunt holding her husband close, rocking him back and forth.

Miguel is frightened and cannot sleep. He lies in bed focusing on the small slit of light coming in from the doorway. He doesn't understand why he hasn't seen his father and mother all day. His aunt and uncle seem so different, they are behaving so strangely. It is like all the adults are lost.

In the morning, his grandmother comes to the house. Seeing her immediately makes him feel more secure; she is always in control. She tells him that they are not going to the hospital, they are going to the funeral home. She explains that that is where they take people when they have died and asks if he understands what that means. He nods. He has seen people die on TV, they become still and their eyes close and people are sad. His grandmother explains that his mother's body is asleep at the funeral home but her spirit has gone to be with God. She explains that the spirit is the part that makes a person who they are, it is the part that loves, it is the part that speaks and laughs and creates and remembers. His aunt leaves the room in tears and his grandmother helps him to get dressed.

The funeral home is not a house. It is a big official-looking building with a steep marble staircase and shiny wooden doors. His uncle carries him up the steps, and on the second floor he takes him into a big, dimly lit room filled with fold-out chairs. People sit whispering in small groups. A ghostly murmur hovers in the air. In the corner of the room, hundreds of flowers are crowded together, like a secret garden hidden in the middle of this cold and polished building, their perfume overwhelming. In the middle of the flowers rests a long wooden box on two stands. He sees his father kneeling down next to the box like an abandoned child, scared and alone.

His grandmother nods for him to go to his father. Miguel walks over tentatively, terrified of what will happen next. His father reaches for him, clings to him with all his strength. Suddenly Miguel, too, is crying, uncontrollably.

The rest of the day is a blur. He doesn't understand the resignation of the adults. To him death is like the bogeyman; it sneaks in during the middle of the night and steals your spirit away from inside of you, squeezes it into an empty jam jar and leaves behind the empty body. He doesn't understand why his mother had waited at the hospital for death. He's angry that she didn't hide away somewhere safe.

The next day, hundreds of people gather in church to pray for his mother. But even the prayers of hundreds do not bring back her spirit, so they take the box that contains her body and bury it. He remembers at school they had planted a bulb in the ground, too, and a few months later it blossomed into a flower, so he believes that they are storing her body safe in the ground until they are able to recover her spirit from death. Then she will reappear like the flower, her frozen body warm again.

Only months later will he realise that death is a permanent separation, and he will mourn her again, crying in his grandmother's arms for hours.

On his fifteenth birthday, his grandmother presents Miguel with a letter. It is from his mother, written shortly before she died, a note really, scribbled in a lazy script inside a note card with a picture of some red roses on the front: *"I've been going over and over in my head what I want to say to you in this letter. It is my only link to you in the future and I could write a novel if I had the time. But I know my time is nearly up, so what to tell you, son? What is important? Walk through life with your eyes open. Be conscious. Make your own decisions and believe in yourself. Live life passionately to the end.*

Death is just the moment when living stops. If you have lived, then Death can hold no fear for you. But some people stop living long before Death, some never even start. That is the real tragedy. I wish I could tell people how nice it is to die of cancer because I now see Death up ahead and I know that I am living. Cancer, with all its indignities, has shown me my beautiful life—which I will squeeze and hold onto until the end. Live your life like that, son. Every day look Death in the eye and rejoice in your glorious life."

CHAPTER NINE

Miguel walked through the school gate and checked his watch—8.15 a.m.—exactly on time. He could see Mr. Quigley pacing up and down behind the glass double doors at the main entrance.

"Bang on time! I'm impressed," Mr. Quigley said when Miguel pushed through the doors. "So how are you feeling?"

"Good."

"Nervous?"

"No, should I be?"

"I'd like to say no, but I wouldn't want to lie to you. In less than an hour, this place will be overrun with about four hundred teenage girls; it's no wonder I've lost half my hair!"

All week, Miguel had wanted it to be Friday already. He had wanted time to go at double speed, but the opposite happened. It became gelatinous, the hours stretching out long and viscous as he trawled the mire of savage acts that the Tribunal was investigating. Thankfully, today promised a complete change of air.

He was curious to see what kind of teacher he'd make. He always imagined he'd be good at it—he fancied himself as someone who could inspire others. And if he were honest with himself, he was curious to see Laura again, too. He'd caught himself looking out for her as he walked home from the bus stop every evening, exhausted after a day at the Tribunal, hugging his jacket to him as a shield against the biting evening air. Apart from the Quigleys, she was the only face in this small community of strangers that felt familiar. The disappointment poured through him every night when he rounded the corner of the Chinese place, into the alleyway, and up the stairs to his empty flat without having caught a glimpse of her. But now he didn't have to wait and wonder—she was probably behind the very door that they were walking towards.

Just as they reached the staff room, there she was, coming out of it with a pile of jotters in her arms. She was wearing a brown woollen skirt that hugged her hips, following the line of her long legs until the ankle and a dark green, high-necked jumper that traced closely the silhouette of her narrow waist. There was a collage of faces behind her looking in his direction, and he had the vague notion that they were smiling at him, but for now they were all merely a backdrop to her.

"Hi, welcome."

"Laura, it's good to see you again."

"You too, have you managed to get yourself a lock for that bike of yours yet?"

"No, but I have paid a year-eight student ten pounds to skip class for the day and watch it for me." This earned him a tiny smile, and a slight flush of pink in her cheeks. He'd forgotten how pale her skin was.

"I forgot you two already know each other," Mr. Quigley said.

"Laura has been helping me with my English."

"That's right. Listen Martin, I have to miss the morning meeting. I'm meeting the public speaking group. But maybe you can do me a favour and explain to our friend here what a pantomime is." She winked as she walked past him and out the door.

Mr. Quigley looked delighted by the mention of the pantomime. "Come meet my fellow player," he said, and ushered Miguel into the room, deep into the sea of faces and towards a man that Mr. Quigley introduced as Leo Breslin.

"Leo was my uglier sister in last years' production of Cinderella, and the year before that we did an alternative version of Old Mother Goose and he played my husband," Leo looked to be in his late forties. He had a small pot belly, rosy red cheeks and hair so shiny and black it could only be chemically enhanced. It all seemed very strange. A show where Mr. Quigley dressed up as a woman and, by the sounds of it, possibly had love scenes with another teacher? And it was shown at Christmas?

"And this year, it's *Puss in Boots*," Mr. Quigley went on. Puss in Boots, Miguel thought this sounded stranger and stranger by the minute. He smiled and nodded as they talked about plans for this year's production and tried not to look confused, all the while praying that they didn't ask him if he could act.

Teaching didn't come as easily to Miguel as he had expected. Mr. Quigley gave him a lesson plan for each class, basically a point of grammar or topic of conversation to cover—thrilling things like "mealtimes across Europe," not exactly the deep philosophical or political discussions he imagined. But that wasn't the problem; it was the girls. All they wanted to do was interrogate him, in English, about Colombia. Class after class, they bombarded him with the same stock questions: "Is it safe?" "Do you eat spicy food?" "Are there a lot of drugs?"

He just rolled out his standard answers: "It's not dangerous, you just need to be street-smart in the big cities," "No, that's Mexico," and "Not that I've seen, Colombia might be one of the countries that produce the stuff, but it's the U.S. and Europe that consume it."

54

Finally at 3:45 the final bell rang, so he made his way though the crowds of giggling girls to the staff room where he'd arranged to meet Mr. Quigley for a debrief and where hopefully he'd run into Laura. There was an air of chaos about the room as the teachers, obviously frazzled by a long week of power struggles with the girls, rushed through their final tasks before the weekend. He'd just started chatting with Mr. Quigley when Laura floated in, again with a pile of jotters hugged to her chest, and picked up her coat and left. She moved as if encased in a celestial bubble, set apart from the everyday scene around her. She was out the door before he realized he should seize this opportunity to talk to her, otherwise another long week might go by before he got the chance again.

"Martin, can we do this in five minutes? I just need to run to the bathroom." He was already up and making his way to the door before Mr. Quigley could respond. He probably looked like an idiot, desperately running out to the toilet.

Out in the busy hallway, he looked for her up and down, but she was gone, vanished like a master thief escaping onto a crowded street. She was obviously keen for her weekend to commence, unlike Miguel, who had absolutely nothing or no one to rush home for.

He turned and walked back into the staff room. Mr. Quigley's warm smile hit him like a beam as soon as he entered the room. "I'm heading to Charlie's Place this evening, will you join me for a pint?"

"Sure, why not?" Miguel said, relieved not to have to spend another evening looking at the bare walls of his flat.

Laura pushed through the throng of girls leaving the school. She didn't have much time. Catherine was coming round at five and she wanted to buy some wine and run to the florist to pick up a bunch of flowers for the house. Nothing too fancy, just some fresh-cut roses to give the impression that the house was cared for, that the people living there enjoyed life. She knew she shouldn't care so much about appearances, Catherine was supposed to be her best friend after all, ever since they were schoolgirls. But things had changed so much in ten years—Catherine was really going somewhere now—she worked in a PR department at a big investment bank in London and had recently bought a flat. Laura on the other hand, felt like she'd been standing still for years. And most of the time she was just fine with that, until Catherine showed up and reminded her of an alternative existence that might have been hers.

At home, Laura set about tidying up, arranging the flowers and wine glasses on the kitchen table. In her bedroom she changed out of her long woollen skirt and high-neck jumper. It had been a mistake to wear that outfit today. She saw the Colombian looking her up and down this morning. He obviously thought she was some uptight schoolmistress. He was probably used to being surrounded by sexy Colombian women showing everything, and there she was covered from the neck down.

She pulled on jeans and a simple black t-shirt and short grey cardigan—only marginally better. She was pulling on her boots with the small heel when she heard a knocking at the back door. There was no way her father would answer it, so she quickly zipped up her boots and raced down the stairs, through the living room where her father was sitting very still, pretending to be transfixed by a story about EU subsidies for pig farming, and into the kitchen.

"Hi honey," Catherine said, throwing her arms around Laura. As always, she looked stunning. Her shiny black hair hung in thick curls over her shoulders, and she was wearing tight dark trousers, chunky jewellery, an expensive-looking woollen coat and enormous high heels. Over Catherine's shoulders, Laura saw a middle-aged woman waiting in the backyard.

"Chrissie, c'mon in, would you. Laura, you remember

my aunt, don't you."

Laura had met Chrissie a couple of times when Catherine was home visiting, but only briefly. "Yes of course. Chrissie come in. It's nice to see you."

"You wouldn't believe it, but Chrissie has just moved in next door. I've been running around lifting boxes for her since I got in this morning." Catherine said.

Chrissie stepped into the kitchen and closed the door. "Don't listen to this one, Laura. She's more a hindrance than a help, I can tell you. We made the mistake of unloading the mirror first, so she spent half the day in front of it," Catherine swatted Chrissie with her hand.

"Anyway, sorry for intruding on your night like this. Catherine insisted that I tag along. And here, I brought something for you." She thrust a bottle of vodka and a brown paper bag into Laura's hands. Laura peeked inside the bag, it was filled with vine tomatoes, bulbous and wholly red.

"I wanted to bring something, only thing worse than showing up unannounced is showing up empty-handed. I bought those tomatoes at the farmers' market. Don't know why it has to be called a farmers' market these days, I suppose 'cos everyone is obsessed with organics. I remember back when it was just the plain old market. Anyway, I just saw them and thought they look pretty damn perfect and I bet you they're properly sweet, not like those excuses for tomatoes you get in the supermarket. And well, if you're anything like Catherine here you'll like a tipple, so I thought you might like to squeeze some juice from them and make yourself a Bloody Mary. Have something pure to drink, you know. Wine is full of acid and no good for you in the long term, no matter what they say about those antioxidants. Whereas tomatoes, well that's a health food."

"Sorry Laura, there's an express highway with no red lights between Chrissie's brain and her mouth, so there's nothing to stop her saying exactly what she thinks the nanosecond she thinks it," Catherine interrupted. "If you hear a constant whirring noise from next door, don't worry. It's just Chrissie talking to herself or, worse still, the dog."

"You are a cheeky madam!" Chrissie slapped Catherine on the arm.

"Don't worry, Chrissie. I don't take anything Catherine says seriously."

"I'll just go through and say hello to your Dad quickly," Catherine said. "Chrissie, come in with me and meet your new neighbour."

Laura wasn't sure this was a good idea. Her father was used to seeing Catherine on her odd visits home, but she wasn't sure how he'd handle her wandering in there with Chrissie. Although what could she say to stop them?

"Oh, is your dad home?" Chrissie asked. Laura caught Catherine's glare at Chrissie. It was a fair question, why should Chrissie remember her father's "condition," if you could call it that? Chrissie wasn't to know that he was now little more than a breathing statue.

After the town gossips had finished chewing over her mother's death and moved on to other news, probably no one gave her father a second thought. It should have been a comfort to know that in a small town that passes daily commentary on everyone else's business, sometimes the family shames that you'd rather people forgot, really were forgotten. But that thought just made the situation more hopeless, Laura thought, for if her father's attempt to escape the outside world was no longer the source of local chat, then he'd clearly been successful.

Catherine marched off into the living room, taking Chrissie with her, before Laura could think of an excuse to stop them. Laura waited in the kitchen, listening.

"Hello Mr. Kennedy."

"Well hello there Catherine, Laura didn't mention you were coming home." That was a lie, she'd told him last night over dinner. It was probably the only piece of information they'd shared during the whole meal.

"I'm just home helping my aunt move house."

"Hello Peter."

"Chrissie. Hello." It seemed they already knew each other, and Chrissie quickly provided the answer to Catherine.

"We both worked in the nylon factory—oh, moons ago now."

"So you've moved in next door?"

"Yes, I don't know if you heard, but my parents passed away last year. Both of them within a month of each other. And well, I sold up the family home, heartless hussy as I am, and put my name down for a council house. So I'm your new neighbour. God, the move was some piece of work …"

From the kitchen Laura listened to Chrissie babble on about the move for a few minutes more. With Chrissie there was no need to *make* small talk *with* her; she was capable of spinning a conversation out of thin air all by herself—much like the emperor's tailors when he needed some new clothes. It was probably for the best, Laura thought; her father was more than a bit rusty when it came to social niceties. When Chrissie finally stopped talking, Catherine awkwardly wrapped up the conversation and they said their goodbyes and came back to join Laura in the kitchen.

"Would you like some wine or vodka?" Laura asked, keen to play the good hostess.

"No, shall we just head to the pub instead?" Chrissie said "Get in and get a seat before it gets too packed."

Laura was relieved not to have to entertain Chrissie and Catherine with her father listening at the other side of the wall. "And have we decided where we're going?"

"Charlie's Place, of course," Catherine said.

CHAPTER TEN

Charlie's pub was originally a boarding house and, apart from the sign outside, it still looked like any other old house. Miguel followed Mr. Quigley through the sprawling maze of low-ceilinged rooms, each filled with dated tables and chairs and sofas, none of which seemed to match. In every corner, a crackling log fire burned strong, coats and jumpers were piled up in every nook and cranny, and the place was packed with people laughing and talking over each other. Miguel pulled off his coat too, and tried to keep up with Mr. Quigley as he shimmied through the throng.

Finally they arrived at a room at the back, which looked like it had once been the kitchen but had now been transformed into the bar area. Miguel felt the other men's eyes bore into him as he sat down next to Mr. Quigley on the last two free bar stools. Unlike the noisy crowds in the other rooms, the men here looked like lone drinkers cradling their pint glasses in silence and watching the goings-on around them.

"Martin, how are ye?" the bartender asked. He could easily have been in his seventies, but he still looked to have loads of energy.

"Miguel, this is the eponymous Charlie; Charlie, this is that young fella from Colombia I was telling you about."

"Welcome, son—how are ye finding it? Bit different from home?"

"I'm enjoying it—so far, so good."

"And how's business doing these days?" Mr. Quigley asked.

"I can't complain, and even if I could, sure who would listen to me? How's life up at the school—are the nuns treating ye well?"

Miguel listened to the two of them chat—the way they spoke was lyrical, rhapsodic, always on the point of bursting into poetry or song. Quite different from the conservative, American English he had learned in Bogotá.

"And so you'll be helping Martin here with Survivors' Stories?" Charlie asked.

"Yes, I've already started working at the Hudson Tribunal, and in a few weeks' time I'll start interviewing some people."

"He'll be meeting people from all sides and with very different viewpoints," Mr. Quigley interrupted. "It's not been easy, some people object to us treating the families of IRA men killed by the army the same as other victims. Y'know they say those people aren't victims because their loved ones were criminals and got their just deserts. But a woman who's seen her nineteen-year-old son shot down in a field is still a victim, doesn't matter what they say he was up to when he was shot. But then you have the hardliners who say the killing of policemen or soldiers or anyone, in fact, who had 'collaborated' as they say, isn't murder, and so we shouldn't be treating their families as victims, which of course is just as ridiculous. It's always a challenge to get people to open up, but it might be easier, you being an outsider. They might find it easier to speak to you."

"I don't know why you bother Martin," Charlie said, "you know, I find most people, and I admit I probably get more people from one side of the house than the other in here, but anyway, most people are proud of the peace we have now, and asking people to bring their pain back to the surface just so you can record it, well, with all due respect, won't that just do more harm than good? Can't we just start fresh and forget all that nonsense we put ourselves through for all those years? Look at the here and now instead?"

"Charlie, you're entitled to your opinion as much as the next man—but you're wrong. We can't just sweep it all under the carpet. Truthful and lasting peace can only be founded on recognition and reconciliation—telling these stories is the first step. It's because we haven't faced up to our history together that Belfast is still on a knife-edge, where riots can erupt over anything, and we still have the dissidents trying to pull us back to the dark past."

Miguel was impressed with the force of Mr. Quigley's argument. It was amazing how easily he moved from bumbling teacher chattering away about pantomimes to a serious advocate for his beliefs.

"I happen to agree with that," said one of the other men at the bar. "Who was it that said those who cannot remember the past are condemned to repeat it?"

Miguel had heard this quote before. "It's Jorge Santayana," he said.

"Actually I think you'll find it was the Irishman Edmund Burke who coined the phrase first with something like, 'Those who don't know history are destined to repeat it.'" Mr. Quigley butted in—the muscles in Miguel's face hardened a fraction; he was convinced that wasn't right.

"I've read about him, but I thought Burke was English," the man at the bar said.

"Typical," Charlie laughed. "The Brits claim everything good as their own." Miguel opened his mouth to say he really thought it was Jorge Santayana, but Charlie spoke first to put a stop to the conversation altogether. "Now gentlemen, that's enough seriousness for one Friday night. How about something we all agree on, like cricket." The men all groaned.

"The town had a terrible season this year," Mr. Quigley informed Miguel.

"The town has a cricket team?"

"Yes, a lot of towns in the North do—regardless of their religious affiliation. At least the English left something good."

Miguel had only a vague image of what cricket was like garnered from Merchant Ivory films. He found it hard to reconcile this genteel game and its archaic rules with the relaxed and fun-loving community that he found in Northern Ireland, but judging by the impassioned conversation going on around him, love it they did. He tried to feign interest, but all the talk of wickets and golden ducks left him quickly confused, so he turned his attention to the doorway.

He couldn't believe his timing—there was Laura, standing by the door struggling to take off her long green coat. He smiled, hoping to catch her eye but she just looked past him. She was with another strikingly well-put-together girl in her twenties and a more mature lady old enough to be their mother. The older lady waved at Charlie and motioned that they were heading upstairs.

They settled themselves away from the crowds in one of the little rooms at the very top of the house with a view of the stairs and then Chrissie headed downstairs to get the first drink. Catherine immediately started talking about herself.

"My God, Laura, work is just crazy these days. I had, like, four black-tie receptions last week, and I had to sit next to my boss in all of them—it gets so boring."

Laura nestled back in the chair and prepared to spend the next hour nodding and listening to Catherine's alleged "problems."

CAROLINE DOHERTY DE NOVOA

"Pinch me."

Laura was suddenly thrown, she'd only been half listening. "What? He pinched you? Really?"

"No, you pinch me! I think I'm dreaming," Catherine whispered through smiling, gritted teeth. "I can see Chrissie coming up the stairs with a man, and he's not bad looking. I must be hallucinating, am I still in our town?" She was already repositioning herself to sit taller, moving her head so her dark curls tumbled down in front of her shoulders.

Laura turned her head just in time to see Chrissie ducking through the doorway carrying her drink, followed by Miguel with two glasses in his hands.

"You are a darling," Chrissie said as she set her glass down on the table and turned to relieve him of the others. "So girls, I was downstairs struggling with these three vodka tonics when, sorry, what was your name again?"

"Miguel."

"When Miguel offered to help me. Miguel this is Catherine, my niece, and this is our family friend, Laura."

"Hello Catherine, nice to meet you. Laura, how are you?"

"I'm fine, thanks," Probably too curt a response, but what else was she supposed to tell him? I'm well, but the more Catherine goes on about "having" to go to black-tie dinners, the more bitter I feel that this is the highlight of my month? And the more bitter I feel, the more I hate myself for feeling that way—so then I'm just bitter about feeling bitter, bitter squared if you like. No, he probably didn't want to know how she was. 'How are you?' was probably just something he'd learned to say in English class, knowing the phrase didn't amount to the sum of its parts. 'I'm fine, thanks' would do.

"Oh, I didn't realize you two knew each other," Catherine said.

"I think this is maybe the third time we are introduced now."

"Miguel works part time at the school," Laura said by way of explanation.

"Well sit down then," Catherine said, already pushing Laura down along the seat into the corner so that there was room for Miguel to sit at the other side of her. "Laura didn't tell us that there were any new teachers this year. I'm guessing from your name and accent that you're not from round here?"

"That's right. I'm from Colombia."

"Colombia? Really? And what brought you here?" Catherine patted the seat next to her again and Miguel dutifully sat down. Catherine's ability to control the people around her was always a source of wonder.

"I'm here working at the Hudson Tribunal. Have you heard of it?"

"Of course, it's been on the news a fair bit, it's so important for those families to understand what happened to their loved ones. God bless their souls."

Laura thought this was glib. It was one thing knowing the details of what happened, but it was quite another to really understand it.

"And what will you be doing exactly?" Catherine asked.

"I'll be a liaison for the victims and their families. I'll spend most days with them, explaining the process, taking them through the kind of questions they should expect to be asked, explaining to them the legalese used by the Tribunal. And I suppose sometimes I'll just need to be there to listen to them. It's going to be hard on them."

"How many people died in the bomb?" Catherine asked.

"Thirty-one, and seventy-five injured."

"Jesus. Imagine how lucky you must feel escaping something like that." Catherine gasped, sounding surprised, as if she hadn't grown up here with all the killing and violence.

"I know what you mean, after 'dead,' 'killed' or

'murdered,' the word 'injured' seems so mild, lucky, even doesn't it? But it's nothing of the sort. That's one thing I've learned this week. Yesterday, one of the victims visited the offices. He came with his wife. They were newlyweds just back from honeymoon at the time of the bomb. They'd gone out that Saturday afternoon to buy curtains for their new house. They both survived the blast, but he was left severely disabled. His legs are now, how do you say? Completely useless?"

"Defunct," Laura murmured.

Miguel went on, as if he hadn't heard her, addressing his words to Catherine. "He can still move his arms from the shoulder, up and down and around. Although the nerves inside his arms were destroyed, so he can't control his fingers. They just hang limply at the end like they are mocking his still-functioning arms. They're a great couple, chatting and joking the whole time, but when they started talking about the bomb, when they went back to when they were just newlyweds, you could see it in her eyes that this wasn't the married life she'd planned."

Laura looked at Chrissie and Catherine, waiting for them to speak—they lifted their drinks at the same time and took a sip, both, for once, at a loss for words.

"I'm sorry. I shouldn't talk about these things, especially not in the pub on a Friday night. I, uh, I suppose it made a big impact on me, and when you asked me about the Tribunal it all just came tumbling out. Sorry."

His tanned skin looked momentarily ashen. So he wasn't as cocky as Laura had thought. His overconfident friendliness had seemed like a shiny veneer lacking in substance, but she'd been wrong.

He put his hand on the table as if reaching for a comforting glass, something to sip from to fill the silence, but there was no drink in front of him.

"Do you fancy a drink?" Laura asked. He looked up and smiled.

"I'll get it," Chrissie said, already up.

66

This activity seemed to shake Catherine back to life. "So tell me about Colombia."

Laura listened as he spoke about the beauty of Colombia and its variety. She was impressed by his ease; the eloquence in the way he spoke was unusual even in native English speakers. He made small grammatical errors, but his vocabulary was extensive. There was a fluidity and command in his speech, a certain formality that made an impact regardless.

Within no time, Chrissie was back with more drinks, and she and Catherine settled into a steady rhythm of interrogation, broken every now and then by Chrissie disappearing off downstairs for yet more drinks. Every time Laura thought of a question, Chrissie or Catherine got in there with it first. So Laura just sat there, her head getting fuzzier with each vodka, completely dumb, nodding and smiling and growing more frustrated with her lack of participation. He'd probably go away thinking she was incredibly dull—he probably thought that already— she'd not made a great first impression on him in their first few encounters.

"So was there anything else that made you want to come here, or was it just the work? I mean, did you know what you were getting into? That they would be sending you to this wee town for six months?" Chrissie asked.

"Well, it's an experience living in a small town after Bogotá, and I suppose I've always had a fascination with Ireland, and the North in particular."

"Why?"

He shrugged. "I studied the troubles in university, and I've always liked Irish music. From the North I quite like Van Morrison."

"Van Morrison?" Chrissie and Catherine cried in unison, making Laura smile at the family resemblance. It was a natural question; she didn't expect someone so young to like Van Morrison either, especially someone from so far away.

"Yes, you are surprised?"

"Oh, I hate his music," said Catherine.

"I love it, the early stuff more than anything. It's so magical, transcendental even."

"Transcendental." Laura repeated the long word automatically. Miguel glanced over at her and she suddenly realized that she sounded like she was mocking him.

"You know, 'Into the Mystic'?" he asked, ignoring her. "I always wondered what kind of place inspired that song."

"My favourite has always been 'Brown-Eyed Girl,'" Chrissie said.

"Yes, wonder who inspired that song?" Catherine said, fluttering her eyelashes over her own chocolate-brown eyes.

"You know, I heard a rumour that Northern Ireland *had* some of the most beautiful girls in Europe."

The most beautiful girls in Europe? Laura thought, he was either completely insincere or a total sap—or a terrible mixture of both.

Chrissie, though, seemed enthralled. "Is that right?"

"Really, they don't say that, do they?" Catherine asked, probably thinking whoever started that rumour must've seen a photo of her.

"Yes, had some of the most beautiful girls in Europe until the Vikings came and stole all the beautiful ones and shipped them off to Iceland."

"Hang on, they took the beautiful ones and left the others? What does that say about us, ladies?" Chrissie laughed, and Catherine, obviously realising he'd been teasing her, slapped him playfully on the arm.

It takes a lot of courage and charm to openly insult three Irish women and make them laugh at the same time, Laura thought.

"For God's sake, Chrissie. I thought it would be you keeping me and my staff from our beds and corrupting these young people. Off home with you, woman,"

Charlie's voice boomed from the hallway.

Laura looked at her watch. It was nearly one. She hadn't realized it had gotten so late.

"Charlie, you grumpy git," Chrissie stood up to greet him as he stepped into the room, "every time I come in here, you look older and grumpier. Come on children, I suppose we better leave this old man to his cocoa."

"I should go, too," said Miguel. "I just live up around the corner. Will you ladies be okay catching a taxi, or would you like me to wait outside with you?"

"We'll be fine. Charlie will call us one, won't you, handsome. And if we're good, he'll even let us wait in here in the warm until it comes with another wee vodka tonic for the road."

"You do push it Chrissie—anything to get rid of you, I suppose," Charlie turned and made his way downstairs again.

Miguel stood up and put on his coat. "It was very nice to meet you, Chrissie. Catherine, I hope you have a safe journey back on Sunday, and Laura, well, I suppose we'll see each other next Friday?"

"What are you up to the rest of the weekend?" Catherine asked.

So Catherine had obviously liked what she saw, and if Catherine set her mind on something, or someone, she had no qualms about unashamedly pursuing her target. It was a character trait that Laura admired and feared in equal measure.

"If you're not busy, why don't you join Laura and I for lunch tomorrow."

"Yes, I'd love to."

Of course he would, Laura thought, he was obviously enthralled by Catherine, but it was a bit cheeky of Catherine to drag her into it—she probably didn't want it to look like she was asking him out for a date—but then in the morning, Laura would get a message from Catherine asking her if it was okay if she didn't come after all, say she was sick or something.

"Let me take your number, then." Catherine pulled her BlackBerry from her bag and punched in her password. "Oh no."

"What?"

"I forgot I have a conference call tomorrow afternoon. I have no idea how long it's going to go on for."

Miguel caught Laura's eye, he looked stricken.

"Maybe we can meet after?"

"No, it's impossible, but you two go ahead."

Of course, Laura suddenly realised what Catherine was playing at. She should have known Catherine wouldn't be interested in anyone living here in town when she had all those men in London running after her. But that still didn't change the fact that he was obviously keen to see Catherine again.

"Don't worry," Laura jumped in, hoping to save him the embarrassment of having to find an excuse, "there's not really anywhere good to meet for lunch anyway. Catherine, this isn't London, you know."

"There must be somewhere, don't any of the pubs do food?" Miguel asked.

"No, they don't." Didn't he realise she was trying to give him a dignified exit from the trap Catherine had sprung for him?

"Well, maybe I could make us lunch at my place. Would you like that?"

"No, it's fine."

"Really I want to. Let me write down my address. Oh, I don't have a pen."

Before Laura had a chance to respond, Chrissie produced a pen and paper from her handbag. He handed her the note with his address. "One p.m.?"

Laura nodded. He leaned awkwardly over the table towards Catherine first, then Chrissie and finally he came to Laura, kissing her lightly on the cheek.

"Our little town is becoming very cosmopolitan," Catherine remarked when he was gone.

"Not sure one foreigner qualifies as cosmopolitan."

"I reckon he came here to find himself a nice Irish girl. Don't you think, Laura?"

She ignored Catherine and stared at the smoky embers dying down in the fireplace. She might have known Catherine would do something like this. She'd been talking about how she wanted to "find a good man" for Laura for months now. The poor boy hadn't been ready for Catherine's ambush and now he was stuck having to make lunch tomorrow. Maybe she could cancel, she looked at the note in her hands, he hadn't included a phone number, so to cancel she'd have to contact Mr. Quigley to get his number from him and she didn't relish the idea of explaining to Mr. Quigley why she needed it. There was nothing for it—she'd just have to go. He obviously didn't get to do enough *pro bono* work during the week—now he was taking on charity work at the weekend too.

CHAPTER ELEVEN

"¡Bienvenida!" It was a true welcome. His Spanish floated like a song, so different from his quite formal English. He helped her off with her coat and showed her through to the living room, which doubled up as a bedroom, telling her to make herself at home as he disappeared back into the hallway and off to the kitchen at the other side of the flat. Laura perched herself on the edge of the small sofa and looked around. The first thing that struck her was how homely it was. He'd only been here a week or so, but there were houseplants everywhere: tall plants with big leaves stood proudly in two corners of the room, little cacti huddled together in glee on the windowsill, trying to get warmth from the cold winter sun, plants snuggled up next to each other on the bookshelves and tumbled down the side of the fireplace. He had done away with overhead lighting, opting instead for carefully placed lamps to complement the greenery. The effect was wild and beautiful. The ceiling and the walls reflecting in shadows the plants back into the room, creating a wonderful dappled effect.

With just a few simple clues, the place quite firmly established who he was and what he was interested in.

There was a handful of books along the top shelf of the bookshelf: "A Dirty War: The Conflict in Northern Ireland," "A Testament of Hope: The Essential Writings of Martin Luther King," "The Mythology of Latin America," a book in Spanish called "El Conquistador" and finally a battered old copy of "To Kill a Mockingbird."

Above the bed was a huge film poster, a curvaceous woman with long blonde hair stood in the foreground of the picture, in front of a smoky royal blue background. "La Dolce Vita" was emblazoned in incandescent yellow across the bottom.

There were a few photo frames dotted around with friendly faces smiling into the room, and on the floor next to the desk lay a small record player and box of records. Without even being in the room, he had revealed so much about himself to her in just a few short moments. Her room, on the other hand, said so little about her, the only behavioural residue the books piled up next to her bed, waiting to be read. Did she really have so little to say about herself? She really didn't even have knick-knacks or mementoes, just that one photo of her mother on the desk taken just before she died. In it, her mother was standing on a rock by the sea, in long black trousers and a pretty white shirt. Her hair was covered with her favorite polka dot scarf that looked about to fly off. She was striking a pose with one leg slightly out to the side, hand on hip and her head slightly dipped. She must have been smiling, but she was wearing oversized glasses that obscured most of her face from view.

Laura had once read that there is a point in time when character becomes fixed forever, and that the tastes adopted then stay with us as the world changes around us. Our likes and dislikes act as subtle road signs in an increasingly new world pointing out the way back to the person you really are. She wondered what her tastes said about her. Whilst she had always liked film and books, she had studiously avoided becoming a fan of anything. She didn't even have a favourite novel, as if to express such preferences might be limiting. What was really limiting, she now thought, looking round the room, was to avoid liking anything too much, to avoid having a passion.

The door flung open again and Miguel reappeared with two tumbler glasses of red wine clasped together in one hand and the bottle in the other.

"No fancy glasses, but red wine is better this way, no? Held close like this. And, as you may have also noticed, I have no table, no chairs, no fancy tablecloth and no napkins."

"Mmm, do you have cutlery?"

"Yes madame! I do have cutlery, and along with the good wine, we have good music and some good food, or we shall see about the food, I suppose."

He handed her a glass and put the other one on the desk with the bottle.

"Now, music is what we need. How about we start with a local? Perhaps Van Morrison is a good place to start—or do you hate him, too, like your friend?" He sat cross-legged on the floor and flicked through the box of records.

"That's fine. To tell you the truth, I only really know a couple of his songs."

"Great, and maybe after that, I will fly you across the water and play some Colombian rhythms like cumbia, or back in time to the 1960s for some Curtis Mayfield."

She had never heard of him and bit her lip apologetically when he looked up to see if the name rang a bell.

"You will love him. Funky, soulful, political … ah, ha, here it is." He pulled a Van Morrison record up from the pile. The words "you will love him" struck her. It was compelling—the familiarity with which he assumed her tastes.

He teased the record from its sleeve and dusted it with

a soft cotton handkerchief. "I brought my iPod and dock, as it has thousands of songs on there, but I do love vinyl. I love the connection, the ritual of removing it from the sleeve, dusting it off, placing it on the turntable and then so carefully touching the needle down in the right place, enjoying that few minutes of crackling silence before the music starts. My record player and this small handful of records were among the few luxuries I shipped from Colombia. All great music should be listened to on vinyl, don't you think? Or am I sounding like a crazy person?"

"No, not at all." She watched him put on the record—she couldn't quite understand why, but the care he took, the gentle way he wiped the dust off the record first and the way he softly touched the needle down, made her feel safe.

"What does that sticker on the box mean?" she asked, pointing to a red and yellow sticker on the record box that said '*Colombia es pasión.*'

"It means 'Colombia *is* passion' it's a symbol of my country, a message. Basically it is who we are. They had a branding expert study Colombia, and passion was the word he decided defined us."

"And what do you think defines Northern Ireland? Is it conflict?"

"I wouldn't say that. Although people here do seem to enjoy a healthy discussion and exchange of opinions."

"Are you calling us argumentative?"

"That's your word, not mine! But I'm not going to disagree with you, just in case. Excuse me, I'm going to get the food."

Laura offered to help, but he told her to relax so she was left alone again amongst his few sacred possessions to ponder who this man whose food she was about to eat actually was. Feeling restless, she got up and walked to the window. On the windowsill, there was a photo of a young woman in a silver frame, sitting cross-legged on the grass with what looked like thousands of red roses in full bloom growing on a small hillside behind her. Laura couldn't help picking it up and examining it more closely. The girl was beautiful, glowing. Her hand was covering her mouth but you could tell from her eyes that she was smiling, and her smile was directed at the person on the other side of the lens.

Miguel came back into the room carrying two plates piled high with spaghetti Bolognese. Laura quickly placed the photo back on the windowsill. "Sorry, I was just admiring the frame."

"It was a gift."

"Who is she?" Laura wasn't sure why she'd come out with that question. What did it matter who she was?

"That's Natalia—just an old friend. Shall we eat?" He came up next to her and handed her one of the plates. Laura took it from him and returned to the sofa. As she was sitting down, she noticed him move the angle of the frame slightly so that the sun shone directly on it, catching the silver and making it shine.

Over lunch, she soon found out that her worries about them having nothing to say to each other were completely unfounded. He asked a lot of questions, and for someone who had said the Irish were argumentative, he had an opinion on everything. Passion was a word he used a lot. He had a passion for football, a passion for politics, a passion for music, a passion for Colombia. He talked about Colombia at length. He described it as a place full of joy and magic and colour. It sounded like a fantasyland.

Laura had not been so engaged in a conversation in a long time, and it was only when he asked her about growing up in Northern Ireland that she faltered and lost her way.

"What was it like? You know, growing up during the troubles?"

"I don't know. You just grow up wherever, don't you? You don't think about it."

"But the town must have been so different just fifteen or twenty years ago."

She shrugged.

"Did it affect you at all? Did you know anyone that was hurt—or anyone who was involved?"

"No. Probably. I mean, I couldn't name anyone, but God knows who was actually involved."

"That's the thing, isn't it? Everyone in a small town thinks they know everyone else, but when that level of underground activity permeates society, people really have no idea what kind of double lives their neighbours are living."

She didn't respond. All she could think about was how 'permeates' was such an elegant word for a non-native speaker. "When did you start learning English?"

"I've always been learning English. One of my earliest memories is my mother speaking English to me at breakfast."

"Really? You learned English from your mother?"

"No. Her English was terrible. Although at the time, of course, I thought she spoke better than the Queen."

"And why at breakfast?"

"I don't know, but that is the only time I can remember her speaking English to me. Breakfast was our time together. My father always stayed in bed as long as he could. He's always been impossible to wake up. So we would sit at the breakfast table, just her and me, and she would teach me English. I think breakfast was the only time of day that was suited to the few English phrases she knew. For example, 'Good Morning,'" he was now speaking in a slow, deliberate accent that was stronger than usual. "'How are you? Would you like eggs? Corn flakes? Juice? Have nice days.' She didn't know much more than that. But it was very sweet of her to pass on what little she knew."

"She must be very proud of how well you speak it now. Does she think it's all down to her?"

"I'm sure she probably is proud, wherever she is. She died when I was still quite young."

Laura's cheeks flushed red. "I'm sorry," she said instinctively. It had happened to her a few times when she started university—someone wouldn't realise and make some reference to her mother as if she were alive, and Laura would have to tell them that her mother had passed away and then wait for the inevitable 'I'm sorry.' It used to anger her that people had the arrogance to assume that both her parents were still alive and well, and then after they had blundered their way into her private life, they would quickly try to back out with a glib 'I'm sorry,' as if those two words would make everything okay.

"I was very young, but at least I have some memories of her, like the breakfasts in English. I can still hear her say 'Muff-een?' It's funny, the things you remember."

"That's true. Sometimes I'll hear a song and I won't have a clue who the singer is, but I'll know all the words because my mother had listened to it so often in the house."

"What kind of music did she listen to?"

"Country music, you know those songs that sound upbeat, but when you listen to the lyrics you realize they're about heartbreak or death or poverty or some kind of tragedy. She loved those, the sadder the better. And she liked traditional Irish music, too."

"Yes. That reminds me, we need more music!" He jumped up and put on another record, and suddenly the energetic fiddle and drums of a traditional Irish jig filled the room. "Mr. Quigley gave me this one—so what is it that you people call dancing?" He started jumping furiously up and down, probably making the people in the takeaway below fear for their lives.

"Yes, that's exactly what we call dancing," she laughed, "have you been taking lessons?"

He flopped down on the sofa next to her. "I think you might be making fun of me."

"What gave you that idea?" Laura asked, feeling herself relax further back into the cushion behind her.

As the afternoon turned to evening, a blue-black darkness settled in around the flat and Laura found herself feeling more and more snug in the corner of his sofa, facing him as he mirrored her pose just a foot away. He was quite entertaining. He had developed a mock Northern Irish accent, which sounded more like the West Country of England, but he seemed so proud of it she didn't mention this, and he used it to do hysterical impersonations of Mr. and Mrs. Quigley's bickering over Sunday lunch about whether the potatoes were cooked properly.

The hours passed with laughter and wine and gentle chitchat until somewhere in the far off distance, a phone started to ring. At first Laura barely noticed the noise, but it persisted, advancing closer, chopping through the protective haze that surrounded them until it struck her like a slap on the face.

"That's my phone. I have to get that," It could be her father calling. She jumped from the sofa and ran from the shadowy living room to the fluorescent hallway. The phone had stopped ringing by the time she pulled it out of her coat pocket. There were two messages from her father, one at five o'clock and another at seven asking her to pick up meat for tea that evening. The clock on the phone said it was 8:55. In the orange glare of the hallway, everything felt different; there were no stylized shadows to play in, and she felt a shudder of reality course through her. She walked back into the living room. The sofa was still firmly rooted in the centre of the room with the rest of the furniture sitting in its place, staring impassively on. So they hadn't drifted off to sea buoyed up on his tiny sofa with wine as their only provision after all.

"Miguel. I'm sorry. I'm going to have to go."

"Is everything alright?"

"Yes. It's just I didn't realise it was so late, and I should be getting home." Catching herself with her coat already on, she realised how rude it looked fleeing like this. "I mean, everything was wonderful, and I'll stay and help you tidy up, but I should go then."

"No, it's fine it's just a few dishes."

"No, really let me help," she said, gathering up the plates.

He took them from her. "I insist. You are my guest. How about I walk you home instead?"

"It's fine. Don't worry. I'm going to walk up to the main road and hail a taxi there." She really just wanted to get back home as soon as she could. Her father was no doubt sitting alone in the semi-darkness with only the flicker of the TV for comfort, probably worried sick that she'd been gone all day without getting in touch.

"Well at least let me walk you up the main road." He said, already reaching for his coat. Laura opened her mouth to protest again, but nothing came out.

As they passed through the town centre, he marvelled at the simplicity of the names: Main Street, Back Street and Riverside. "Don't you love how the names all describe exactly what they are? They're so honest. It's not like they're called Sycamore Street and there isn't a Sycamore in sight."

Laura had never really thought of it that way. "I think they just have boring names to reflect how boring it is around here," she said. "I remember my mother telling me she and her friends would spend their Saturday afternoons walking up Main Street, down Back Street and then along Riverside, until they hit Main Street again, and then they would turn and retrace their steps back along Riverside, completing the loop again and then turning."

"Why all the turning around?"

"She said they thought they might miss something happening behind them if they kept walking in the same direction all afternoon."

"How funny. It sounds like a musical with the chorus of townspeople spinning around at regular intervals to catch the potential excitement behind them, and in doing so, ironically, they miss cars smashing or lovers kissing in the direction they'd just turned from."

She smiled at the image, "I don't think there's anything to miss out on in this town."

They turned to walk along the river. It was black and shiny in the moonlight. A long-winged bird skated over it, the only other movement in the still night apart from their synchronized steps. Laura hugged her coat around her to escape the evening chill. She stole a glance at Miguel walking just a foot away—it now seemed impossible that they had been sitting so cosy and relaxed on his sofa less than half an hour before. They were almost at the bridge, which led to the main road out of town towards the housing estates—soon they'd be saying goodbye.

"Do you mind if we stop quickly?" He stopped at the end of the bridge and pointed across the road. "There's a picture that I've been wanting to take since I arrived." Following his gaze, she saw the epic bronze and steel structures that stood dominating the busy junction. There was a fiddler, a flautist, a drummer and two dancers standing sinewy and tall at eighteen feet.

"You know they've been here for so long you just get used to them. You start to not see them any more."

"They're magnificent. I see them from the bus every day going to and from work. Each time I pass them I see something new; their flat metal faces seem to change with the light. But don't you think they look at their happiest now, dancing and playing by moonlight?"

He was right, they did look happy.

"C'mon." He ran across the road to the middle of the roundabout where the structures stood and waved at her to follow. Laura stood on the edge of the footpath as car headlights spun around the roundabout. Miguel was just visible in the darkness in the middle, jumping up and down and calling to her. She felt something tremble inside her veins and she took a deep breath to still herself.

At the next break in the traffic, she stepped out and ran to meet him in the middle of the circle. She stood next to Miguel in silence, staring up at the giant dancers and musicians surrounding them, with the stars strewn across the sky behind them. Miguel moved away from her and started to gather a few rocks into a small pile at the edge of the circle.

"What are you doing?"

"You'll see." He said, perching rocks on top of each other. "Stay where you are." He got out his small camera and balanced it on top of the rocks, moved behind the pile and lay on the ground to look through the viewfinder.

"Do you carry that thing everywhere?" She called over.

"Yes, you never know when you might have a moment to memorialise."

"A moment?"

"Okay. All set," he said, clamouring up, brushing himself down and rejoining her in the middle of the circle. "Can you hear the music?"

"No. I can hear the cars, but that's it."

"You're not listening right. You have to listen past that. Are you ready for a moon dance?"

Laura looked at him and he held out his hand to her.

"No," she laughed.

"Why not?"

"Because, well, the cars and …"

"And what?"

"Well, this isn't what I do."

"Well it is now." He suddenly grabbed her hand and spun her out away from him and back in towards him.

"Miguel, no."

He held onto her hand even tighter and persisted to twirl her around, with gentle pushes in one direction and then the other, humming as he did it, a song that she thought she recognised.

He spun her out from him again and then back in, this time much closer than before, and he wrapped his arms tight around her waist, so that their cheeks were almost touching, as they swayed together from one foot to the next. She could feel his breath tingling on her ear. "I seem to find the happiness I seek when we're out together dancing cheek to cheek."

She pulled her face back and looked him in the eye. She knew those words. She opened her mouth to speak but, before she could say anything, he was kissing her and the words, all words, were forgotten.

And all the while, in the corner, every minute or so his camera clicked, capturing the steel structures bathed in moonlight, illuminated in parts by the passing traffic, and the two figures dancing in a blur at their feet, recording, as all photos do, a moment that is gone even before the shutter snaps closed.

CHAPTER TWELVE

Laura meets Cormac at a party Catherine throws when her parents are in France. It is the summer before their final year at school, and they are both seventeen. He spends most of the evening talking to both Laura and Catherine. There are four boys in his family, all close in age. The other three boys take after their mother and are darkly handsome, with a swarthy, gypsy look, but Cormac takes after his father instead, with dusty blond hair and eyes and skin so pale they are barely distinguishable from each other.

By two a.m., the party is dying down, with mostly couples remaining, taking advantage of the free house to disappear into bedrooms, bathrooms, cupboards; any quiet corner they can find. She tells Catherine she is going home, and to her surprise, Cormac offers to walk with her.

As they stroll along chatting, he moves closer to her. His advances are clumsy, at one point almost knocking her off the pavement. Just before they turn into her estate, he grabs her hand and pulls her into a dark alley way. She follows him, unsure what else to do, and there he wraps his hands around her waist and she feels his face lean closer to hers. His mouth tastes fresh like mint, and she remembers that he was chewing gum as they walked. She wonders if he has swallowed it or if he has saved it in his hands. They kiss for about half an hour, and then he walks her to her house, where they kiss again outside her front door.

They arrange to meet on Monday after school, and they walk around town chatting idly about nothing in particular. Over the next few weeks, Laura starts going to his house in the afternoons. His younger brother is always entertaining girls in their bedroom and his mother watches quiz shows in the living room, so they hang out in the kitchen. Now they barely talk, they mainly fumble around, feeling inside each other's uniforms, like the blind getting to know new and strange places by touch alone. At first he jabs at her, like he his urgently trying to find the right button in a panel of thousands. She knows what he is doing feels wrong, but she doesn't know how to direct him; even if she did know, she'd be too shy to say.

At the end of the school year, he accompanies her to her formal dance. She gets ready at Catherine's house, with Catherine's mother and aunts fussing around them. Her mother would have loved this moment; she loved dressing up.

Laura thinks Cormac must know what happened to her mother; the whole town does, but in the time they are together, he never mentions it. Nor does she. They never talk about anything important.

That summer, they get their A-level results, and Cormac doesn't do as well as expected; he doesn't have the grades to get into a university closer to home, so he has to go to England. They promise to write and call and see each other as much as possible. Before he leaves, he asks her to transfer to his university. She tells him she can't afford to go away. She knows as she says it that this is not the real reason.

Six weeks later, it is all over after a five-minute phone call from the hallway of his university halls. She never really expected much more.

During university, Laura kisses some boys at house parties, but it never goes any further. She occasionally stays over with friends who live near university on a Friday or Saturday night, but she never leaves her father alone for more than one night at a time. Always, no matter how hung over she is, she rises early and gets the first bus home to have a silent breakfast with her father.

There are always drugs at the parties: ecstasy, speed, sometimes acid. Drugs are readily available. They say that in the newfound peace, the country has become flooded with them, but this place was always fuelled by a narcotic paranoia. She is too afraid to try any of them, though. It's best not to take the chance. There might be some mental illness asleep in her brain, something genetic, that the drugs will wake up. Something that might cause her to do what her mother did.

At one party, a girl starts throwing up in the corner of the living room. Most people walk out in search of another room to party in. Some people don't even notice. Laura finds the girl a bucket, gives her some water and tries to clean up the mess, but the girl continues to wretch and shake. Laura goes to the kitchen, where most of the party has congregated, to find someone to help. The scene is reminiscent of a Munch painting: long faces, eyes wide and lifeless, chins dropped open to one side, the scream of narcotics roaring through their brains. She notices someone in the corner of the room drinking a beer. He's handsome, athletic, and looks just a little drunk, but otherwise he looks to be in control. Laura pushes through the crowd and asks him to help. Together they carry the girl into a taxi. The driver warns them that if she throws up in the taxi, they will have to pay for it.

They sit together in the hospital waiting room. He tells her his name is Ian. He is a trainee optometrist. He teases her about her plans to start teacher training after the summer. He laughs at the idea of her being a school ma'am, about having to be a good example for young minds. The doctors eventually return and tell them that the girl will be fine. When they leave the hospital, it is light outside. Ian invites Laura to walk with him through the city; he knows a good greasy spoon that will open soon where they can get an Ulster fry up. The city on an early summer morning is quiet and still. Halfway across the bridge, Ian points out a naval base much further down the river. He tells her the story of the German u-boats that surrendered to the British at the end of World War Two and sailed up the river into the base. Laura can't make out the base in the early morning mist, so he pretends to examine her eyes; he asks her to look up and down, left and right. He marvels at how her eyes change colour with the light, from blue to grey and back again. Then he tells her to close them so he can check the lids. With a rush of his breath, his lips brush her eyelids and move down and take her mouth. They do not go to breakfast; they go back to his house.

He quickly makes the bed, throwing magazines and clothes off it onto the floor before they fall into it, entwined together. Laura lets him take the lead and does not tell him that she has never been this close to anyone before.

For the rest of the summer, Laura's life becomes polarized between the silent hours at home with her father and those delicious hours in bed with Ian. She will be starting teacher training soon, and a life of her own suddenly feels possible.

The first month of teacher training is exhausting. There is so much reading to be done. On evenings that she spends at Ian's house, she has to study. She sits on his bed surrounded by her books and waits for him to come back from the pub or up from the living room where he is watching sports with his housemates.

One Saturday he finally takes her to the greasy spoon

for the breakfast he promised her that first morning. There, over a full Ulster fry, he tells her that it's not working, that he wants out, that they both knew it was always going to be just a summer fling, that she should concentrate on her course. He finishes his fry up with relish as her own remains untouched, congealing on the plate with a bundle of napkins stained with her tears resting on top. Afterwards Laura walks alone through the city, along the walls that have been witness to so much bloodshed.

In the coming years, there are occasional dinners, afternoon coffees and even a couple of blind dates, but when they touch her, all she feels is a clammy hand or a heavy arm. There is no adrenaline shot accompanying the touch until she meets Miguel.

CHAPTER THIRTEEN

It was incredible how fast she'd fallen. Even after a month, it was still happening, the inevitable force of gravity pulling her down. It felt exhilarating, like flying, but she could see the ground rushing up to meet her, and eventually she would hit it with a wallop. The impact was sure to be painful, but that's the thing about falling, once you start, you can't stop.

Random memories of their first month, strung together, were like a montage in a film. Although Northern Ireland didn't offer the most cinematic of backdrops: there was no sweeping park surrounded by skyscrapers, no tall buildings with observation decks and no star-filled observatory. There was, however, a great soundtrack, Miguel always made sure of that. "Rhapsody in Blue" was swirling through the air when they first cooked together, just six days after that first lunch.

Miguel pulled a bag of rice from the cupboard and started studying it, reading the packaging intently. Laura looked up from the carrots she was chopping, "Everything okay?"

"Yes, I'm just checking how this works."

"How it works?"

"You know, if you need hot or cold water."

He set the rice down and came to stand behind her, his arms around her waist. She could feel him rest his forehead on the small of her neck. She went to turn around but he held on to her, stopping her from moving.

"I have a confession to make," he murmured.

"What?"

"I have no idea how to cook," she loosened his grip and turned to face him, his head hanging in mock shame, and she could see a cheeky smile on his face.

"Come on, that's not true, that lunch you made me was delicious."

"Beginner's luck." He stepped back from her and leaned against the fridge. "I was so terrified about having to cook for you."

"Then why did you offer?"

"Because I really wanted to see you, and I didn't want to have to wait another week, so when Catherine mentioned lunch, I jumped at the chance, and I couldn't believe my luck when she dropped out. But then you, madam, start rambling on about how there's nowhere to eat, so I had to do something."

Laura revisited their conversation in the pub in her head. It was so strange to see it again now from his point of view.

"As soon as I got home from the pub, I called my grandmother to get a recipe. It was the middle of the night here, but I couldn't wait. Colombia is five hours behind, so if I'd waited until the next morning, it would've been too late."

"You called your grandmother? What did you tell her?"

"That I'd met a pretty girl and I needed an idiot-proof recipe to impress her. I'm sure her eyes popped right out at the idea of me cooking, they probably rolled along the floor like marbles, wide in amazement." He made a funny little gesture with his hand, chasing the imaginary wide-eyes along the floor.

"Can you believe it, twenty-eight and I needed to phone my grandmother to find out how to make spaghetti Bolognese —it's embarrassing, huh?"

"How come you never helped in the kitchen?"

"We always had maids—we still do."

Laura thought maids sounded like such an aristocratic word; she couldn't think of anyone she knew actually using that word, except maybe her mother, who used to ask "what did your last maid die of?" when her father asked her to make him a cup of tea.

"Oh… Well, you're learning now. Anyway, its no less embarrassing than me, about to turn twenty-six, and still living at home."

"Nothing strange about that. In Colombia, people often don't leave home until they get married."

Laura turned back to the chopping board. She wasn't at home because she was waiting around to get married.

"Did you ever think about getting your own place?"

"Not really. It's convenient living with my father," she lied. She picked up the bag of rice. "Now, shall I show you how this works then?"

"Why don't you go ahead—you seem like the expert, I'll just watch and learn," he smiled, leaning back against the fridge again. "Oh, and I meant to ask you."

"What?" Laura said. She didn't like surprises.

"When's your birthday?"

"Twenty-fifth of January. What about you?"

"Twenty-third of July. I'm a summer baby. I'll be back in Colombia by then." Laura felt his final words linger between them, as if watching her to see how she would react. She chose not to. She started to pour the rice into a saucepan.

"So you were born on the cusp," she said.

"On the what?"

"On the cusp of Cancer and Leo. It changes on the twenty-second and twenty-third of each month."

"Interesting. I was actually due on July twentieth, but I

was five days late, which is uncharacteristic. I've never been late for anything since then."

"So have you ever wondered what would have happened if you had been born on time? How would your life have been different if you had been born a Cancer instead of a Leo?" Laura asked.

"No, never. I don't believe in astrology. But you obviously do."

"No, not really."

"Yes, you do! Now tell me, how would life have been different if I'd been born a Cancer instead of a Leo?"

Laura folded her arms in front of her and thought for a moment, she'd read an astrology book last year and she tried to remember the characteristics of each sign. "Well, not that I really know anything about these things but Leos are supposed to be creative, and enthusiastic, and generous, and loving. Whereas Cancerians can be moody, and difficult to predict, and don't take responsibility for their actions. My father is a Cancer, but you are definitely a Leo, that must be why you hung on for those extra days."

"¡Mi pitufina! ¡Te adoro!" Miguel moved towards her, wrapping his arms around her like a duvet on a cold winter morning. She hadn't quite understood what he said but she knew that her answer should be "I adore you, too" but she couldn't bring the words out. So she kept her head on his shoulder and stayed quiet, hoping the words unspoken were enough. She felt him shift and snap back to life, and in her stomach she sensed another question coming.

"So what made you want to become a teacher?"

Laura moved back to the counter and picked up the saucepan of rice to fill it with water, her back to him once again.

"If you plan to work in a small town, teaching is an obvious profession," she said.

"And you always planned to stay?"

"I never looked to go anywhere else."

"Do you think you'll ever leave?" He was back on a roll

with his questions. Laura turned to face him. "Why did you become a lawyer?"

"Because I like to get to the truth, and I think the witness is avoiding my question."

"I'm not a witness, and don't I ever get to ask any questions?" she snapped.

"Fair enough, well, I enjoy the tasks that make up being a lawyer, the research, the writing, investigating, pulling pieces of information together, searching for the answer, finding evidence to support my proposition. And I suppose I had this idea that it was a noble profession."

"It is noble, what you do at the Tribunal, especially the way you help the victims. I know it was quite controversial that it took so long to do a proper inquiry, and not just a short inquest like they did at the time, but I suppose in a way it's easier for the victims to talk about it now that ten years have passed. Time heals all wounds, right?"

"No."

"No?" How could he disagree with that statement? Maybe he hadn't understood, she thought.

He moved closer and then reached behind her to pick up their glasses of wine. He handed Laura hers, and looking her straight in the eye, he clinked their glasses together. "Time doesn't heal anything," he said, "it's what you do with the time that matters."

CHAPTER FOURTEEN

At three o' clock in the afternoon, on the first Friday of December, night suddenly descended and the storm blew in from the Atlantic. Peter, alone in the living room, listened to the rain pounding down outside—it sounded like a thousand desperate joggers in tap shoes all running on the spot.

He pulled back the net curtains an inch and looked up at the brooding sky, then he let the curtains fall back in place and turned his gaze back in towards the living room. He'd lived in this council house since the day he was married.

When his mother died, being an only child, he had inherited the family home, and Diane had wanted to use the proceeds from the sale of his mother's house to move out of their rented council house and into a private development. But Peter preferred to stay where they were and stow the money away somewhere where it could grow steadily. They had argued about it for months. At the time, he thought he was sensible saving the money for the future. He couldn't have known that there would be no future, and that the only thing the money would finance would be him doing nothing at all.

He sat down on his chair and tried to ignore the howling of the wind outside. It felt like it was blowing the walls in, surrounding him, so that every detail of the room came into sharp focus—every hairline crack in the walls, every rusty hinge, every inch of the now-dated carpets Diane had picked out well over a decade ago, was achingly familiar—he knew it not through observation but through osmosis. Even now, images of Diane in these four walls haunted him—far-off looks, cryptic lines scribbled in a diary, an expectant smile, whispered phone calls, and they were everywhere he looked. But no matter how often he studied the clues, he could never locate the moment it had all gone wrong.

He often thought he should have taken Diane to Australia. In the year before she got pregnant with Laura, she read an article in the *Northern Ireland Enquirer* about a group of young couples who, tired of the troubles, had immigrated to Australia. For six months, she obsessed over the idea, going to the library to read all she could about Australia and nagging him to do more overtime at the factory so that they could save enough money for the visa. He was not so keen, though. It all sounded grand: the sunshine, the opportunity, the peace. If he had really killed himself doing overtime, he could probably have saved the money in about eighteen months. But he didn't want to go.

It wasn't that he minded the work and the saving, or even that he minded leaving his family and friends, but he worried about what would happen to them in Australia. In Northern Ireland, she was Mrs. Kennedy, there were witnesses to their marriage, but who knew who they would be if they left? He had procrastinated and stalled until she eventually gave up.

At the time he thought she'd forgotten about it, but in later years, she brought it up often, telling Laura that she could have been born in Australia. She constructed a whole parallel life for their daughter where the sun shone every day and they lived in a big detached house with a pool and ate outside from the barbecue as a family instead of on plates balanced on their knees in front of the TV. "But your father preferred this," she would say, sweeping her hand around the living room, looking at him like he had robbed them all of some better life.

She seemed to thrive on the feeling that she'd been hard done by, that someone else was living the life she deserved. It was never more obvious than when she was talking about the other side. Diane had no Protestant friends but still thought she was an expert on how they lived and, according to her, they all lived better than the Catholics. By some birthright, they all had bigger houses, better decorated, with nicer cars and fancier holidays simply because of the religion they had been born into. She resented silly things, like the bonfires on eleventh of July. "They shouldn't be allowed to light those fires," she'd grumble.

"I don't really care—as long as they don't come marching past my window throwing stones tomorrow, they can light all the fires they want," he had told her.

"It's what it all stands for, Peter. They are out there celebrating their tyranny over us."

"It's just an excuse for a party. That's all. Like us on St. Patrick's Day. We should get out there and celebrate the twelfth, too, you know, join the party."

"Do you think they'd let us, even if we wanted to? Which I don't, by the way. And take those bonfires. If I decided to take that sofa out and burn it in my own backyard, I'd have the police up here in a shot, telling me to put it out. But they're burning all sorts, left, right and centre, wherever they want. We don't have the same liberties as they do."

"Oh my God, woman. Are you trying to tell me that you want another new sofa?" He had joked, not that she'd seen the funny side.

"You don't understand, do you?" was her typical

response.

It was true, for almost twenty years they had woken up next to each other, sat across from each other at dinner and switched off the lights together at night, but he'd never known her. Rather than looking for the answer to their problems, he just tried to keep a lid on them. It was like the British policy of containment they used to talk about on the news. When things got bad, all he was capable of was restoring the impression of calm, and he was blind to the pressure that continued to build up underneath.

The hours passed, and the storm simply became more furious. Laura didn't arrive home at half six from work as usual. By eight there was no sign of her, so he decided to make himself some dinner. When the ten o'clock news started and the house still shook from the assault of the wind and rain and he still hadn't heard from her, he decided to call her mobile.

He put the phone to his ear and started to dial. Suddenly there was an almighty crack. In the same instant, the lights went out, plunging him into darkness and the phone burned red hot against his ear. He threw it from him and collapsed into a sitting position at the bottom of the stairs. He could hear a loud ringing in his ear. His hands were shaking. His heart was racing.

He pulled himself up slowly and went to the kitchen and felt around in the drawers for candles and matches. He examined his ear by candlelight, using a saucepan as a mirror—it looked okay, but he couldn't be sure.

He might need a doctor, but he wasn't going to touch the phone again, and who would he call anyway? He'd have to wait for Laura to come back, and then they could decide together what to do.

He sat down on his chair in the living room and stared into the darkness. He picked up a newspaper and tried to read it by candlelight, but it was useless; he couldn't concentrate enough to read a full sentence. As the hours passed, the noise in his ears subsided. He stopped worrying about himself and became more and more worried about Laura. She rarely stayed out all night, and when she did she always called him.

Dreadful thoughts started to race through his mind: car accidents, lightning, burst riverbanks, drowning. Peter had been here before, sitting up all night—waiting, watching the front door that never opened, listening for the turn of a key.

At six a.m., he heard Laura walk up the path to the house. When she came in, she looked surprised that he was still up.

"Where've you been?" Peter immediately heard his fear crystallise into anger.

"I couldn't get a taxi. With all the fallen trees no one wanted to come out, so I stayed with a friend. What's the problem?"

"And you didn't think to call me, to let me know not to worry."

"Well, I tried, but every time I called I just got an engaged signal. There must be a problem with the phone lines."

He remembered the phone lying off the hook in the hallway. "And you didn't think there might be something wrong here?"

"Was there something wrong here?"

"No, but you normally call, and on a night like last night especially."

"You could've called me if you were so concerned."

"Well according to you, the phone lines were down." He wasn't making much sense—he knew that.

"What would you have had me do instead? Walk all the way home just so you don't worry? I couldn't get through on the house phone! If you had a mobile maybe I could've contacted you, but what would be the point of you having a mobile?"

He knew what she was getting at. A mobile was useless to someone who never left his own house.

"That's the last time I'll lose any sleep worrying about you. Ungrateful wee bitch." The words were out before he could moderate them—he got up and walked straight past her, being careful not to look her in the eye. On his way through the hallway, he picked up the phone and gingerly replaced it on the receiver.

"For God's sake, why do you have to be so difficult?" she screamed, but he was already up the stairs, and the only way he could respond was to slam his bedroom door like a frustrated teenager.

CHAPTER FIFTEEN

After the fight with her father, Laura climbed the stairs and collapsed into her bed, not bothering to close the curtains or get undressed. She lay there listening to the small creaks of the house. She could hear her father move around in the next room, but she might as well have been in a hotel with a stranger padding around next door for all the comfort that gave her.

Outside, it was completely calm, with just a few wispy clouds floating across her window, giving no clue of the carnage of the night before. It had been such a stupid argument. Not really an argument, in fact, more like an attack. He had obviously been sitting there in his chair all night, plotting what he was going to say to hurt her. Anger started to build in her chest like a primal scream waiting to be unleashed. He was completely pathetic. She was his only link to the world. Didn't he realise that? Without her he'd be completely lost. Ungrateful? He was the one that should be grateful. She felt like shouting that through the thin walls. There were some truths he needed to hear. He needed to know that he couldn't just take her for granted. He couldn't assume she'd always be there to take care of him no matter what. She opened her mouth but the weight of her words choked her and the scream turned into tears.

As she struggled to catch her breath, her mobile started to ring. She reached for it from her bedside table—it was Miguel. She didn't want him to hear her in this state—she was happy when she was with him and she didn't want any nastiness contaminating that—so she let it go to voicemail, but it immediately started to ring persistently again.

"Hello," her voice crackled, hopefully he'd think it was because she'd just woken up.

"Hey. I thought you were going to call me when you got home. All okay?"

"I'm fine. I've been trying to sleep but I can't."

"I know what you mean, I've been missing you. I hated it that you had to leave so early this morning." That wasn't what she meant, but she didn't correct him. She hadn't yet had a chance to savour the memories of last night. "Why don't I come over to your place and I'll make you breakfast?" he said. "How does some smooth Colombian coffee, eggs scrambled with tomatoes and onions and thick chunks of French bread sound?"

"It sounds divine, but I'm not really that hungry."

"Is everything okay?"

"Yes."

He fell silent. Hopefully she hadn't sounded too sharp. Her father's bedroom door opened and then the bathroom lock clicked shut.

"I don't know. It's such a nice day outside. It would be nice to get out," she said.

"I'll tell you what, I'll ask Mr. Quigley to lend me his car and maybe we could take a drive to this famous Giant's Causeway that I've heard so much about."

A day by the coast sounded like a great way to clear her head. Miguel had borrowed Mr. Quigley's car a couple of times on the weekends now to drive to various tourist spots nearby. With Miguel as her guide, Laura felt like an explorer discovering a new land for the first time, even though she'd been to most of the places they visited many times before. Like Malin Head, the northernmost part of Ireland—a strange place of wonder and desolation. They had spent an afternoon walking hand in hand along the sweeping sand, under the white arctic sky, as Atlantic waves pounded against the shore.

"Yes, let's do that."

"I'll pick you up in a couple of hours then, hopefully they'll have cleared the fallen trees by then. Be ready," he said.

"I can come to you."

"No. It's okay. I'll be in the car, I'll pick you up. See you soon."

Laura was ready with thirty minutes to spare and sat watching out her bedroom window for him to arrive. Her father had gone back into his room a while ago and he hadn't made a sound since. As soon as she saw Miguel, she raced down the stairs and opened the door just as he was lifting his hand to ring the bell.

"¡Hola guapa!"

She had no idea what this meant, but it sounded joyous.

"Let me just put on my coat and we can go," she turned around to grab a coat from the hat stand behind her.

"That's a beautiful picture," Miguel pointed to the painting hanging on the wall behind her.

"Oh that? It's been there forever."

He stepped in past her to take a closer look. It was an oil painting of a lighthouse shining white and tall on top of a dark cliff, with a stormy sky in the background. The lighthouse looked almost ethereal in front of the dark, threatening clouds. In the bottom corner, on top of the sea, instead of the name of the artist a few lines of poetry had been scratched in black ink. He read it out loud:

"Nor fog, nor rain, nor stormy weather shall prevent
You shine
A straight strong arm of light
For me to reach out to
I forever Thine"

"Powerful. Where does it come from? Who painted it?"

"I don't know, it's been there for years." Laura shifted towards him, trying to get him to step back outside, but he didn't move.

"And you've never wondered? You never asked your parents?"

"No, well, maybe, I don't remember."

"And the poem, did the artist write that?"

"I don't know. Sorry. Shall we go now?"

"Yes, your carriage awaits."

In the car, Miguel announced that he wanted to take a slight detour on the way to the Giant's Causeway as Mr. Quigley had recommended they go to Greenan Fort, too. Laura didn't think the Fort was worth the detour, but she was happy just to be out of the house. On the way there, Miguel chatted aimlessly about some new band that he had just "discovered," leaving Laura to rest her mind. By the time they arrived at the Fort, she was no longer wound tightly like a ball of wire wool. Miguel had worked his magic.

They parked up and got out of the car. By the exit from the car park to the footpath, they stopped to read the information board. Miguel stood behind her, his arms around her waist and his chin resting over her shoulder. He was barely an inch taller than her, and his warm breath tickled her neck. The sign claimed the Fort was originally built sometime between 3000 and 1200 BC.

"Can you believe this has stood here for so many thousands of years? Look at it!" He pointed up to the Fort on the height, an almost perfect circle of imposing stone walls five metres thick and five metres high. "I can't believe it's so well preserved after all this time, that's amazing."

Laura didn't have the heart to tell him that it must've been restored in recent years by an overzealous tourist board. She had visited it as a child, and there were more imperfections in its construction back then, more holes in the walls and one part of the circle had been missing altogether.

"Mr. Quigley told me it was supposed to be on top of a mountain."

"It is on top of a mountain." She joked.

"In Colombia, that's a hill. I could walk up there in less than ten minutes."

"You think so?"

"I'll show you." Miguel kissed her on the side of the neck and started striding up the hill. Laura followed, climbing much more slowly, watching how he moved as he raced ahead; he took long, confident steps. He was strong, wiry, with defined muscles and a narrow waist.

The images of him naked on top of her last night came flooding back. They'd spent the evening talking and laughing and sampling his small selection of Irish whiskey, glasses of deep gold liquid cradled in their hands, letting the homely aromas of peat and cherry wood intoxicate them as the wind howled outside. It had happened so gently. He moved so easily around her with his lips, from hand, to neck, then further down, dispensing with her clothes with such light fingers. He took his time, building the anticipation until he was inside her, moving intuitively, banishing her thoughts with his touch. Remembering it now her cheeks flushed red and hot against the cool breeze.

"Can you believe that these walls have stood in this spot since before Christ?" He said when she finally reached him at the top. "Since before a time when there were Catholics and Protestants, before there were any

Christians at all?"

She'd never thought of the Fort as a relic from some magical time before history began. "And what do you think they used the Fort for?" she asked.

"To protect themselves."

"From who? They were all the same back then."

"No they weren't. Some people were out here and some people were in there. That makes them different. Sad, isn't it?"

"And what's even worse is, that was four thousand years ago and things have hardly changed since."

They wandered around the inside of the fort, climbing its walls and taking in the sweeping countryside views around them, and then soon she was back in the passenger seat next to Miguel, relaxing back as he drove them along the bendy costal road.

"So when is your next interview for Survivors' Stories?" she asked.

"Next week. I'm meeting a Catholic woman. When she was seventeen, she went out with a local policeman. Someone put a car bomb under his car when he was round at her parent's house for Sunday lunch. He died instantly."

"That's awful."

"It gets worse. Apparently she was standing waving him off and was hit by some shrapnel and lost an eye. You know what the worst part is? After it happened, people in the town used to jeer at her and call her Popeye because they still hated her for having gone out with a Protestant policeman. Isn't that sick?"

"I don't know how you do it. I don't know how you can hear these things day after day and not get totally screwed up."

"Of course it affects me. I'd be lying if I said it didn't. But it gives you some perspective on life, too. You can't let the world get you down, there's too much in life to enjoy."

Laura made a noncommittal sound in response and

stared at the road ahead. Miguel went on, "I mean, there are so many small moments of absolute bliss that remind you no matter what happens, it's good to be alive. Like the sound of coffee bubbling in the morning, for example."

"Bubbling coffee tells you something about the meaning of life? Really?"

"Yes, aren't there any small moments when you just think yes—this is what life is all about—these moments."

"I don't know."

"After my mom died, they found her agenda and instead of appointments she had a long list of simple things that brought her joy. She would add to it each day: the cheesecake from the bakery on Eighty-first Street, watching people walk their dogs in the park, the sound of the waterfalls close to the country house where my grandmother grew up. There were hundreds of them."

"And what's on your list?" Laura asked, satisfied that they were in the realms of the trivial.

"Well, off the top of my head? Let me think ... Listening to a song over and over until I'm almost sick of it then, months later, accidentally hearing it fresh again and falling in love with it all over again. Eh, what else? Taking a really good photograph just seconds before the light disappears ... Hearing Colombians speak proudly about their country."

Laura racked her brain for something similar that she could offer up to him, some small insight into her psyche. "I suppose for me it would have to be browsing in bookshops."

"I've noticed, you go through more books in a week than I do in a year!"

"That's not true. I wasn't always such a big reader, though. When I was young, I never really read that much—I used to watch old black-and-white films on TV every day after school. Fred and Ginger were my favourite."

"You know, Fred and Ginger made less than ten films

together."

"That can't be right, it must have been closer to a hundred, they were always on TV when I was growing up."

"And what was the big attraction?"

Laura fell silent, recalling the afternoons she spent with her mother after school watching those films. When she got home from school, her mother would make a pot of tea and they'd eat chocolate biscuits and sit on the sofa together, watching and singing along when they knew the songs. Her mother could never stay until the end, because she always had to rush off to the twilight shift at work that started at seven p.m.

It was the apparent simplicity that was the best thing about those films. They presented such a deliciously uncomplicated view of life where the boy always gets the girl and everyone has a wise one-liner up their sleeve for every occasion. Where it is so easy for people to say, "I love you." Laura smiled just thinking about the escapism of it all, as if she needed any escapism back then. She wondered if that was why her mother had also enjoyed them so much.

"So?" Miguel prompted.

"I suppose the music, the dance, the art deco sets, the glamour, Ginger's glorious dresses. I just loved how they used to glide around together in complete harmony."

"I don't think it was all that harmonious—truth of the matter is that he was a bit of a nightmare to work with, you know it took days of practice and hard work and quite a bit of camera trickery to make it all look so effortless."

"And I thought I was the realist out of the two of us!" Laura laughed, "stop ruining it for me by telling the truth!"

By the time they arrived at the Giant's Causeway, the cool morning sun had given way to a gloomier afternoon. The coastal wind hit Laura with a bitter slap as soon as she got out of the car. She wasn't sure if it was such a good idea, visiting the Causeway in winter. To really appreciate it, you had to climb quite far out to the edge by the sea, and the weather was so changeable this time of year, if the wind picked up speed they could find themselves being beaten by the high waves. Miguel looked so eager, though, and they had travelled all this way, so she kept quiet and hoped for the best.

Almost halfway out, Laura stopped to take in the waves ahead, dark and unrelenting. "Maybe we should just turn around here," she said.

"Go back now? But we've come this far."

"I know, but I don't like the look of things up ahead. Look at those waves."

"Don't worry, it'll be fine. I'll protect you."

Easier said than done—if she fell in, he might or might not be brave enough to jump in after her, but what good would that do? She was sure they'd both then end up being beaten against the rocks like raggedy dolls.

"It's okay, follow me," he said, coaxing her along. "I just want to get a bit further out so I can get a good picture of the causeway looking back towards the land."

Miguel was already far too close to the edge. It was no use, though. There was no talking to him, so she ignored the sick feeling in her stomach and walked on. When he finally came to a stop, they were barely six feet from the edge, and the rocks beneath their feet were wet and slippy, but Miguel didn't look remotely concerned about their proximity to the sea, he just snapped away with his camera.

"It's like a work of modern art isn't it? So uniform," he enthused.

"It doesn't feel natural, does it?"

"So tell me, how were these odd geometric shapes formed?"

"Finn McCool." It was the only explanation that she knew. Miguel gave her a questioning look. "The Giant Finn McCool. He built it, hence the name Giant's Causeway," she went on, "Finn had a great rivalry with another giant, Benandonner, across the sea in Scotland. The two giants were always shouting at each other across the water, you know, acting the big men that they were. So one day Finn challenges Benandonner to a fight, but Benandonner says he can't swim across."

"Ah, the old 'I'd whip your ass if only I could swim across there' line."

"Exactly. Not such the big man if he can't swim. But then neither could Finn, so Finn starts grabbing pieces of volcanic rock and throwing them out into the sea to create a pathway for Benandonner to cross over."

"That was very generous of him."

"So anyway, there was no way Benandonner could say no to the challenge then. But while Benandonner was on his way across the sea, Finn ran back to his house and dressed himself up as a baby. When Benandonner got across and saw the size of Finn's supposed baby, well he freaked out thinking how big Finn must be if that's his baby, and he fled all the way back to Scotland, destroying the causeway as he crossed the sea to prevent Finn from following him. Benandonner never bothered Finn again, and the remains of that walkway are what we're standing on now."

"So you Irish aren't as stupid as people think then, are you? Although I have just one question."

"What?"

"If Finn used his bare hands to pull up the rock, why are the rocks hexagonal and not like giant hand shapes?"

"Always the lawyer, aren't you? Asking questions and trying to find holes in the story. Why can't you just accept this as historical fact?"

"Mmm, I think I might need to talk to someone in Scotland about this, just to get both sides of the story."

"Huh, last time I go to the effort of teaching you anything!" Laura turned her back to him, feigning disgust, with a smile on her face. Suddenly she felt Miguel rush towards her from behind, throwing his arms around her in a massive bear hug. At the same time there was a whoosh of the waves right next to them. The weight of his affection was too much, and they both lost their footing and fell forwards on to their knees.

"God, Miguel. Be careful. I knew we'd come too far. You nearly knocked me in!"

She looked around. Miguel was sitting on the rock behind her, almost soaked from the spray. And he was laughing!

"Oh, I do love you when you are angry. In fact, I love you all the time."

Where had this come from? "Ugh, right," Laura said, struggling to get up without slipping again. Miguel stayed where he was.

"'Ugh, right' wasn't exactly the reaction I was hoping for," he smiled up at her.

This was her chance, she could recover the situation. She could smile and tell him she loved him back. She looked out past him towards the sea. Her face was frozen still, a few droplets of the salty spray splashed across it.

"Listen, forget I said anything," Miguel got to his feet. He looked angry, but what did he expect from her? It was easy for him, he could come here and say and do what he liked; none of it mattered to him, this wasn't his real life.

"C'mon, let's get back to the car," he reached out for her hand and she took it, letting him guide her back towards the shore in silence, leaving the waves to thrash the rocks behind them.

He was just in front of her, clasping her hand in his, but it felt like he had run far ahead of her, well out of earshot.

CHAPTER SIXTEEN

Miguel rubbed his eyes and looked up from his papers. In front of him, Aoife's long red hair tumbled down her back. They were the only ones left in the office. Everyone else had left for the day, their computer screens blank, their identical blue chairs pushed under their desks, which had been cleared, and their documents locked in the large case rooms down the hall. Despite the clear desk policy, the remnants of the day's investigation was all around in the colourful timelines drawn on the whiteboards, marking out with horrific brevity the basic chronology of that day. Numerous handwritten observations scribbled with marker pen on yellow Post-it notes had been stuck on the walls in neat rows. From where Miguel sat, it looked like a patchwork quilt, a seemingly pretty mosaic that recorded the details of the carnage.

Miguel still had his folders piled high in front of him. He'd been stuck at the same page of the hospital reports for about half an hour. Convoluted medical terms floated in front of him. It was all just more information waiting to be elevated to the status of fact, assuming it even made its way into the Tribunal's final report by way of a footnote or an exhibit.

An old TV show came into his mind. It was about a group of law students, interns at a big New York firm, who were always instrumental in solving the case for the partners. The opening credits showed hundreds of files in boxes with the eagle-eyed interns rifling through them. In the show, the key to the case was always hidden in some document. The interns would run around talking to witnesses, checking out the scene of the crime, and then suddenly remember some inconsistency with something they'd read and that would crack the case. They'd go through telephone records or bank statements with a highlighter pen marking out patterns, finding some undeniable, empirical evidence that would stump the lying witness at the end and force them to confess. Miguel had always been attracted to this idea of being able to find the one fact that everyone else had overlooked that would throw open the door on the truth.

The reality of being a lawyer was very different, though. Especially at the Tribunal, where there were never any answers, just greater and greater levels of detail, leading to more and more questions. As far as Miguel could see, the Tribunal had no budget to constrain it; it had unfettered rights to delve as deeply as possible into the facts, looking at the minutiae of every second of that day. It wasn't going to make a difference if he finished reading these reports today or tomorrow, or ever. He shut the file and sat back in his chair. Aoife was pulling photographs from a box, glancing at them and then throwing them into another box at her feet.

"So, tell me, who's idea was it to get a bunch of lawyers—many of whom charge by the hour—and tell them to leave no stone unturned?"

Aoife stopped what she was doing and turned to look at him. "Not you as well."

"What?"

"Investigation fatigue. Everyone gets it at some point."

"It's just depressing to think I've been here now for

nearly two months and we've not had a breakthrough. I heard the other day that they think it's going to be another two years before they start writing the report. I'll be long gone by then."

"Stephen has a theory that they want this to be never-ending, so by the time we publish our findings, the world will have moved on. That's why it took so long to constitute the Tribunal and agree on its scope, and why we've committed to looking at every single damn shred of so-called evidence that comes our way."

"Sounds like you have investigation fatigue, too."

"Maybe," she muttered and returned to her pile of photos.

Miguel stood up and went over to her desk. "So what's keeping you here until this time then?"

"The world may well have moved on by the time we publish – but the families won't. Here, look at this." She threw a photo of a young, smiling bride on the table in front of him. She looked so excited, gripping onto her father, a gleaming white dress to her feet and purple flowers in her hand. Miguel recognized the street scene behind her. The back corner of the red car was just visible in the background.

"Did she …?"

"No, the bomb went off just seconds after she walked into the church. But she's suffered post-traumatic stress for years. And she's one of the lucky ones."

"Let me give you a hand," Miguel stood up and started looking through the photos. He looked at about five or six photos in a row and dismissed them all as irrelevant. They were all of the wedding guests. The photographer had obviously asked them to pose as they arrived at the church.

"A, what exactly are you looking for? They're all standing with the church behind them, so they must be facing the site of the bomb."

"How long are you going to call me A?"

"You're name is too hard. I'm going to start a

campaign to get some eastern European languages to donate some consonants to Gaelic. Maybe you can help by giving up those excess vowels you have in exchange."

Aoife smiled up at him and leaned back in her chair, pulling her hands through her hair. "I don't know what I'm looking for. All these people are sending us stuff, wanting their experience of the day to be heard, and it just seems important to acknowledge it. But you're right, Aideen McHugh's wedding photos don't prove that the police knew about the bomb two weeks beforehand. They don't show that cuts in the ambulance service meant there was only one available locally that could get there in time. It doesn't tell us the names of the bastards who did this. Let's just call it a night."

Miguel went to place the photo in his hands back in the box when he noticed something, a man standing at the edge of the photo carrying a video camera.

"Who's this guy?' Miguel said, pointing at the picture.

"Dunno, a guest, I suppose."

"Did we get his video?"

Aoife stood up and started rummaging through the box on her desk. "Nope, all we have from the bride are these official photos."

"Do you think he might still have the video?"

"Dunno, I suppose—aw, Miguel, don't go searching out more of this crap for us to look at."

"You were just trying to convince me how important it is to look at everything."

"Well don't start listening to what I say!"

"It's a line of enquiry. A, we have to follow it."

"No we don't, we're not police officers investigating a crime. We're gathering facts, learning lessons. And anyway, the wedding started at one p.m. We know the car was already there by then, we know it was driven in earlier that morning. Please, I have enough on my plate as it is. Like you were saying, the more we know, the further from the truth we get."

"Well I didn't put it like that … but," she looked at him, pleading with her big green eyes, "Okay, you're right."

"So you'll drop it?"

"Yes."

Aoife eyed him with suspicion. "Promise?"

"Promise."

She smiled at him and started clearing her desk.

"Listen, why don't you go make me one of those amazing Irish cups of milk with a dash of tea in it and I'll help you clear up," Miguel said.

"Okay, fair deal." Aoife stood up and headed out the double doors towards the kitchen. Miguel watched her go. As soon as she was out the door, he grabbed the notepaper that had come in the box with the bride's contact details and stuffed it into his pocket.

CHAPTER SEVENTEEN

The next morning, Miguel sat at his desk with the phone at his ear. Light poured in from the windows up near the ceiling, and around him, the daily symphony of the Tribunal played. Some interns leafed through documents and murmured into Dictaphones, all following the same dull melody, others tapped out notes on their keyboards, the photocopier humming in the corner provided the base and the clinking of teaspoons in cups and the occasional frustrated slamming of the door was the percussion. Miguel watched the door, willing the bride to pick up the phone before Aoife arrived back from the morning biscuit run.

Finally there was a click on the other end of the line. "Hello."

"Mrs. McHugh?"

"Yes."

"I'm calling from the Hudson Tribunal."

"Oh, did you get the photos okay?"

"Yes, thank you."

"Did you want me to come in and give another statement? Like I said, I didn't see anything unusual. It was my wedding day. I was too busy looking at my daddy—

hoping he wouldn't cry—he was such an old sop. But maybe there's something significant that I haven't thought of."

Miguel tried to interject, but he wasn't quite sure what to say. It was so much easier when people were close, when he could reach out his hands to them.

She went on. "The limo driver mentioned that there had been a bomb scare—but he said not to worry as it was way up the other end of the High Street—but people could still get in down the church end. I remember seeing crowds of people just milling about when we pulled in to the street. Sure, we were so used to bomb scares by then— I never thought it would go off—not then—not when the peace process had been going so well—and then just as I'm starting down the aisle, boom, it goes off just across the street—where we'd just passed all those people in the car. So many of those faces that were just a blur to me, just background on my wedding day, well, they were gone." She stopped and drew a long breath.

"So …" Miguel could see Aoife walking down the corridor towards the kitchen with the shopping bag in her hand. He needed to wrap this up quickly, but how could he get down to the business end of the conversation without sounding insensitive? "Thank you Mrs. McHugh. I think the statement we have from you is sufficient, but we'll keep that under review." He sounded like a robot. He had heard other people placate witnesses with meaningless phrases like that, and now he was repeating them. "The reason for my call is that I was wondering if you might have a film of the wedding? I saw one of the guests holding a camcorder."

"Yes, my uncle Tommy did take one, although in the end it was just the guests as they were arriving. I tried to watch it once a few weeks after the wedding, but I couldn't bring myself to. He's been saying for ages that he must put it on DVD for me because there were lots of nice messages on there. If you think it would be helpful, I'll get a copy."

"Yes, umm, please do that." Aoife was now coming back into the room. Thankfully, she stopped to talk to a girl who was just heading out the door. "Can I give you another address to send it to? Do you have a pen?"

Miguel gave Mrs. McHugh his home address, speaking as quietly as he could without arousing Mrs. McHugh's suspicions. She seemed to accept his explanation that it might take some time for them to sort it and classify it before it got to him at the Tribunal, so it was better to send it to his home address so he could review it faster. He quickly said his goodbyes and put the phone down just as Aoife was getting back to her desk.

"Hope you got the chocolate chip cookies this time," he said.

"Of course," Aoife said, "anything for my favourite colleague."

Miguel picked up the phone and dialed Laura's number. He was done being mad at her, he wanted to see her now and tell her about his day at work. Their trip to the Giant's Causeway had been only two days ago, but he looked back on it now with new eyes—he could see her standing on the shorefront terrified and shaking. He could see now that it hadn't been the right time or place for grand declarations, but there was a place where she might be more comfortable, a place he'd been meaning to take her for a few weeks now. He willed her to pick up, but her phone just rang and rang until it eventually clicked to voicemail.

CHAPTER EIGHTEEN

"There's a bus at half four today to Derry. Can you be on it and I'll meet you there?" Laura deleted the message and dialled Miguel's number. No answer, he was probably in a meeting, but she hung up and tried again anyway—still it just rang and rang. She snapped her phone closed and gathered her things for her last class of the day.

It was with her A-level group. She checked her lesson plan; today they were going to discuss Gatsby's relationship with Daisy. It was about time they changed the curriculum, Laura thought. She'd been having this discussion since she was sitting in their place studying for her A-levels.

Laura kicked off the discussion and then sat back and let the girls debate it out between them, whilst she let her mind wander to what Miguel might have in store for her today. He'd been distant and brooding in the car on the way back from the Giant's Causeway, and she hadn't heard from him yesterday, but his message had sounded easy and casual, which is how she liked it.

"Please Miss, can you tell her that's ridiculous."

Laura focused in on Chloe, who'd just called to her.

She realised in her daydreaming about Miguel she'd completely lost the thread of the conversation. Hopefully, she'd nodded a few times so the girls would at least think she'd been paying attention.

"Well every opinion is a valid one, and the examiners are looking for independent thought, so I can't tell you what's right and what's wrong." It was the perfect escape from a potentially very embarrassing situation. Hopefully, today was not the day the girls started taking her advice. The examiners, for all their talk of independent thought, had a list of interpretations that they considered to be correct. If it wasn't on that list, then it really was wrong as far as they were concerned.

"But he's not just trying to prove something. She's his first love; he'll never love in the same way again. Isn't that right, Miss? You never get over your first love."

"Well, in a sense Daisy does represent an ideal for Gatsby that he can't quite give up on." Laura drew in a deep breath; all the girls were staring at her waiting for her to go on, they didn't look convinced. She knew she sounded like something straight out of Cliff Notes, but how was she supposed to give an honest critique of the lives of fictional characters when her own life had less dimensions than the one on the page?

"But she's more to him than just a symbol, she's a part of his identity," Chloe whined.

"We're going to have to pick that up tomorrow, Chloe. I've got a dentist appointment, so I need to finish five minutes early," It wasn't a complete lie; she did need to finish early if she was going to make that bus.

As the bus pulled into the station, Laura saw Miguel's happy face distinguish itself from the hundreds of layers that he had wrapped himself up in.

"We Colombians are not engineered for this cold!" He said when she got off the bus. He pulled down the scarf that was masking his smile and moved close to kiss her.

"And you think we are?"

"Okay, no one is engineered for this cold—we should get moving then." He grabbed her hand and steered her left out of the bus station into a small cobbled side street. Strings of delicate white Christmas lights zigzagged across the street above their heads, lighting their way.

"You look pretty today. I like that scarf. The colour fits your eyes," Miguel said. Laura picked up the ends of the green and white polka dot scarf she was wearing. It was silk, so not really designed for winter, but it kept her covered up.

"Thanks, it was my mother's. She loved this scarf, she wore it all the time." Laura remembered finding it hanging over the radiator in the living room after her mother had died. Her mother had handwashed it the day before she killed herself. It had always struck Laura as strange that someone who was about to end her life could concern herself with something so trivial as laundry. She shook the thought from her mind. Now wasn't the time for wondering what her mother might have been thinking as she planned her own death.

"So are you going to tell me where we're going?" Laura asked. She'd never been up this way before. Without the festive lights, it usually just looked like a dark alleyway that was best avoided.

"Patience." He turned around and walked backwards up the hill so that he was facing her. "All I can say is that I'm taking you to a little place that you probably know already, but I want to introduce you to someone there who you may not know."

"It all sounds very mysterious. You're taking me somewhere to meet someone who I may or may not know—got any more details than that?"

"No, not right now. It'll all become clear very soon." He looked like he was enjoying keeping her in suspense.

At the top of the hill, Laura saw a small sign for the International Café jut out from the city walls. Miguel pushed open the door and motioned for her to pass. Inside, she was immediately warmed by the sweet-smelling air in the cosy café.

"Is this new?" Laura asked.

"Apparently, it's been open over ten years."

Embarrassingly, Laura had studied four years in Derry, which was really just a big town, and she'd never come across this place. She slipped off her coat and stood, taking in the place, as Miguel unwrapped himself from his various layers and hung them on an old hat stand by the entrance. The café was tiny. It had five bright red tables with white Formica chairs. Along one wall, there were large black and white prints of famous landmarks around the world. The other wall was lined floor-to-ceiling with bookshelves with various sliding wooden ladders reaching high up to the books at the top. In the right-hand corner was an alcove with a hand-painted sign that said "Reading Room" hanging over it. In the back left-hand corner was a narrow counter with a gleaming coffeemaker. A man stood frothing milk, and in front of him on the counter sat a line of inviting cakes decorated with citrus-coloured icing.

The man waved at Miguel and turned off the steam. Miguel guided her towards him. "Laura. I'd like you to meet François —François this is Laura."

"Lovely to meet you," François said in a velvet French tone, coming out from behind the counter to greet her with two kisses. "You are freezing! You must have something to warm you up fast! One of my regular customers kindly brought me back some Masala Chai from a trip to India. Would you like to try?" François took up his place back behind the counter and went on. "It all sounds exotic, but guess who makes it? Tetley!" he announced pulling the familiar blue package down from the shelf behind the counter. "But it's much better than the Tetley tea here, it has ginger and clove and cinnamon and all kinds of spices, perfect to warm you up on a miserable day like this."

"It sounds delicious," Laura said, instinctively reaching for Miguel's hand. Even though they'd just come in from near-freezing temperatures outside, Miguel didn't feel cold to the touch. No matter what, he always radiated a comforting warmth.

"Go on through to the Reading Room. I'll bring it through."

Miguel prompted Laura to go ahead in front of him. She stepped through the low-ceilinged alcove, tilting her head down to get through. On the other side, it opened out into a huge room with a high glass ceiling. Laura walked around the edge of the room. The walls again were lined with books, not quite as high as the glass ceiling but still high enough to necessitate a ladder to reach the top shelves. There were clusters of lounge chairs and coffee tables dotted around the room. Each cluster was separated into its own private space by standalone bookshelves that formed protective fences around each seating area. A few lone students lounged in the chairs, lost in reading with empty coffee cups on the tables in front of them. The early evening moonlight falling in from the glass ceiling was complemented by reading lights, which stood behind each chair, peeking over the readers' shoulders in silent curiosity.

"This place is gorgeous," her voice was almost a whisper.

"I thought you'd like it. Have you never been here before?"

He looked so proud.

"No. God, I didn't even know it existed! What a find!"

François came in, left a tray of tea on one of the tables and slipped away quietly.

"It's nice. You can browse, you can sit and read a book here in the reading room and have coffee and cake. With your passion for literature, I thought you'd enjoy it."

Was she really passionate about literature? She'd dedicated a lot of her life to reading, studying and teaching it. But what did it mean to have a passion for something? She moved around the edges of the room, lightly touching the rows of books that surrounded them. She felt Miguel's eyes on her; he was beaming. It was like he'd conjured this place up to order especially for her. And in a way, it felt like he had.

Laura studied the titles of the books. None of them seemed to be in a language she understood. "So does this place sell any books in English?"

"Well I guess it's mainly for foreigners. I hunted this place down because I started missing reading in Spanish. And it's not that I'm lazy—well maybe a bit—but it's just so much more pleasurable reading in your own tongue, you can get lost in the story without having to concentrate on the meaning of the specific words all the time. But don't worry, there are English translations hidden amongst the melting pot. François can find them."

Laura sat down where François had left their tea tray. There weren't any teacups on the tray, just tiny glasses with an emerald rim, so she poured the rich gold tea into them. She picked up her glass and sipped it slowly, enjoying the fragrance that came with each sip. Miguel fell down into the huge armchair opposite her.

"You know, you would love Bogotá."

"Really? Why's that?"

"Well, there are hundreds of reasons actually. But I was still on the subject of books. Bogotá was the world capital of books a few years ago in recognition of our world-class libraries. Also, there are literally thousands of bookstores—one on every corner—just like pubs here."

"That I don't believe."

"You're right, there's nothing like pubs here. But there are a lot of bookstores, although come to think of it, it's nearly impossible to find books in English or any language for that matter that's not Spanish. We could do with a place like this."

"No good for me then, I guess."

"Well, until you learn Spanish, that is."

Laura looked up at the ceiling. Outside it was covered in sparkling droplets of rain tumbling down the glass panes. "Looks like the rain is getting heavier. It's a good thing we got in just before it started." Her eyes dropped to Miguel opposite her—he was staring, like he was searching her face for something. "François seems nice. Is that who you wanted me to meet?"

"No." Miguel shook his head and blinked, as if waking himself up. "Come with me." He took her glass from her and sat it on the tray and led her to a bookshelf on the other side of the room. "This" he said, waving his hand up and down a section of the wall "is Gabo."

Laura scanned the section of the bookshelf Miguel was stood next to. It was dedicated to one author— Gabriel García Márquez. There were copies of his books in about ten different languages.

"This is our Nobel prize winner."

"I have heard of him, although I'm afraid I've spent far too much time studying English literature, it's given me tunnel vision. I've never read any of his books."

"Pick one and I'll get it for you—an early Christmas present."

"How do I know what I want? I don't understand any of the titles?"

"If you pick one of the Spanish titles, then I'll ask François to check in the storeroom for the English translation."

"But you're missing the point. If I don't understand it, then how will I know which one I want?"

"I guess you will just have to judge the book by its cover. No?"

Laura smiled and moved closer to the bookshelf, running her hand along the multicoloured spines. Her fingers came to rest on the title "El amor en los tiempos de cólera." She recognised the word "love," but she couldn't make out the rest of the title. She eased the book out from the tightly packed row and examined it. The cover was of a young woman lying naked in a garden, staring out at the reader with passive brown eyes. The garden was thorny and wild and overgrown, and in the background was the figure of a man in a dark suit peering into the garden through a black wrought iron gate, watching the girl from a distance. She found the cover image disturbing and was about to return the book to the shelf when Miguel snatched it from her.

"Excellent choice. Your instincts are very good."

"But I'm not sure yet."

It was too late; Miguel had already disappeared with the book into the other room. Laura took her seat back at their table and waited, drinking in the tea laced with ginger and spices.

A few minutes later, Miguel returned and handed her a book, "Love in the Time of Cholera." On the cover was a huge red rose, with petals falling on to a black background and the tiny figure of a naked woman lying almost hidden in the corner amongst the petals.

"Interesting title. Is this a love story?"

"Yes, well it's a book about love—in all its forms—but mainly it's about unrequited love. Y'know … love sickness."

Laura studied the book for a moment, reading the short synopsis on the back and the first and last lines.

"Have you ever suffered that?" Miguel asked.

"What?"

"Love sickness."

Laura heard her own nervous laugh bounce off the walls, and she noticed one of the students look up from their book to stare at her.

"I'm serious!"

"That's just a construct of fiction."

"You're wrong, love sickness is very real, it's just modern medicine doesn't know how to treat it, so it pretends it doesn't exist. Before the eighteenth century, love sickness was accepted as a natural state, something we were all capable of suffering. But then industrialisation and advancement meant that if we couldn't explain it, if we couldn't find some rational means of quantifying it, then it wasn't an illness."

Laura was suspicious as to where he was going with this. "And what are the symptoms?"

"Well, they range. They could be insomnia, preoccupation, tearfulness, even mania. And all for love."

"I never pictured you as the Jane Austen type."

She hoped he wasn't going to mention what had happened on the Giant's Causeway. She didn't want to be reminded of the declaration of love she'd thrown back in his face. Anyway, he hardly looked preoccupied or lacking in sleep because of her.

"Okay, maybe I'm sounding dramatic. But I'm a Latin. Drama is in our blood! You know, I first read this book when I was at school. I thought the main character was a fool, running around expressing his undying love at the drop of a hat. It'll be interesting to see what you think. To me, it's not even clear if the woman ever really loved him."

"You said it was an excellent choice!"

"It is."

"So what changed your mind?"

"The book came back to me years later, and when I read it then, I realised that it was more foolish to feed the love sickness than it was to take a leap into the unknown, to at least try. Life is too short not to at least try."

Laura looked squarely into his eyes. There was so much they didn't know about each other. Maybe she could prise some of his secrets from him. Maybe with a few careful questions she could illuminate the road that had brought him here, to a hidden bookshop, drinking exotic tea on a wintry afternoon in Northern Ireland, talking about unrequited love. But then he would want to cast a spotlight over the journey she'd been on, a journey that took her absolutely nowhere. Just like her mother when she was a girl, wandering around town in endless circles. So she didn't ask the obvious question. Instead she just said, "I'll let you know what I think when I'm done."

CHAPTER NINETEEN

Natalia is the daughter of a golfing buddy of Miguel's father. After his mother dies, Miguel and his father spend more time with Natalia and her parents than ever before. Her mother usually takes them both out shopping with her each Saturday whilst their fathers play golf. The high-end shopping centres of Bogotá are their playground. Two happy children playing hide and seek between the clothes racks, getting caught splashing in the decorative fountains and nagging her mother to buy them ice cream. When they move on to high school and no longer need supervising, they still meet frequently, hanging out in each other's houses listening to records or watching television. Filled with the divine laziness of adolescence, they flop on their fronts on the floor, hands resting on chins, watching Sunday afternoon films interspersed with seemingly endless commercial breaks—no real cares in the world.

Then, when they are fifteen, he walks onto her terrace one evening as the sun is packing up the day and as she stands to greet him she raises her slender arm to her forehead to shield her eyes from the final few rays, exposing her honey coloured birthmark on the tiny round bone jutting out at her wrist, casting a small shadow over her face, giving her an alluring air of mystery. He has seen her thousands of times before, but in this moment, he looks at her with new eyes, and as the sun slips past the horizon, Miguel's heart gives itself over to her.

That is when the sickness takes hold. They remain friends and outwardly nothing about their relationship changes, but the landscape of his heart is altered forever. He starts thinking about her all the time, and struggles to maintain an interest in anything else. When he is not with her, he finds ways of mentioning her in every conversation, just saying aloud her graceful name gives him pleasure. Everything she does takes on a new enchantment for him, and he stores up visual memories of their smallest moments to replay later in his head. Like the image of her on the terrace that evening, or the picture of her lying serene on her bed lost in a book with a box of chocolates by her side, each one individually wrapped in bright smiling colours.

Throughout the rest of school and into university, their friendship remains strong, and to the outside world is as platonic as when they were eight-year-olds racing around the shopping centre. Miguel keeps his love very still and quiet. He fears that if he tells her how he feels, she might feel nothing but betrayal. To her, he would be just another man vying for her affection, a player of the worst kind, one who has masqueraded as her friend. He is terrified removing the mask would set the stage for the final act in their friendship. Most of all, he is terrified she will not return his look of love. And so Miguel dutifully welcomes each new boyfriend as any good friend would, and listens to her highs and lows as she learns the ways of love with others.

In moments of optimism, he tells himself that the best course, the only course of action is to wait for her. He imagines that in the end there will be no dramatic unveiling to surprise her—she will create the moment. If he waits long enough, one day she will reach across and with the slightest of touches gently remove his mask herself and toss it aside forever, and so he does nothing.

At the end of their second year at university, they start seeing each other less and less. Miguel suspects that she might have met another boyfriend, but then if she has, he reasons, surely he would have met him by now. Towards the end of August, she calls to say she is on her way over because she has something to tell him. She says she knows he hates those words, but she assures him it is good news. Within half an hour she is at his doorway, throwing her arms around him in excitement and telling him that she is happier than she had ever felt possible. She asks him to promise not to say anything until she has finished speaking. "You have my word," Miguel tells her.

She proceeds, breathless and excited, to tell him about Pedro. Pedro is a DJ at a local radio station who she met a few months earlier. Usually she is keen for Miguel to meet her new boyfriends; usually his opinion matters, but not this time. This time the feelings are different; she says she wanted to keep them just between Pedro and herself for as long as she could. But now there is good news to share, she says. Miguel senses that something so monumental has happened that it will be impossible for him to ever confess his love.

He waits, without breathing, willing her not to go on, desperate for it to be something else, but it isn't. Jumping with excitement she confirms his fears—she's pregnant and they plan to get married in a matter of weeks.

Miguel has been hiding his emotions for so long that it has become second nature, and so his customary act as her best friend takes over his external persona, sharing in her joy, but inside he is in turmoil. The metronome that keeps his internal music on a steady beat has stopped mid-swing, and the notes are now stumbling over each other, fighting for attention and clanging louder and louder in his ears.

She tells him that her parents are beside themselves. He can understand why: she's leaving university to get married and become a housewife. She's pregnant to a man fifteen years her senior, and not even to a professional who will kiss her goodbye in his suit and head off to his office each day.

It takes time for her parents to come round, but no one, not even Miguel, can deny that there is real love in the registrar's office on the Saturday morning that they wed. Just six months later, they have a gorgeous baby girl and her fairytale is complete.

Miguel tells himself that if he really loves her then he should be happy for her, that it would be selfish to feel any bitterness about her new family, that he must forget his feelings for her. But the river of love that has bubbled beneath the surface for so long fills his chest, immoveable like a lake.

At her daughter's first birthday, she pulls him to one side as the grandparents fuss over the birthday girl. "We're moving to Brazil. One moment I'm excited, the next I'm terrified. I've never been out of Colombia, well, except for a couple of trips to my aunt in Miami. Can you believe it? A wife and mother, and I've barely had a chance to use my passport!"

"Why?" is all he can say. "Why?"

Pedro has decided that, after spending years playing other people's music, he wants to make his own. He's been invited by a music collective in Rio to join their new studio. The plan is to make money teaching rich kids the art of mixing, scratching and various other DJ tricks. According to Pedro, this is quite a lucrative business, and the cool and moneyed young middle classes of Brazil provide the perfect market. In his spare time, Pedro and his partners will produce local talent and play their tracks in the clubs and bars of Rio. Miguel thinks that between the teaching, producing and playing in clubs, Pedro won't have much time to be a husband, never mind a father. But as always with Natalia, he holds back and doesn't tell her what he really feels.

Two days before she is due to fly out, Natalia arrives at Miguel's apartment alone and unannounced, carrying a shoebox.

She looks tired. She tells him it's from all the chaos of the move.

"Now that we're leaving, I finally had to go through all those boxes that I brought with me to Pedro's place when I moved in after the wedding. Ironic isn't it, that leaving the country has forced me to unpack! I should be packing stuff away, but it feels like every time I turn my head more and more things appear, like I'm sabotaging my own efforts!"

Miguel remembers that before the wedding she procrastinated for so long that it was only on the afternoon before the big day that she finally got round to clearing out her room at her parents' home. He had tried to help her organise her things, but her form of packing involved simply throwing the contents of whole drawers and cupboards straight into cardboard boxes without stopping to think what she really wanted and needed to take. She said she would unpack and sort it all when she moved into Pedro's apartment, but then the baby came and, apart from a suitcase of clothes and shoes, she never did get around to unpacking her old life and sorting it into her new one. So the boxes remained sitting in the corner of the nursery, waiting patiently to be unpacked, every day they have remained unpacked adding to the sense that whatever was in them has now become obsolete.

"Here," she says, handing him the shoebox, "something to remember me by."

Miguel looks down at the shoebox in his hand. "Something to remember you by? That's a bit dramatic—

I'll see you again, won't I?"

"Of course, silly—I just found these and thought you'd like them." She flops on the sofa and motions for him to join her. "Open it!"

Miguel takes a seat next to her, so close that their legs are almost touching, and lifts the lid. Inside is a pile of photos, a hundred at least. He pulls them out and starts going through them as Natalia watches over his shoulder.

All of them are of Natalia and Miguel, from young eight-year-olds, standing by the entrance to their fathers' golf club, looking straight-backed and serious beyond their years, to the photos of the first time they got drunk together at fifteen, giggling, their foreheads cut off at the top of the picture or a thumb in front of the lens, to their senior trip together to Cartagena, Natalia cradling a sloth in her arms. She remarked at the time that they looked like an odd family, Miguel, her and their lazy bear baby. It is all there: beaches and horse riding, his birthdays, her birthdays, dancing the waltz at her Fiesta de Quince (sweet fifteen), dancing on the tables at the famous "Andres Carne de Res" in Bogotá. They study each one together, travelling through their shared history of over fifteen years, laughing at their past selves, at the clothes and the haircuts and their youthful antics.

"What a life we've had together," she remarks, "you've always been there with me through everything, and now we'll be separated. You know my mother always said that we'd end up together. I think this is the first time she's ever been wrong about anything."

"Really? I always thought your mother just saw me as the naughty little eight-year-old that used to lead you astray in the shopping centre. I suppose she's relieved not to have me as a son-in-law."

"No, she would've been delighted if we'd got together. She only ever wanted to see me happy, and you made me happy," Natalia holds his eye for just longer than an instant and then gets up. "What am I doing here? I should be at home packing." She grabs her coat and makes for the door, her eyes averted, unable to meet his gaze again.

He follows her to the door, she opens it and then turns around and throws her arms around him in a bear hug. He holds her close, feeling her warm breath on his neck. She pulls away and she turns to leave. As she does, Miguel notices a single tear trace the side of her beautiful profile and drip on to her bare shoulder. "Nati," he calls after her, but she is already running down the corridor and doesn't look back.

In that instant he realises unrequited love is a sham, an impostor that convinces you that love can only ever be that way—that you have no option but to accept the pain. Maybe she does not love him now, but she could have— he thinks perhaps she always did. Suddenly, their whole history together is revised. He was always so afraid of losing her friendship that he never risked asking her if she loved him back. But what has he been protecting? Wasn't it inevitable if he didn't play for the big prize early in the game that his safe hand would eventually get chipped away, leaving him with nothing in the end? Sometime in the past, there was a fork in the road, and he chose the path of unrequited love. And so Miguel realises, far too late, that not unrequited love but regret is the cruellest of human emotions. Now the possibilities of love with Natalia can only be glimpsed in the roads too far away in time to reach. Regret is as merciless and unrelenting as unrequited love, but it has one advantage; it teaches you to do things differently. In the future, he decides, he will be honest with himself and those he loves. He will live his life truthfully and passionately to the end.

CHAPTER TWENTY

Laura stood at the kitchen sink drying and putting away the few plates that she and her father had used that day. Her cereal bowl from breakfast, her father's plate for his toast, a couple of teacups, her father's soup bowl from lunch, two saucepans and the dinner plates. It only took five minutes to clean up each day; such was the small life they lived.

Suddenly she heard a scream from the dark night. She rushed to the back door and flicked on the outside light. Something cold and furry brushed past her feet. Laura turned and saw Harry, Chrissie's dog, bounding through the house. His big paws skidding along the linoleum floor as he tried too quickly to make the sharp turn through the door into the living room, narrowly avoiding thumping into one of the kitchen cabinets as he went.

"Jesus Laura, I'm sorry."

Laura squinted out into the night—it was Chrissie, trying to open the gate and let herself into the backyard.

"I don't know how he managed to get out of the yard. Have you seen the size of that fence I've had put up? I let him out there for two minutes and I come out and he's in your yard. There's no way he could jump that fence. Don't know how he does it."

"Should we be calling him Harry or Houdini?" Laura smiled.

"Houdini the Hound, I like it. Where the hell is he?" Chrissie was now next to Laura at the back door looking over her shoulder into the kitchen.

"He's in the living room. C'mon in and get him." Laura held the door wide open for Chrissie, but she seemed to hesitate at the threshold.

"Harrr…eeee!" Chrissie screamed.

"Just go on in and get him."

"Harr…eee!"

Laura looked round but there was still no sign of Harry. Chrissie rolled her eyes in exasperation and edged past Laura into the kitchen and over towards the door to the living room. Laura came up behind her and looked over her shoulder. Harry was curled up on the mat at her father's feet with his front paws stretched out in front of him and his head resting on them with both eyes closed, feigning sleep. Laura noticed a small crooked smile on her father's face as he reached down to pet Harry on the head.

"Jesus, Peter I'm sorry for the intrusion," Chrissie said, "he's been standing at the back door whining for about half an hour. I thought he was desperate to go for a walk, so I let him out for a wee walk around the yard, and when I go to get him he's in your yard and now look at him. I'm sorry."

"Don't worry. Isn't that right, Daddy?" Laura said. Chrissie seemed to be being overly apologetic.

"Aye. That's okay, Chrissie. Laura, why don't you get this man a biscuit."

Laura went back to the kitchen and took the biscuit tin from the cupboard. Chrissie didn't move, she was glued to the spot just under the doorframe, Harry's lead in her hand. Laura wondered why she didn't just go on in and put him on the lead. Was it because she was afraid to be in the same room as her father? Chrissie looked like she didn't want to get too close. Like she was afraid of the local recluse, Laura thought. As if he were Boo Radley.

Laura popped open the biscuit tin and started to shake out a digestive from the packet—Harry was at her feet within two seconds.

"Sorry again Peter," Chrissie said backing into the kitchen. "I suppose I better take this mutt for a walk. Burn off some of that energy of his before bedtime."

She looked into the living room. Her father had gone back to staring blankly at the TV, a walk in the fresh air sounded tempting.

"Let me grab my coat. I'll join you, if that's okay."

Chrissie looked delighted. "God, Laura, that'd be great. I hate walking the roads by myself on these dark nights, and he isn't much of a bodyguard, I can tell you, unless he can lick someone to death."

It was a clear evening, so they decided to walk along the riverside. When they got on to the embankment, Chrissie let Harry off his lead. Laura watched him rush ahead of them, turning back on himself every now and then to hurry them along with a loud yelp. It reminded her of her childhood summers—Laura and her mother had shared many long afternoon walks along the river with their beloved old boxer Edward. Poor Edward, who they had to put down when he got a tumour when Laura was thirteen.

She could remember those walks vividly; Edward showering them with river water as he sped past, the smell of the wet dog, the grass-like green slush clinging to her school shoes. Her mother was always asking her about the future, about next year at school, about what she wanted to be when she grew up. Laura tried to remember the plans her younger self had spoken of or the dreams she confessed to on those walks, but she couldn't. Perhaps, she thought, the mind has a way of managing your memories to avoid disappointment.

"So, how are things with you and your young man going?" Chrissie asked.

"Good. It's good."

"Oh, that's it? It's good? I was hoping for some details."

"I don't really know what to say. It's going well. I like him …"

"But?"

Laura thought for a moment. In one way there was no "but;" Miguel was wonderful, he had brought some much needed fun and laughter into her life. Although it was only temporary—she supposed that was the "but."

"It's fine. We're having a nice time."

They walked on in silence, treading through the long shiny grass, which looked almost purple in the darkness. Laura stole a glance at Chrissie's profile bathed in moonlight, charging along next to her, constantly watching for Harry. Chrissie seemed so vibrant and open; she'd become the pulsing heart of their little street since she moved in. She always had a smile for everyone, she was always happy to stop and chat if you saw her in the street. But what was Chrissie like, Laura wondered, when she closed the door on the street and stepped into her house all alone?

Laura's phone started to ring. She pulled it out of her coat pocket. It was Miguel.

"Hey."

"Hi, gorgeous. What are you up to?"

"I'm just out for a walk with Chrissie—you remember Chrissie, don't you?"

"Yes, of course. Tell her I said hi. Listen, I won't be long, then. I'm going to do some shopping tomorrow after work, and I just wanted to check what I should get your dad for Christmas."

"My father?" Laura caught Chrissie glance over at her with a concerned look so she waved to indicate everything was fine, but obviously the tension in her voice showed.

"Yes, for Christmas. I can't show up at your house on Christmas day empty handed."

"Oh, about that, why don't we talk tomorrow?"

"What's wrong?"

"Umm, nothing." Laura knew the conversation that was coming and she didn't want to have it in front of Chrissie.

"If there's nothing wrong then we can talk about it now."

There was no arguing with the truth of his logic, it was infuriating.

"It's just my father and I have such a simple Christmas day. It's so boring, just lunch and then TV. I thought it'd be nicer if we celebrate just the two of us on the twenty-fourth. Isn't that how you said you do it in Colombia?" She said, trying to keep her voice normal. Chrissie stood a few feet away wrestling a stick from Harry's mouth.

"Yes, but I'm not in Colombia," he said. " If you don't want me to meet your father, you should just say so."

"No, it's just I'd rather it be just the two of us."

Laura smiled at Chrissie who was now staring over, not even bothering to pretend to play with Harry anymore.

"Is it because I'm Colombian?"

"No, don't be ridiculous."

"Ridiculous? What's ridiculous is your, your... Ugh— *me falta el inglés*—the way everything is such a secret with you."

Laura was sure Chrissie could hear Miguel loud and clear by now. She dropped her voice to a near whisper. "I'll explain tomorrow, okay?"

"Fine." He hung up.

"Are you okay?" Chrissie asked.

"Sure," Laura forced a smile.

"Do you want to talk about it?"

"No, we're just making arrangements for Christmas,

there's nothing wrong."

"Is it something to do with your dad?"

"It's fine, Chrissie. It's nothing. Let's keep walking, or we'll be out here all night." Laura was thankful that Chrissie couldn't see how flushed her face was in the darkness.

"Okay, but I'm here anytime you want to talk. I'm just next door."

"Thanks."

"Can I just say one thing? And I hope you don't think I was eavesdropping, but I couldn't help but overhear."

"Go on." Laura said, thinking of course Chrissie had been eavesdropping.

"Maybe you should give him a chance. Let the boy into your life. Open up to him a bit more—you never know how it could work out."

"I know how it works out. He leaves at the end of March and then I'm left here."

"Maybe not," Chrissie started, but Laura didn't want to hear it so she cut her off. "Yes Chrissie—that's exactly what's going to happen, so I might as well just enjoy it for now and try not to treat it like it's something bigger than it is."

"But isn't it better to at least have a go? Let yourself fall in love with him and see what happens? And if it doesn't work out, isn't it better to have loved and lost and all that?"

"No Chrissie, I don't buy into that—I think it's better to be …" she searched for the word, "pragmatic."

"Pragmatic?" Laura winced at the way Chrissie screeched out the word. "God, you are the opposite of me. I sometimes think I'd happily fall hard as anything and risk cracking my head right open just to feel that way again—even if it was only for a short time."

"Again? So you've been there before—and how did it turn out for you?"

"Well, obviously I'm alone, so not too great in the

end," Chrissie said.

"Chrissie, I'm sorry, I didn't mean to pry."

Laura couldn't work out Chrissie's true expression in the semidarkness—she hoped she hadn't offended her.

"Don't be silly. You're right; there's me an old spinster lecturing you, what do I know?"

"That's not what I meant."

"Where did that dog go? Haaaarrrry!" Chrissie called, turning her back on Laura.

They stood waiting for Harry. There was complete silence apart from the gurgle of the river. Harry was nowhere to be seen or heard. "Bloody Houdini—doing his disappearing act again. Where is he?"

Laura heard a splash and Harry suddenly leapt up from the river onto the embankment next to them, his tongue slopping out one side of his mouth, his black eyes glinting sheer happiness as he shook himself vigorously, spraying them both with icy river water, causing them to shriek and start running away from him. Laura watched Chrissie run ahead of her, still feeling guilty that she'd touched a nerve, but Chrissie seemed to have forgotten and was now laughing and playing with Harry again.

"C'mon Laura," Chrissie called.

Laura ran to catch up with her, forcing a smile to her face as she grabbed the stick that was hanging from Harry's mouth. On the outside at least she looked relaxed and happy, even though the pending discussions with Miguel were still weighing heavy on her mind.

CHAPTER TWENTYONE

They arrived just as the choir was finishing the opening hymn. Laura cast her eyes around for somewhere for them both to sit. It was midnight mass on Christmas Eve and, as usual, the place was packed to the brim. Normally she'd just squeeze into the edge of the last row, but then normally she was alone.

The chapel had been built in the 1960s and was a functional, low-ceilinged red brick building. Unlike traditional Catholic churches that arranged the congregation like an army in straight rows lined up in front of the altar, this one had the altar in the middle and the seats formed semicircles, radiating out from it on an incline. Because of this unique design, you could see nearly the whole congregation from most seats. Laura remembered that it was one of the things her mother had enjoyed most about mass, looking at the gathered crowd and, between prayers, commenting in a low whisper in highly unchristian terms on what people were wearing.

Laura pointed towards the corner. "Shall we just stand by the back wall?" she whispered. Miguel shook his head and pointed with his lips towards the front. It always made her smile when he used his pout to signal things off at a distance. She looked down in the same direction; there was some empty space on the third row. "But we have to go all the way down there."

Miguel ignored her and started striding down the centre aisle. Laura waited a beat and then followed, keeping her eyes on the marble floor in front of her. Her head was slightly fuzzy, and she suddenly remembered that her lips were stained purple from all the mulled wine she'd had at Miguel's earlier. Hopefully no one would notice them come in.

Throughout the mass, Laura's eyes cast around in all directions for people she knew. A lot of her school friends who had left the town to go to university were back for their annual visit home. Some of them worked in Belfast and England, although she'd heard that a few of them had moved further afield to America or Australia. She couldn't imagine where life might have taken her if leaving had been an option. It seemed unfathomable. Next to her Miguel stared ahead, following the priest's every word intently and bowing his head down in concentrated prayer when they had to kneel. She hadn't imagined he'd be so devout. She'd thought, like her, that he had wanted to come to Christmas mass simply for the tradition, but he actually seemed to be praying.

Laura stared straight ahead, past the altar. In the front row, just opposite, a little brown-haired boy, probably four or five years old, was playing with a bright red truck. Laura's eyes wandered to his mother, who smiled over. Laura knew her, they'd been in the same class at school. She racked her brain trying to remember her name. Lisa, maybe. It was true; Laura was not the only one who had stayed behind. There had been a few people from her class who hadn't bothered to go to university or anywhere. Their lives seemed just as foreign. though. They'd bought houses of their own ten minutes drive from their parents and now apparently some even had school-age children of their own. 'What have I been doing for the past eight years?' Laura thought.

The priest gave the usual homily about how Christmas was such a joyous time, a time to celebrate the birth of Christ with family and loved ones. Then he asked the congregation to remember those people for whom Christmas is difficult and lonely, those who don't have anyone to share it with, for whom Christmas is just another day facing the wall. Laura felt Miguel's warm hand lift hers and hold it tight within his. She glanced over at him. He was still staring straight ahead, listening intently to the priest, as if his reaching for her hand had been a completely unconscious act, something his heart had done naturally whilst his mind was engaged with the act of listening.

After midnight mass, they strolled leisurely down the main road chatting idly about Christmas in Colombia, doing their best not to let their teeth chatter too much in the freezing cold. It was going on one o'clock in the morning when they arrived at Laura's house. At the garden gate, Miguel pulled her into a bear hug and kissed her forehead.

"So this is where I leave you. But not for long. What time should I come round tomorrow? Or later today, in fact."

"Come at 12:30 and we'll have lunch at one."

Miguel cupped her face with both hands and kissed her firmly on the lips. When he pulled away she could see his smile, wide and bright in the moonlight.

"I'm looking forward to finally meeting your father."

"Yes, he can't wait to meet you," she said, hoping her lie wasn't obvious.

"See you in a few hours then," he kissed her once more and left.

She watched him walk down the street until he reached the corner and then she turned towards her house. The place was in complete darkness except for the twinkling of the Christmas tree lights visible through the living room windows. In less than twelve hours' time, Miguel would be back here expecting a fun-filled family Christmas. It had been two weeks since she relented, promising to finally introduce him to her father over Christmas lunch, and now it was less than twelve hours away and her poor father still had no idea. She cursed herself for having procrastinated for so long.

She opened the front door and stepped into the darkened hallway. With a sense of panic, she realised that he might already be in bed and she wouldn't be able to tell him until morning. She went into the living room to turn off the Christmas tree lights—it looked pathetic. Her mother had always insisted on a real tree. Each year she'd bought a monster of a thing that dominated the whole room and spent an entire day decorating it, although she was never happy with the result. There were never enough lights, or it was too bushy or too sparse. All those allegedly imperfect trees of her mother's were far superior to the twisted bundle of plastic and glitter that now apologetically adorned the living room.

Laura had bought it the second year after her mother's death. The first Christmas it hadn't seemed appropriate to have any decorations. Laura couldn't now remember how exactly they had spent that Christmas, as if her mind had anesthetised itself, knowing that any memories created from that year would prove far too painful to look back on, it hadn't bothered to hit the save button.

She could remember clearly though the following year when, in mid-December, her father had given her his bank card and PIN and told her to go get a tree. At 17, with no license or car, she had no hope of lugging back a full-sized tree all by herself, so she'd gone to the supermarket and bought a lightweight fake tree that came in a box, and they'd used that ever since.

Laura reached under the table and flicked the switch, putting an end to the manic blinking of the multicoloured lights for the night, then she started to make her way upstairs. Halfway up, she heard a noise in the bathroom. Her father must be getting ready for bed. She paused at the top of the stairs and waited, watching his shadow dance around in the small strip of light under the bathroom door. She took a deep breath, going over in her head what she was going to say, what she should have said long before now. She heard him tap the sink with his toothbrush three times, that was usually the last thing he did before coming out, and sure enough, a second later, the lock clicked and the light from the open bathroom doorway streamed into the darkened hallway where she was waiting at the top of the stairs.

"Hi Daddy."

"Jesus, Laura you scared me. I didn't hear you get home. I wasn't sure what time you'd be back."

"I've just been to midnight mass."

"Good mass?"

Laura nodded.

"Right, well, I'll see you in the morning." He moved to go into his room. She had to do it now.

"Actually, about tomorrow. I wanted to talk to you."

His head spun round, "You'll be here, won't you?"

"Yes, of course."

He looked at her questioningly.

"It's just, I'd like to invite someone over for Christmas dinner if that's okay."

"Is it Chrissie?"

"No, she's with her sisters. It's someone else. A friend. He's not from the town, and he doesn't really have time to go home for Christmas." The words raced out, finally released from her mind after all the ruminations of the past two weeks.

"Oh, is it that boy you've been seeing?"

"Yes, how did you?"

"Laura, I'm not blind, or deaf."

"So, do you mind?"

"Do I have a choice?"

Laura looked at the ground and then back up at her father. His jaw was set hard in a show of strength. She was about to speak again when her eyes fixed on his hands, he was scratching each thumb with his index fingers. It was something he did when he was nervous. She shouldn't push it, she knew he hated having to deal with other people, and here she was landing a total stranger on him on Christmas of all days. But even so, there was a part of her that wished, just for once, he could be normal.

"Would we even have enough food?"

"Yes, of course, we have a whole turkey defrosting down there just for the two of us. But if you're not happy, don't worry, I'll just make other arrangements."

"No, there's no need to go running off to his house for dinner."

"I wasn't planning to, I just meant …"

"Laura, it's fine. Okay?"

She waited. She wasn't sure what 'it's fine' was supposed to mean.

"He can come to dinner."

"Really?"

"I suppose I ought to meet him sometime, he spends enough time hanging out by the gate waiting for you, It's about time he came in so I can get a proper look at him."

"Thanks, Daddy."

He smiled at her and turned to go into his room and then stopped.

"And what's his name?"

"Miguel."

"Is he Spanish, then? I didn't think he looked like he was from round here."

"No, he's Colombian."

"How did you meet?"

"At school, he teaches Spanish on Fridays. "

Her father nodded. She prepared herself for a deluge of questions.

"Okay, well good night. Happy Christmas, love."

And that was it! He shuffled off into his bedroom and closed the door behind him. Laura felt every muscle in her body slowly start to uncoil, and she was suddenly overwhelmed with the desire to lie down and dream.

CHAPTER TWENTYTWO

Laura hauled the hoover upstairs and dropped it at her feet. Catching sight of herself in the landing mirror, she scowled. Her clothes were shapeless and grubby, she had a yellow glove on one hand and cleaning products in the other, and a stub of a ponytail stuck out from her head—she looked so much older than her twenty-five years. She'd spent the morning spinning around the house like a disoriented cyclone, cleaning, trying to spruce the place up. She only had the bathroom left and then she could finally make a start on herself. She didn't have much time; Miguel would be arriving soon. But the bathroom door was shut, just as it had been for well over an hour.

"Daddy, are you going to be much longer?" she waited, no answer.

She went into her father's bedroom and laid out the jumper she'd bought for him the previous Christmas, alongside a freshly ironed shirt and a pair of dark blue jeans. She searched in the wardrobe for his black shoes, they were lying next to a big cardboard box at the back behind his coat—she pulled them out and dusted them off. She hoped he'd get the hint and wear them instead of his old slippers, if he still fitted into them; he'd not worn his black shoes since her mother's funeral—from that day on, he'd had no need for outdoor footwear at all.

She walked back out to the landing and looked at the closed bathroom door. Her stomach lurched as she pictured Miguel arriving and her having to explain to him that he couldn't meet her father because he'd decided to barricade himself in the toilet.

Feeling frustrated now, she lifted her hand to knock the door, just as her father opened it from the inside so her hand, swinging down, almost punched him in the chest.

"Don't worry, I'll be ready. No need to get violent!"

"Sorry."

He shuffled past her towards his room—years without sunlight had made him look old. He looked like the invisible man.

An hour later, Laura ran downstairs tugging at her black pencil skirt, hoping the white shirt didn't make her look like a waitress. As she raced through the living room towards the kitchen, she noticed her father's shoes laced up on his feet, and she smiled to herself.

Looking over the instructions that Chrissie had scribbled down for her, Laura checked the turkey and potatoes roasting in the oven, and the ham and vegetables boiling on the stove. There were never usually so many pots bubbling away on the hob; so much to manage, it was all a bit overwhelming. Condensation dripped down the walls and steam covered the windows, masking the outside world.

Laura flung open the top corner window, letting in an icy breeze, but it was no match for the swelter of the kitchen, so she stretched her face up towards it, gulping in the cool air. Suddenly the trill of the doorbell reverberated through the house and Laura sprang into action, rushing through the living room, past her father, before he could even stand up.

She took a deep breath and quickly checked her features in the mirror, and then pulled open the front door to a smiling Miguel.

"What's that look? Are you okay?" he whispered.

Laura reminded herself to smile. "Everything's fine! Great. Come in."

She turned and walked into the living room and motioned for Miguel to follow, realizing as she did that she hadn't even bother to greet Miguel properly or kiss him.

"Daddy, this is Miguel."

Her father stood up, reaching out his hand. Miguel grabbed it and shook hands with his usual overconfident vigour.

"Happy Christmas, it is very nice to meet you, Mr. Kennedy"

"Yes, you too."

"Thank you for having me over."

"It's no problem …" her father trailed off and cast his eyes downwards as if searching the carpet for something.

"I brought something for you, Mr. Kennedy."

"Call me Peter, please."

Miguel pulled a large photo album from his bag and passed it to her father. "I made an album for you of some of my favourite photos of Colombia."

Her father took the album and opened it and Miguel went over and stood close to him. Laura, not really sure what side to stand on, flitted around them until she eventually came to rest in the middle behind them.

Her father leafed through the first few pages containing photos of pretty colonial towns as Laura peered through the gap between their heads. He stopped for just enough time to show he'd looked at each, but Laura was worried that he wasn't reacting, he wasn't speaking or engaging. The photos of old town squares gave way to glassy, futuristic office blocks and still he said nothing.

"What's that?" Laura asked.

"That's Bogotá's financial district."

"Isn't that nice, Daddy?"

"Yes, very good," he mumbled.

There were a few more pages of modern architecture, which was probably Bogotá and then the photos changed to pictures of nature—huge waterfalls surrounded by lush green countryside, and snow-capped mountains that looked down onto paradise-like white beaches. Still her father didn't react.

"Isn't that gorgeous."

Miguel glanced at her but didn't say anything; her father just kept leafing methodically through the pages.

The silence was excruciating. Looking at the two of them, Laura estimated that they both probably stood about an inch taller than her. Miguel was thin and muscular, and she could almost see the energy coursing through him like car headlights on a superhighway at night, even as he stood still, unspeaking. He didn't have much time for sport, as he was so busy with work, so it must have been the synapses in his quick mind that burnt the huge amount of calories he consumed each day. Considering the sedentary life her father led, he didn't look so bad, she thought. He had a rounded belly like all men his age, but his arms and shoulders still looked strong and hadn't withered from lack of exercise. For a fleeting moment, Laura wondered if he could have found a new love, if he hadn't cloistered himself away after her mother's death, but she quickly dismissed the thought.

"And what's that?" Laura asked. It was a picture of a black cavernous room with an enormous, neon-lit crucifix carved into the wall.

"That's the salt cathedral; it's cut into a salt mine."

"How do they do that, then?"

"Not sure, I think they use explosives and then start carving—I'll take you there sometime, it's not far from Bogotá."

Laura felt her cheeks flush, "isn't that interesting how

they've got a cathedral in a mine Daddy, isn't it?"

"Umm," was his only response.

Laura glanced down just as her father was turning over the final page, a picture of a street vendor selling exotic fruits by a busy crossroads, and then he was closing the album. All that effort Miguel had gone to, and her father had barely said anything.

Laura could hear the pot lids tinkling in the kitchen, gently threatening to boil over, she knew she should go turn them down, but she couldn't leave them just staring at each other. She opened her mouth to speak again, to say something complimentary about the album, but her father spoke first. "It looks like a lovely country."

"Oh, it is. We have so much diversity, the mountains, the ocean, the Caribbean, the rainforest, it's as if we have an entire continent." Miguel never needed much of an excuse to talk up his country.

"And you took all these?"

"Yes, I did."

"They're very good, I must say."

Suddenly there was a crash in the kitchen. The men turned towards her, both sets of eyes looking at her—one of the pot lids she'd left half on must have slid off.

"I'm going to go check on the food."

"Can I help you?" Miguel offered—she was tempted to say yes, so she wouldn't have to leave him alone with her father, but she didn't want him hovering over her either, crowding her in the kitchen.

"I'm sure Laura has it under control," her father stepped in. "So you like photography, then?" he said, turning back to Miguel.

It was oppressively hot in the kitchen so she worked quickly, cutting the turkey and ham and draining the vegetables, all the time with her ears trained on the conversation in the living room. Miguel was now talking about "the light" in Northern Ireland and how good it was for photos—she'd heard him enthuse on this subject before, and her father was at least feigning interest.

Laura pictured her stomach, constricted with nerves, and mentally she told it to relax—like she'd seen at the end of a yoga class once, that one class she'd taken. It's all going okay, she told herself, but it didn't help.

Finally she was ready to call them in to the kitchen.

"Everything smells wonderful," Miguel effused.

"You did a good job, love," her father added. Laura smiled, he said thanks all the time for the things she did around the house, but it was the first time he had praised her in years.

"Well, you haven't tasted it yet."

"Exactly, that's why we're complimenting you now, when we can still be honest," Miguel said. Laura slapped him playfully on the shoulder and then looked to her father, who was smiling.

With the hob and oven turned off, the temperature in the room became more comfortable. The three of them munched quietly, the only other sound in the room the forks and knives tapping on their plates.

"It's delicious," Miguel said, "honestly."

"I think I left the potatoes to boil for too long, they're all soggy."

"No, really, it's delicious."

"Don't worry, love," her father said, "it's only a few spuds."

"Peter, there's something I've been wondering about. I thought you might be able to help."

What burning question did Miguel have for her father? Whatever it was, she was sure he couldn't answer it.

"Maybe I should've mashed them."

Miguel put down his fork and looked at her quizzically.

"The potatoes, I should've mashed them."

"Stop fussing Laura, everything's grand," her father said, stuffing a big fork of potatoes into his mouth.

"So I was just wondering," Miguel went on—in typical

stubborn fashion, he hadn't been distracted from his thoughts, not that her potato talk was much of a diversion.

"What's all the fuss with cricket? They're all mad for it down the pub and I just can't see the attraction."

Inside, Laura breathed a sigh of relief. Something trivial; this was fine.

"I quite enjoy it. I think you need to understand it before you can appreciate it," Peter replied.

"Do you go watch the local team often then?"

"Daddy's not really that into local cricket. You prefer the international matches on TV, don't you?" Her father looked over at her, as if trying to read her face.

"I imagine they're a bit more exciting," Miguel said "but to me it all just seems like baseball on Valium."

"You know, one time when we were just newlyweds, I took Laura's mother to see the local team take on Pakistan. They were doing some kind of tour. God knows how they ended up here. I remember it was such a hot day, and there was a real carnival atmosphere about the town, and so she agreed to come along to see what all the fuss was about. Diane always thought cricket was more a game for the other side, if you know what I mean."

Miguel nodded, but Laura wasn't sure if he really had understood what "the other side" meant.

"And so we go and take our seats," her father went on, "and I'm ready for all the questions, because she has no idea of the rules. But she just sits there in silence, staring at the play and I thought, what luck, she seems to be getting into this—then after about two hours she turns to me and says 'Say, when do they start?'"

Miguel laughed, "I suppose that was the first and last match."

"Yes sir, it was."

Laura looked up and smiled at her father. Maybe it was the heat in the kitchen, but his cheeks looked flushed with the colour of life.

Suddenly, through the open window, Laura heard a loud knocking from across the street. She got up and peeked out through the net curtains. It was Chrissie knocking on the MacPhersons' door. Laura didn't know what she was doing there; Chrissie was supposed to be spending Christmas with her sisters. She opened the back door and called over, "Chrissie, are you okay?"

Chrissie turned round, "Yes, fine thanks," and then turned back and continued knocking.

"Chrissie, I think the MacPhersons are out all day, over at her mother's house." Laura stood shivering at the backdoor as Chrissie knocked a few more times with no success, then she turned and crossed the street. "Are you okay?"

"I'm fine, I just … I've bloody locked myself out, and the MacPhersons have my spare set. I was with my sisters, but then they all have the in-laws to visit, and I thought I'd just come back to my own wee house for the evening."

"We're just about to have dessert, why don't you come in and join us? You can wait here until they're back."

Chrissie came into the yard but then hovered by the back door. "Sorry everyone, I don't want to intrude."

"Come on in, sit down," Laura said. Chrissie hesitated and then took Laura's chair at the table. The room suddenly seemed very crowded.

"Coffee anyone?" Laura asked, and Miguel and Chrissie both nodded.

Laura started to fill the kettle.

"So, Miguel, how is work going at the Tribunal? Have you figured out who did it yet?" Chrissie asked.

"Well, we're not really supposed to be investigating that part."

Laura turned around and caught her father's eye.

"What Tribunal's this?"

"The Hudson Tribunal," Miguel replied.

"The one looking into the bomb?"

"Yes."

"But Laura told me you worked at the school."

"He does, Daddy, but only on Fridays."

"I thought you were a Spanish teacher."

"Not exactly."

"So what are you?"

"I'm a lawyer."

Laura cursed herself for not mentioning the Tribunal last night, but it just hadn't come up, and really, what did it matter if Miguel was a lawyer or a Spanish teacher?

"What are you doing at the Tribunal, exactly?"

Laura didn't like her father's accusatory tone.

"Mainly I'm liaising with witnesses. We have to take our time with them. It's quite an emotional thing for them to give evidence. For them, it's all still so fresh, even if it was ten years ago."

"Some damage can never be repaired, no matter how many years pass." Chrissie said, not really to anyone in particular, and Laura wondered if she'd had much to drink at her sister's house. Her eyes did look a bit glassy.

"There's quite a lot to piece together, and we still need to track down some eyewitnesses who weren't interviewed for the original inquiry."

"Maybe they haven't come forward because they were involved themselves," Chrissie said. Laura wasn't sure, but she thought she saw her father's back stiffen further.

"That's a possibility, I suppose," Miguel said, "or perhaps they've moved away, or died even; anything could have happened to them in the past ten years."

Laura stepped between Chrissie and Miguel to put their coffee cups down in front of them. "Here we go, neither of you take sugar, do you?"

Miguel smiled up and shook his head. She knew he didn't take sugar. Chrissie just ignored her, looking straight at Miguel, and went on talking, "Are they going to prosecute anyone?"

"No, the purpose of the Tribunal isn't really to prosecute. It's just to get to the bottom of what happened.

To find an official truth."

"But they do have an idea of who it might've been, don't they?" Chrissie put the question to Miguel almost as if it were a fact—much in the same way a prosecutor might cross-examine a witness. Laura had heard the same rumours, that the police knew who'd been involved but they didn't have the evidence to prove it. Or some conspiracy theorists believed the police could in fact prove who had done it, but that would involve revealing how much they knew from their sources beforehand and would leave them open to the accusation that they should've prevented the bomb.

"I don't know," Miguel said, "there are a couple of names mentioned on the quiet at work, nothing official, but it would have taken quite a big team to get everything in place. And maybe some of them just expected it to be a warning shot, or some kind of financial hit, but the bomb went off too early and the warning referred to the wrong part of town, so the cost of life was much greater."

Laura still stood between Miguel and Chrissie, looked across the table at her father—he seemed to have excluded himself from the conversation and was picking at the final pieces of turkey on his plate.

"But can you believe it," Miguel went on, "that there are some people out there, just living their lives, sitting down with their families for Christmas lunch, probably sat in the front row at mass this morning, all the time knowing that people died because of them? I don't know how they can live with themselves."

"Well maybe some of them couldn't," Chrissie replied.

Her father suddenly stood up. "I'm going to watch the news," he said.

"But Daddy, it's Christmas Day, what news can there be?"

"I'll tell you when I've watched it."

Laura watched him walk into the living room without even a backward glance at their guests. Her cheeks burned with embarrassment.

"Laura, thanks for the coffee, but I think I'm just going to walk over to Kitty MacPherson's mother's house and get my keys back, leave you to your Christmas." What was left of their Christmas, Laura thought. She couldn't believe her father couldn't have made more of an effort to engage with Miguel, and Chrissie, too. These were people she cared about.

"No, don't go, what about dessert?" But Chrissie was already up and putting her coat on.

"I just want to get my keys and get into my own wee house. I'll see you."

A gust of cold air shot into the house as Chrissie exited the back door and into the darkening evening.

Laura was unsure of what had just happened, why her father and then Chrissie had decided they'd had enough of her attempt at Christmas dinner. She looked over at Miguel. "So, I guess there will be extra pudding for me then?" he said, making her smile—he could always make her smile, no matter how weary she felt.

He stood up and started rifling through his pocket.

"Here," he handed her a small box. "Open it." She tore off the wrapping paper. Inside was a box with an MP3 alarm clock. "I've already added lots of music to it. Lots of inspirational stuff to help you kick-start each day, and don't worry, you don't need to know how to use it; my ongoing technical and musical consultancy services come with it."

Laura smiled at him, amazed at how fluid she was, like the liquid she'd seen on a science programme that became solid with impact, she hovered between emotions until something forceful, like Miguel's affection, solidified her feelings, making her feel one emotion at a time—the present one being sheer gratitude that he was here, replaced very quickly with terror as she remembered how soon it was until he would be leaving again.

CHAPTER TWENTYTHREE

Laura woke early to the sound of a piano racing a saxophone, the instruments getting swept up and entangled together and then tumbling apart. She blinked as her eyes became accustomed to the new day. According to the electric blue writing scrolling across the screen of her alarm clock, the sounds came from Alice Coltrane and the date was January third.

She lay there listening to the music, letting the saxophone sweep her away on a magic carpet, twisting and turning, flying back on itself and then shooting out in another direction, as the piano flowed beneath it like a fast-running river. She felt exhilarated by the crazy sound and jumped out of bed, ready for the first day of the new term.

The pupils were not back for another week and Laura was looking forward to having some time to plan her lessons, but during the morning meeting, Sister Mary Margaret (the "boss" as Laura called her) announced that she had allocated each teacher a special task to complete before the start of term. When the boss left the room, Laura huddled around the notice board with her fellow teachers scanning the list. No one seemed to be impressed with what they were being asked to do. Laura groaned when she finally found her own name. "Clearing the basement archives: Laura Kennedy and Sister Claire."

A week in the cold and dusty basement seemed like a particularly cruel and unusual punishment, even by the boss's standards. Sister Claire would definitely make the job more fun, but Laura doubted she'd actually lighten the load. Sisters Claire and Margaret were the only two nuns left teaching at the school, the rest were lay teachers like Laura. Whilst Sister Margaret was in at the crack of dawn every day and the last to leave each evening, Sister Claire was not well known for her work ethic.

Laura found her eating some left over Christmas cake in the alcove kitchen.

"Shall we go and ask the boss what clearing out the archives actually entails?" Laura asked.

"Oh, don't worry. I've had it explained to me in detail—over Christmas dinner, no less!"

"God, doesn't the woman take a holiday? So? Don't keep me in suspense."

"They want to turn the basement into cloakrooms so then they can turn the cloakrooms on the first floor into a new classroom."

"I suppose that makes sense." Laura taught most of her classes in a chilly caravan-type room that was supposed to be temporary but had been there since she was a pupil at the school.

"Our instructions are to go through all the rubbish down there and sort it," Sister Claire went on. "We're supposed to get Mrs Carlin to scan any official school documents and then for everything else we'll hold an open day for ex-pupils so they can come and take anything they might want, like old report cards, essays about atoms— that kind of fascinating stuff. Anything left after that we can just burn."

"That doesn't sound too bad."

Sister Claire raised her eyebrows. "You haven't seen what's down there."

There were literally hundreds of boxes stored in the basement, with documents shoved in them in no particular order. After nearly three hours of work, all Laura's positivity had disappeared. It was a huge task, and Sister Claire's scattergun approach didn't help. Laura watched in silent frustration as Sister Claire randomly opened boxes and picked through their contents, ignoring Laura's repeated suggestion to start with the boxes at the back and work their way to the front, sorting the contents into two piles: documents for scanning and others.

"Well, well, look what I found," Sister Claire said handing Laura a single piece of paper.

She looked down at the title of the piece, "Why I hate boys" and then saw her name at the bottom; she'd completely forgotten writing it in first year.

"My, how things change."

Laura's cheeks burned a deep rose. Her attempts to keep her relationship with Miguel discreet had clearly not been as successful as she thought. Sister Claire obviously knew what she was thinking. "I wouldn't worry, this town is small and curious. Everything in this place becomes public knowledge sooner or later. Well, public knowledge to everyone except those involved. He's a very charming young man. If I were ten years younger …"

"And hadn't made a vow of chastity."

"Thanks for reminding me, I'm still allowed to look, though."

"Really?"

"Yes, just don't tell the boss."

Laura crawled over and joined Sister Claire by the box she'd just opened. It seemed to contain various pieces of work belonging to her own year group. Rifling through it, she found a picture of her class just before they left school. She picked it up and took a closer look, quickly finding herself in the front row wearing chunky Doc Marten boots and a skirt that was far too short. It was the same rebellious uniform that half her classmates wore. Catherine stood at the bottom right-hand side of the picture, tall and prim, her blazer buttoned over her knee-length skirt, complimenting perfectly her sensible shoes. A stranger looking at the picture would probably have picked out Catherine as the girl most likely to become the small town English teacher, not Laura.

"What've you got there?" Sister Claire asked.

"My year group." Laura sat on the floor next to Sister Claire so they could study it together.

"Speaking of town secrets, remember those two sisters?" Sister Claire pointed at two blonde girls who sat next to each other in the front row.

"So even the teachers knew? Do you know if Áine and Grian ever found out themselves?"

"It must've been shortly before this picture was taken, when you girls were about seventeen or eighteen that their parents told them. They asked us to make sure they weren't being teased about it at school. But I'm sure everyone else's parents had told them long before then anyway. Gossip that good never gets old."

Sister Claire was right. Laura remembered showing her mother another annual class photo when she was twelve or thirteen, and her mother making some remark about how alike Áine and Grian were. Laura recalled looking at the photo and noticing it for the first time. The same cornflower blue eyes, the same blonde hair, bordering on white, the same straight, narrow nose.

Her mother told her that Áine's father, Eugene, had in his youth looked like a young Robert Redford and was adored by all the girls in town. He developed quite a reputation for the ease with which he moved from one girl to the next. Grian's mother was the first to fall pregnant by him, but he quickly dumped her and very soon afterwards people started seeing him about town with Áine's mother. She also, within a matter of weeks, fell pregnant.

Laura remembered asking her mother how come he had ended up marrying Áine's mum.

"Áine's grandfather," she replied.

At school, Grian always said her father was dead. Laura wondered if Grian knew the truth. "I don't know love," her mother had told her, "but if she doesn't she shouldn't hear it from you. So promise me you'll keep this secret. I can trust you to keep a secret, can't I?"

Looking back on it, that was one of the few times Laura could recall gossiping with her mother as if she, too, were an adult. But she would never be able to experience the special confidences between a mother and her grown-up daughter. Her mother had been taken from her too early, before their relationship had time to mature. Laura looked around her at the boxes surrounding them, all stacked up this way and that. The light was so dim she couldn't quite see the corners of the room. The air was cold and heavy, and Laura suddenly felt the need to get out.

"I'm just going to the bathroom."

"Sure." Sister Claire didn't even look round. She was already ransacking another box to see what interesting artifacts she might find.

Laura climbed out of the basement and stood in the hallway, looking out at the darkening afternoon. She pulled her mobile phone from her skirt pocket and cradled it in her hand. With her thumb she unlocked the keypad and moved to the most recently dialled. All of them were to Miguel. She rested her thumb on the green call button. She didn't understand this urge to call him in the middle of the day. There was nothing to report. Nothing in particular that couldn't wait until this evening. She stared at the phone for fifteen more seconds, locked it again, stuffed it back into her pocket and made her way back downstairs.

At the bottom of the stairs, Sister Claire was waiting for her, looking excited. "Look at this. Turn to page four," she said handing Laura a yellowed copy of *The Chronicle*, the town's local paper, from 1972.

Laura turned the pages, wondering what all the excitement was about. 1972 didn't strike her as a particularly significant year. On page four, there was a large photograph of about thirty people of various different ages under the headline "Winners of This Year's Feis." Laura looked at the rows of strange faces and suddenly drew in a deep breath. There was her mother smiling back at her from the middle of the group, holding up a certificate and a trophy. 1972. Laura did the math quickly in her head. She must have been twenty-five then.

Laura quickly searched the text below. It listed all the winners of the local cultural festival. Her mother's name leapt out at her: *"Winner of the best original poetry category went to Diane Kennedy for her short piece called 'The Lighthouse.'"*

CHAPTER TWENTYFOUR

"So, Cinderella, the ugly sisters have had you locked in the cellar all day." Laura and Miguel were out walking after dinner. The air was crisp and the sky clear, and each of them was bundled up in a big winter coat, complete with hat and gloves. Laura walked a few inches apart from Miguel; she'd been distracted all through dinner thinking about the discovery she'd made earlier that day.

"It's a pretty tedious task. Although," she hesitated, still not ready for the onslaught of questions he'd have, but no longer able to keep the news to herself, "I did come across a newspaper article mentioning my mother."

Miguel stopped in his tracks, "What did it say?"

"Not much. It was a list of winners at the Feis."

"The what?"

"It's an Irish word, it's like a cultural festival."

"What did she win?"

"Best original poem. I never even knew she wrote poetry. Well, who knows, maybe that was the only poem she ever wrote. It probably sounds strange, but for that brief moment, when I first found out, she almost seemed alive again to me. I suppose it's because I learned something new about her after so long."

"I know what you mean. I used to ask my grandmother and father to tell me more about my mother, but they would always just repeat the same stories. Like they had distilled their time with her down into a few moments. But sometimes, randomly, they'd see something that reminded them of an almost forgotten memory and they'd tell me and, I dunno, it felt like a match being lit in a cave, you know, illuminating it for just a few seconds."

"But really it's just a scrap, isn't it? I know something more *about* her, but I don't *know* her better."

"Did you like the poem? What was it like?"

Laura hugged her coat tighter to her to keep out the chill. "I don't even know that much. The article just said she had won a competition for writing a poem, but it didn't publish it.

"And that's it? Nothing more?"

"It said it was called 'The Lighthouse.'"

"The Lighthouse?"

"I know."

"It is too much to be a coincidence, no? It must be that poem in the picture. She must've been the author."

"I suppose she could've been."

"So what about the painting? Did she paint it too?" Miguel was looking animated now, Laura could see his inquisitive mind racing ahead, already coming up with theories and explanations.

"I don't think so, I never remembering her painting. I think she was a terrible artist. In fact, I know she was. When I was eight or nine, I had to do a poster for school of my favourite book and I remember her helping me, or trying to. It was a disaster. She couldn't muster anything better than a few stick people. I think I might've even got angry with her. I was such a mean child."

"Okay, well did someone paint it for her?"

"I don't know. Maybe she bought it because it reminded her of the poem and then added the poem later on." For some reason, this was Laura's preferred explanation, it implied that her mother had acted completely alone.

"Impossible. If that were the case, it would look that way, it would look like an afterthought. But if you study the picture, it's clear that those words are integrated into the original."

Laura didn't say anything, she knew he was right.

"Could your father have painted it?"

"No, absolutely not. Anyway, he doesn't know where it comes from. Remember?"

"Then who?"

Laura shrugged and walked on, her eyes fixed on the path ahead. Miguel caught up and wrapped his arm around her waist. Thankfully he didn't speak, and so they walked on in silence, their breath making ghostly clouds and both of them thinking of her dead mother's secrets.

For the next week, Laura and Sister Claire worked in the basement every day. Sister Claire was infuriating. Sometimes she'd pore over the yearbooks and school reports of favoured years, swirling the memories around like a fine vintage, and at other times she'd stick an orange "rubbish" label on a box with only the most cursory inspection of its contents. Laura, on the other hand, approached the clear-out like an archaeologist. She dusted down every piece of paper and examined it for clues, hoping to catch a fresh glimpse of the woman she only half knew.

If her mother were still alive, scraps of information like her poetry triumph at the Feis would have been a mere stitch in a much greater patchwork. She wouldn't need to scavenge like this in a poorly lit basement. But that was how it had to be.

For all her digging, Laura didn't find much more. Only a picture of her mother playing tennis in the school grounds in a pretty white dress when she was about fourteen and her mother's school report from her final year at school, which read just the same as the school reports Laura now drafted each June, with the same list of meaningless adjectives and phrases.

On the day they finished the clear-out, Laura turned off the lights and pulled the door behind her, feeling cheated that she'd been given a glimpse, a promise of some new knowledge of her mother, and then nothing more. What she didn't know, what she couldn't know until much later, was that Miguel had taken that scrap of information and planned to use it as a clue to further his investigation, whether she wanted him to or not.

CHAPTER TWENTYFIVE

The morning after her birthday, Peter sat in the living room listening to Laura tell Chrissie about the night before. He kept the volume down on the TV, just loud enough to keep up the charade that he was watching it, rather than straining to hear what was being said in the kitchen. He had always loved the sound of his daughter's voice.

In all of Peter's memories of Laura as a child she was talking, chirping away, telling the stories amassed in a typical schoolgirl life. He had adored her zest for living—it didn't matter the topic, she always had something to say. She would interrupt Diane and him when they were talking about grown-up things, like the rise in council rates, or the "Ulster Says No" campaign, or the incessant rain, and she would always have some unique childlike point of view that made him look at the topic in a whole new light. Even with a child's vocabulary, she had a way of matching the words perfectly to the ideas rolling around in her head.

Back then, she was always asking questions—he imagined them as tennis balls being shot out of a practice machine, and he was the tennis player sprinting across the court to hit one back, just as another came flying out and off in a different direction. She'd lost that curiosity, that ability to query everything, long ago.

He wished Diane had written down in her diary more of the funny things that Laura had said as a child. He should have kept his own notebook of her quotes, but he never got round to it, and then it was too late; the years sped through their lives and suddenly she was a grownup and the chirpy little girl was gone.

It saddened Peter to think of what that little girl had become—measured, matter of fact, resigned. Maybe the only way to fight a melting core was to keep a cool steady exterior. He understood that feeling.

Yet as he eavesdropped on Laura telling Chrissie about her birthday, a smile crept across his face, for in the tumbling cadences of her sentences he could now detect just an echo of the enchanting little girl he had thought was gone forever.

"His sense of humour. He really makes me laugh." was Laura's response to Chrissie's hushed question about Miguel's best feature, which to Peter had sounded more of an anatomical query than Laura's answer suggested.

"Sense of humour is very important. I suppose life would get pretty dull sure and fast without one," Chrissie said.

"I know it sounds like such a cliché, but it's true. Sometimes it takes me by surprise. I'll be with him and I'll hear this loud, carefree laughter and for a moment I won't recognise it and then suddenly I'll think, 'My God, that's me!' I'll think, 'Do I really laugh that loudly?'"

"A bit of an out-of-body comedy experience."

Chrissie always had her own unusual way of putting things, Peter thought.

"Now come on, tell me how was last night," Chrissie pressed.

"It was perfect. For dinner we went to the Lobster Pot."

"Oh, very nice," Chrissie sounded genuinely impressed. It had been years since Peter had been to that restaurant. Back then it was just a grotty pub down by the river that only recreational fishermen frequented, but he remembered seeing something in the Chronicle a few years back about someone buying it and sprucing it up. He wondered if it was as good as they said in the paper. From the other room, Laura answered the question for him.

"The food was delicious. The menu changes each day, depending on what's been caught in Donegal that morning. And we had some delicious Italian wine and just sat chatting and laughing all evening, lost in our own world. By the time we finished dessert, it was almost midnight and the place was empty. And then Miguel asked them to call us a taxi and said he had a surprise for me."

"Oh, I love surprises, what was it?" Chrissie asked.

"Well, I'd been expecting that we'd either go home or to the pub. I mean, really, at midnight what else is there to do in this town? So when he asked the taxi to take us out to the cinema, I was a bit confused. I tried to tell him that there are no films on that late here, but he wouldn't listen. So I felt kind of bad for him when we pulled into the cinema and the car park was deserted. You know he'd gone to all that effort to take me out there, in a taxi, and we'd just have to turn around and go back. But then when we got closer to the entrance, I noticed a light on and there was someone sitting in the box office. I expected them to be just cashing up or something and to laugh at us eejits out looking to see a film at that time. But when Miguel asks for two tickets, the box office attendant just replies 'And what film would that be for?' So then Miguel says, 'I don't know. Birthday girl's choice?' and points up to the posters. It's only then do I realise that they are all Fred and Ginger films."

Peter remembered Laura and Diane were obsessed by those films. How could this boy, who wasn't even from around here, arrange that?

173

"Fred and Ginger?" Chrissie's voice boomed through the thin walls.

"Yes! There they were smiling back at me. They'd changed all the posters. Screen One: Follow the Fleet. Screen Two: Top Hat. Screen Three: Swing Time and Screen Four: The Gay Divorcee. 'Take your pick,' he says. 'I told you it's Birthday Girl's choice.' Can you believe it? He'd arranged for them to keep the cinema open just for us, for a private showing. It was amazing."

"How'd he manage that?"

"Charlie. He owns the cinema, too—did you know that? Miguel's always chatting to him when we go to the pub, and well, he said he was happy to help."

"So does this young man have any single brothers for me?"

"Brothers?"

"Or, well, I suppose an uncle would be more appropriate. I quite fancy getting swept off my feet by a handsome foreigner. Maybe he can take a few pictures of me back to Colombia with him, he can show them around, see who's interested. What do you think?"

Peter smiled to himself, imagining Chrissie in Colombia—chatting away to everyone, even if they didn't speak English.

"Sure," Laura said.

"Oh, when does he go?" Chrissie said, sounding delighted with her plan.

"End of March."

"That soon?"

"Yup."

"My God, that's only eight weeks away. Have you talked about what will happen then? Is there any way he can stay here?"

Peter had to strain to hear Laura's response. "No, we've not discussed it. I know he really loves Colombia and he wants to make a difference there. I couldn't ask him to stay here. This work he's been doing at the

174

Tribunal and with Survivors' Stories, well, it's just sort of a one-off. He's on a special visa. And even if he could get a visa, if he actually wanted to practice as a lawyer, then it would take years for him to re-qualify."

"Okay. So go back with him. You can take my picture to Colombia with you and find me a man yourself. Even better."

"Are you crazy?" Laura asked, again her voice just above a whisper. Peter turned the TV volume down a few bars to hear better.

"Well I have heard people say that of me behind my back, but no, I'm not crazy, I'm perfectly serious."

"We've only been together a few months."

"And? Sometimes you need to act, Laura, and not think about these things too much. My mother always said you should know after six weeks whether it's right. That's how my parents did it. They got married within six weeks of meeting each other. Of course, my father was about to go off to war, and she didn't know if she would ever see him again. I suppose during war normal rules no longer applied. That's what I told her when she would go on about how people these days take too long to fall in love, because I never wanted to admit that she had a point. But she did, you know. You need to act quickly or you get left behind."

Peter wasn't sure if he liked where Chrissie was going with this, but it wasn't as if he could intervene and admit he'd been listening all this time.

"I never pegged you as such an advocate for marriage," Laura said.

"Jesus, I'm not telling you to run out and get married! All I'm saying is that if there's real love there, then don't turn your back on it. It might not come along again."

"If it's real love, then maybe it won't matter if he goes back. Maybe eventually we can be together—just now isn't the best time."

"Laura. Get real. Do you really want that to be you? To

spend your life longing, wondering what if? I see how happy you are with him, and it scares me to think what'll happen to you when he leaves."

"Don't worry about me Chrissie, I'll be fine. I knew what I was getting into from the start. I knew it would only ever be for a few months."

It was gone—the melody from her voice had dropped away and been replaced with an all-too-familiar resignation. Peter kept listening, but there was only silence now from the other side of the wall;- the only voice in the house was that of the local NI Assembly rep on the TV talking about the proposals for the new police force.

Leaving the house shouldn't be so daunting. It wasn't like he had a fear of wide-open spaces. It was the opposite, in fact, he was terrified of being hemmed in by all the people out there. This was no life, festering in here all day—no life at all—and now he was robbing his daughter of her life, too. What sort of man was he? It was time to take some action, he resolved, some drastic action, for his daughter's sake.

CHAPTER TWENTYSIX

Chrissie's face ached. The wind was so biting, she could hardly muster the energy to push forward against it, so exhausted was she from the morning shift. She turned the corner and onto her street. Two minutes and she'd be home.

Over the wind, she heard a knocking. She stopped briefly and looked across the street to Kitty MacPherson's house, but Kitty's car wasn't there and the place looked completely empty. Then she heard it again, louder this time, coming from behind her, from Laura and Peter's house. The rapping sounded again, louder this time, like someone was trying frantically to get her attention.

There must be a problem, she thought, for Laura should have been at work and never in a million years would it be Peter, unless there was something wrong, really wrong. She let herself in their gate and rushed up to the back door.

She could just make out the shape of a figure waving at her from behind the yellowing curtains, gesturing to her to come into the house. She felt a shudder within her ribcage.

She flung open the door to find Peter standing in the middle of the room.

"Everything okay?" She asked, bracing herself for the response—getting ready to leap into action to face whatever emergency had forced him to take this drastic action.

"Yes. I just wanted to see if you'd like to join me for a wee cup of tea."

"A cup of tea?"

"Mmm, hmmph," he mumbled.

Chrissie scanned the room, still on the look-out for danger, but everything looked eerily normal.

"Oh, okay." She stepped into the kitchen, immediately wondering why she'd said yes. He pulled out a chair for her at the table, motioning for her to sit down, without quite looking her in the eye.

She watched in silence as he went about making the tea. The faded brown and orange kitchen that had always felt so oppressively small when she was visiting Laura now suddenly seemed vast, like even if she screamed right now at the top her lungs, he wouldn't hear her and would just stay like a statue, watching the kettle boil.

Out of the corner of her eye she watched him—the years hadn't done him as much damage as she might have expected. Underneath his simple wool jumper, his shoulders still looked broad and strong. His black hair had been replaced entirely with grey, so it was wiry but still thick and plentiful, with a hint of a curl despite its short length. She supposed Laura cut it for him from time to time, or maybe he ran a pair of shearers through it himself. That would be better. Chrissie hated to think of him being dependent on his young daughter for absolutely everything.

After an age, he turned around and came to sit opposite her at the table, two cups of tea in hand. This is when he tells me what he wants, Chrissie thought.

"Good day?" he asked.

"So far."

"Busy?"

"Monday's always busy." She lifted the mug he'd set in front of her, and her eyes focussed in on a small chip on the edge of the handle.

"You work at the post office now?"

"Yes."

"Is it still down the Back Street?"

She looked at him, trying to read where he was going with all this chitchat. "No, it moved about four years ago. It's now in Cookson's General Store."

"Oh, so you work with old Johnny Cookson then?"

"No, he died six years back. His son Jack runs the shop now."

"Right. Jack Cookson. I remember him."

Chrissie took a sip of tea and watched Peter do the same. Their eyes met briefly and then she glanced back down at the table. Awkward silences weren't usually a problem for her; she tended to chew through them like a terrier devouring a pillow. But right now the drumming of her heart in her chest felt so loud she could hardly think, let alone speak.

"That dog of yours makes some racket when you leave in the morning."

Was this why he'd dragged her in here? To complain about Harry?

"I'm sorry, Peter. There's not much I can do."

"No. No. I didn't mean that …"

"I've no one else to take care of him …"

"Chrissie, I wasn't complaining. He's no problem. He calms himself after five minutes."

Chrissie took a big gulp of tea. It was nearly cold. He'd put far too much milk in it. She looked up, and for the first time their eyes met properly, long enough for her to remember how green they were—it was unsettling how people's eyes never changed.

"Speaking of Harry, I should probably be going. He's waiting for his lunch." She stood up and Peter stood with her, watching her expectantly as if he thought the next move were hers to make. But Chrissie had no idea what that was supposed to be. Now that she was standing and had announced her intention to leave, she supposed she had better go.

"Thanks for the tea."

"No problem. It was my pleasure."

Pleasure was an odd word to describe the last five minutes, Chrissie thought. She pulled her coat around her, lifted her handbag and sort of nodded goodbye to him and walked to the back door.

"Oh and Chrissie," he said before she was out the door, "maybe we could do this tomorrow again. Same time?"

She couldn't think of an excuse fast enough, so she instinctively said "Sure, see you tomorrow," and nearly ran out the door.

"Have you heard about Father Brendan?"

"What?"

"He's got a recording contract with Sony."

"Really? I've only met him a few times, y'know when he does his visits round the houses. I've not heard him sing," Peter said.

"Lucky you. He sings every week at eleven o'clock mass. I tell myself I must be going to heaven for putting up with that on a Sunday morning—especially on a hangover," Chrissie reached for another piece of cake from the centre of the table. She looked at Peter smiling opposite her. They were sitting in his orange kitchen, which was illuminated with winter sunlight. How things had changed since that first strange morning three weeks ago when she'd come in for two gulps of cold tea.

The next morning she'd been passing by at eleven when she'd heard him knocking again. That morning there'd been an explosion at a nuclear plant in China. It had been on the news all morning, so they'd chatted about that—repeating things both of them had heard on television. It had struck her as odd how much he knew about something at the other side of the world and how yet little he seemed to know about events right outside his front door. And then he'd invited her back again, and the day after that, and so, with the aid of a few global crises, they had somehow relaxed into a daily routine.

Now every morning at eleven he would have the tea ready, waiting for her arrival, and she'd bring some cake from the shop and tell him all the news and gossip she'd picked up that morning. She could see he was starting to reintegrate, to recognise again the characters that he knew from a life long ago. Their talk was light and inconsequential, looking out at the world rather than in. Although, sometimes, when the conversation slowed, she caught a glimpse of the unsteadiness within him, and it seemed like he might be about to tell her something real, something honest, but it would pass quickly and they would return to trivialities.

"When Father Brendan's CD comes out, I'll get you a copy. Do you still listen to a lot of music?" Chrissie asked.

"No, not anymore. In fact, I don't even think we have a CD player. It broke a long time ago," he paused, then suddenly looking brave, he added, "Diane broke it. She knocked it over one night when she was, ummm, not very steady on her feet."

It was the first time Chrissie had heard him mention Diane. The name pierced her ears.

"I always meant to get it fixed, but I suppose I didn't fancy listening to music for a long time after she died and, on CD, all we really have is her country music. All my stuff was on vinyl. I think it's still in the attic somewhere. But Diane threw the record player away years ago in one of her redecorating fits."

It made Chrissie sad to think that even years after her death, Peter still lived in the silence Diane had imposed upon him, with his own tastes suppressed in the attic.

"Doesn't Laura listen to music?"

"She listens to all sorts of weird and wonderful things on that clock radio thing she got for Christmas. I don't really know what it is. I can't say I like it all, but some of it's good. Odd, but good. You know when Diane was pregnant with her, I thought maybe she'd be a musician," he suddenly hesitated, "don't tell her I said that, will you? I wouldn't want her thinking I'm disappointed or anything. I wouldn't change her."

He had used Diane's name again. He seemed emboldened by it, as if realizing that he wouldn't be bewitched to stone if he conjured up a memory of her. Quite the opposite, Chrissie thought, talking of Diane seemed to turn him back from a statue into a man.

"Really, you wouldn't change her? Don't you ever wish she would be a bit more daring? She seems kind of stuck to me."

"You think she should be a bit more like Diane?" Peter challenged.

"No, that's not what I'm saying," Chrissie knew she was in danger of insulting him if she went on, so she retreated.

"You know she's a very good teacher. I heard Mrs. Mullen, the head of the school governors, say the other day how impressed they are with her."

"Thanks."

"For what?"

"For … you know." Peter smiled and lifted his hands like he was about to explain something, but then he just let them drop to his lap and kept looking at her, completely speechless, until Chrissie was forced to look away, embarrassed.

A few days later, Chrissie was at work listening to Mrs. Browne complain about the church choir. It was Mrs. Browne's favourite subject, which was useful as there were no silences for Chrissie to fill and instead she could calculate time. Provided Louise arrived bang on time to take over her shift, and she really ran, she could make it to the bus stop by half eleven. It would take forty-five minutes to get there. That would leave her over an hour to pick it up and make it back for her afternoon shift. She could drop it off that evening on her way home. Laura had mentioned that Miguel was taking her to a concert, which meant she wouldn't be home until at least ten.

Chrissie wasn't sure if Laura knew about their little morning routine. She doubted it. Laura hadn't mentioned it the past couple of times she'd seen her in the street, so Chrissie had decided to stay quiet. Even if Peter had told her, Chrissie didn't want Laura there when she gave him the gift.

The trip to and from Derry went just as planned, and after work Chrissie went straight to his house, rushing through the wintry January evening to get to him. He looked surprised when he opened the door. She hadn't planned what she was going to say, so the words just rushed out before she could review them.

"I was in Derry just doing a wee shop, one of my nieces is getting married at the end of May and I thought I'd go see if there were any nice dresses and so I was in Derry and I saw this, it was on special, half price and for some reason I thought I remembered you liking Handel, so I got it for you."

She drew a breath and shoved the CD, Handel's "Il trionfo del tempo e della verità—The Triumph of Time and Truth," into his hand. It was still inside the plastic carrier bag. She had intentionally not wrapped it; she didn't want it to look like a gift.

Peter took it out of the bag and looked at it. His eyes moved slowly from her face to the CD and back again. She couldn't read him. He was quiet for far too long.

"Shall we listen to it together?" she said.

"Yes, but we don't have a CD player."

She remembered what he had said about Diane

breaking it years ago and it never having been replaced.

"You could perhaps come over to mine. I'm sure you've heard me playing my music until all hours, so at least you'd be listening to something you enjoy."

"I can't. I ummm," he looked beyond her shoulder— he was clearly trying to think of an excuse, it was bloody obvious that he wouldn't come. It had been insensitive of her to ask.

"Why don't we try it on your DVD player?" she suggested, pleased that she'd found a way to recover the situation.

"I never knew you could do that."

Chrissie followed him into the living room. She grabbed the remote controls, turned the TV to the DVD channel and pressed eject to ready the machine. He unpeeled the plastic, loaded the CD and pressed play. She stood a few feet away, watching him.

The music began with a majestic and hopeful overture. Peter folded into his chair, staring straight at the TV. Chrissie reached over and turned off the overhead light, plunging the room into semi-darkness, leaving just the solid navy blue light of the television, which was broken only by the DVD symbol, which ricocheted hypnotically from one side of the screen to the other. Chrissie lowered herself onto the edge of the sofa, captivated more by the still figure in the chair across from her, whose face was now obscured by the shadows, than the music twirling around them. She studied him carefully. He looked so still. Then she noticed a barely perceptible movement of his hands, drifting up and down with the music, light as the soprano's voice. Chrissie followed his hands as they danced and she felt her mind being cast adrift, floating back to another time.

Usually his voice sounded thin like paper, but the voice that emerged from the shadows when the music was over was full and rounded. "It's incredible. Thank you for this. I forgot how beautiful it can be just to listen sometimes."

Chrissie bounced up and turned on the overhead light. Peter was sitting back in his chair with an absolute smile on his face, smooth and almost deceptively youthful.

"I'm glad you liked it."

"What a great recording. So moving."

"You know, if you ever wanted to, I could borrow my sister's car and we could drive to Derry. There's always some sort of classical music event on at the Play House or the Guild Hall. Nothing as fancy as," she picked up the CD case and read the cover "the New York Handel Choir and Orchestra, but they do get some decent acts. I could keep an eye out in the paper if you like."

Peter turned white. Her mind and her mouth were getting ahead of her as usual.

"So you like the recording?" she said, trying to revive the Peter who had been with her just moments before.

"Chrissie, actually, I've been meaning to talk to you."

Her nerves started to jangle. She had been overly presumptuous. She had assumed that he wanted to spend more time with her. Actually, all he probably wanted was nothing more than a friendly chat every once in a while, a mere portal to the outside world, since Laura was spending so much time with Miguel. She had stopped even asking him if she should come over, she just landed on his doorstep every morning at eleven, and how was he supposed to escape her, housebound as he was.

"It was one of the reasons I started asking you over, and I suppose I was just enjoying the company so much that I took my time about asking."

"Asking what?"

"I need your help."

The jittery cells in her body slowed down to a smooth rocking. "Need my help with what?"

"Don't pretend you don't know what I am talking about. I need to … you know. Get back out there."

"Okay," she paused, trying to evaluate what exactly it was he was asking of her, "Peter, you know me, I'm happy to help, but what can I do?"

"I don't know, I just know I can't go on like this, it's not fair to Laura and I thought you … I thought you might be able to …" his voice trailed off.

"Have you thought maybe you need a professional?"

"I'm not crazy, I'm just … Never mind. I thought you would …"

"I'm not saying you're crazy, I'm just saying some things a professional is better equipped to handle."

"I'm not seeing some bloody doctor. Forget I said anything."

"No, listen, I'm sorry. Of course I'll help." She didn't think there was anything she could do to help him, but she couldn't refuse. "What does Laura say?"

"I can't talk to her. Not about this."

"What, you've never discussed your," she grappled for the right word, "situation?"

"What are we supposed to discuss? It's not like I chose this, it just sort of happened, I couldn't face people after Diane … and a few weeks became a few months, and then months became years and we just got on with it."

"Have you never discussed why?"

"I'm not about to burden her, she shouldn't have to go through that."

"I'm sure she wouldn't feel burdened."

"It wouldn't be right," he said, more forcefully than before.

Chrissie had often wondered why Laura lived with this odd state of affairs, reinforcing the status quo by doing nothing. Maybe she didn't want to think about why her father was so ashamed that he couldn't face the world after Diane's death. There had been so many rumours, so many questions asked by the town's gossips—trying to draw a link between the bombing and Diane's sudden suicide. Chrissie hoped for Laura's sake that she'd never heard them.

She looked at Peter, crumpled in his chair. It wasn't

right that he should suffer like this—Chrissie was sure he'd never done anything to deserve this kind of imprisonment. She would help him, the only way she knew how, through the sheer force of her own energy and enthusiasm.

"Let's go for a wee walk then. Just around the block."

He didn't move. "Perhaps tomorrow?"

"I read once it takes just fourteen times to form a habit, and this is just a habit. It can be replaced with a new habit. So we'll start tomorrow. We'll go out to the backyard tomorrow. Then the next day we'll go over to my house. Then the next we'll take a walk around the block, and then the next we'll take a walk down the river. On day fifteen I'll have you walking to Derry!"

"Just a bad habit, I like that," he said, "do you really think that's true?"

Chrissie didn't believe a word she was saying, but she caught the thought before it raced out her mouth. Now was not the time for realism.

CHAPTER TWENTYSEVEN

Peter's eyes crept along the kitchen floor, from his own beaten house slippers to Chrissie's black high heels, and then up to meet her steely stare. She was tapping her bright pink fingernails on the kitchen counter. Even in middle age, she still existed in Technicolor, whereas he had faded to grey. Growing older was inevitable, but looking at her, it was clear that the way one grows old, one's attitude to the passing years, was entirely optional. The tapping grew louder—he needed to move, he needed to stand up and walk.

It had been ten years since Diane's death, but still he knew that people would scrutinise him, watch his every move, analyse his voice, his expressions, his actions.

Chrissie was watching him, studying him. He didn't want this. He didn't want people looking at him, whispering their questions and their theories behind his back. He closed his fists around his sweaty palms. "Maybe you should just go," he whispered, barely able to squeeze the words through the tightening muscles in his throat. "Leave me alone for a bit."

"For God's sake, Peter. I'm only asking you to go out to the back garden." She came up next to him and reached for his arm to help him up. He immediately shrugged her off.

"I'm not a cripple. I can walk by myself."

"Then walk." The room around him began to move and Chrissie was transformed into a purple mass with undefined edges and red hair.

"I'm waiting,"

"Why don't you go, we can do this another time."

"No, to break the habit you have to start."

"I can start tomorrow."

"Today's as good as tomorrow."

"Just go."

She didn't move. "Please, can you get out of here? You're not helping."

Chrissie stepped closer to him so that her feet came into his downcast view, reaching over him for her bag and coat from the chair next to his. Her silence was unnerving. He followed her shoes to the back door, and saw a triangle of sunlight enter when she opened it.

"You're not ill. You can change this behaviour if you want to. I know you, you're not hardwired this way."

Peter kept his eyes fixed on the floor as the walls in his peripheral vision continued to spin. He could feel her cool stare judging him. This had all been a terrible mistake— why did he think Chrissie of all people could help him?

"Fine, suit yourself," Chrissie pulled the door behind her with a thud, erasing the triangle of light as she went. Peter exhaled for what felt like the first time all morning and gasped for new air, trying with each gulp to paint over the red terror in his mind with a thick coat of white.

As his breathing steadied and the room stilled about him, he became aware of a voice outside the window.

"Harry, I won't tell you again. Get up. Home. Now!"

Peter stretched up from his slumped position at the table. Through the window he could see Chrissie standing at his gate, shouting at Harry who was out of view.

"For Christ's sake, dog!" She bent down, disappearing from view and then reappeared looking more furious than before. "Fine. Stay there then you stupid mutt. I'll be back for you when you're hungry."

She stormed off, and a few seconds later the room shook as Chrissie slammed the door next door. Peter counted to five, stood up, and inched over to the kitchen window. There was Harry, in the middle of the yard, fully stretched out, lying on his side facing the house. Peter gingerly pulled down one of the Venetian blinds by a fraction to take a better look and, as he did, Harry's tail started to thump the ground in recognition of the attention. Peter stepped back from the window. He could hear Chrissie slamming cupboards and bashing plates through the thin wall that separated their kitchens. He looked around him, wondering what he should do next.

Alone in her kitchen, Chrissie took out her frustration on the pots and pans and other kitchen appliances as she moved about putting away the dishes from last night's dinner. She was furious at that disobedient dog of hers, she was furious at that ungrateful man next door and she was furious at herself for even thinking she could help. She looked over at Harry in Peter's yard, in which he had made himself at home, sprawled out on the ground. Then she noticed his tail was moving up and down. That was Harry's way of smiling back at someone.

Chrissie grabbed a glossy magazine from the living room and pulled herself up on to the kitchen counter to get the best view possible, with her legs dangling down in front her, like a teenager.

Fifteen minutes passed before she saw Harry stir again. His tail started to twitch, he scrambled himself up and onto his four legs with his tail wagging at treble speed behind him. She got close to the window and craned her neck, trying to get a look at Peter's back door, but it was impossible. Harry was jumping around in the middle of the yard now, lowering his front legs as he raised his behind— his tail wagging so much he looked like a helicopter about to take flight.

Then she heard a voice, which must've been Peter, although she couldn't see him or make out what he was saying. Harry started to yelp with excitement and ran to Peter's back door and then back to the middle of the yard bouncing on his overgrown paws. This game continued for nearly five minutes. Harry rushing to the back door and disappearing out of sight and then reappearing and bouncing around and all the time Chrissie stared out the window, willing Peter to come out of his cave.

Finally, he stepped into view. It had taken him all of three steps to get to where Harry now lay, legs in the air waiting for his belly to be tickled. Could this be a new start for them all? With her entire being she wanted to believe it could be so, but she'd been disappointed before.

CHAPTER TWENTYEIGHT

An unexpected sound hit Laura as she walked in the front door, a whooping cackle of a laugh. She popped her head around the living room door. Her father was where she expected him, in his usual chair by the TV, and Chrissie was on the sofa, dabbing away tears, a small smudge of mascara just below her left eye. Harry started thumping his tail against the floor, but he didn't bother getting up from his cosy spot in front of the fire.

"Laura, you have to see this," Chrissie said.

Laura went and perched on the edge of the sofa, giving Harry an affectionate tussle on the head as she stepped over him.

"Do you remember Father Brendan?" Chrissie asked.

Of course she did. Up until last year Father Brendan had been assigned as school chaplain. He called himself the "Singing Priest," a nickname he encouraged the girls to take up, with little success, and he carried a guitar everywhere in case he found an occasion to sing, which was often. Because of Father Brendan, Laura had developed a phobia of acoustic guitars and all the sing-along jolliness they represented. She shuddered when she saw his cheesy grin smeared across the TV screen.

"You know how he's signed a one-million-pound contract with Sony?" Chrissie asked.

"No!"

"How did you not hear that gossip? It was weeks ago. Anyway, this whole show is based around him, it's called Holy Hit Makers. They've had the singing nun, and the Reverend Al Green. According to this, Father Brendan's going to be huge. I saw he was on, so I came round to tell your dad to watch it."

Laura looked over at her father, who didn't take his eyes off the TV. She wondered how he was coping with this invasion.

"Will you listen to that!" Chrissie said.

On screen, Father Brendan was, in all his priestly humility, saying, "I suppose I'm a marketing executive's dream. If you think about it, my brand is two thousand years in the making."

"Talk about a Jesus complex!" Chrissie added. Laura noticed the corner of her father's mouth rise up into a smile.

The voiceover on the television went on: "Piracy is one of the biggest threats to the music industry, which is one of the reasons Sony have decided to branch out into the religious market with their latest one-million-pound signing. The thinking being that the devout are more likely to buy music than to steal it. There are other advantages too: from a management perspective it is much easier to handle Father Brendan than a young rock star."

"I don't think they realise the prima donna they're dealing with." Peter muttered. Laura looked at her father and smiled.

"Will you look at this fella!" Chrissie screeched. On screen was an old Franciscan monk singing a Metallica song, his brown robe slashed open at the front revealing the pumped chest a man half his age would have been proud of.

"Sit back, Laura, make yourself at home," Chrissie said, patting the sofa next to her.

When Laura came downstairs the next morning, her father was not in his usual resigned slump in his armchair supping tea from his chipped old mug. She passed through the living room and into the kitchen. The back door to the house was wide open, letting a breeze flow in. Like an uninvited guest, the air moved through the rooms, discovering the previously closed off territory. She rushed towards the door to close it, but stopped when she saw her father in the yard standing between the black wheelie bin and the coal shed, hand in pocket, back somehow straighter than usual. She watched him for a second. He could have been a man standing on his back porch in Colorado, surveying the horizon, contemplating the wonder of God's hand in creating such spectacular mountains and lakes for him to gaze upon each morning. Perhaps that was what was in his mind's eye. Although following his gaze, all Laura could see were squat little counsel houses just like their own.

"Morning," she called. He turned around, his weary expression was still there, he had been wearing it for so long his muscles naturally fell that way, but she noticed something right by the corner of his eyes that well could have been a rogue muscle trying to smile. "What are you doing out here?" she ventured, trying to sound light—as if this were a normal occurrence, which it should be, a man having a morning tea, alfresco on his own tiny patch of land.

"Just having my tea," he turned and shuffled back towards the house, and as he passed her in the doorway he said, "And how are you this morning, Olive?"

"He hasn't called me Olive in such a long time."

Laura was with Miguel in his kitchen helping to prepare dinner.

"And why would he?"

"Olive Oyl—he used to call me Olive Oyl when I was a child."

"Because you loved the green, how do you say? Elixir of the gods? As a child you were very healthy! Most kids have a thing for candy instead."

"No! The green elixir hadn't quite taken hold on these shores when I was young, back then we still cooked with lard—when I was a kid we thought spaghetti Bolognese was exotic!"

"And now here I am bringing Latin flavour right to your door, how things have changed."

"Yes, in terms of exotic, I suppose you are a step up from spaghetti Bolognese."

"And how do I compare to carbonara?"

She rolled her eyes at him.

"So, getting back to my very important question. Olive oil?"

"O.Y.L. —not O.I.L. You know Popeye? The sailor man?"

"Ah yes, his girlfriend!" Miguel stood back and examined her. "Tall and slim, big smile, dark hair. Yes, I see it. You never told me that."

"To be honest, it wasn't the nickname that surprised me. It was that he was standing out there." Laura looked up from the carrots she was chopping. Miguel was pulling vegetables from the fridge. He didn't seem to have picked up on what she said. "He hasn't left the house since my mother's funeral."

She studied Miguel's face. "I suppose you already knew that."

"I have heard something like that, yes."

"And you never asked me about it?"

"You never really know what's rumour and what's true,

so I thought I'd just wait. I thought you'd tell me in your own time."

Laura felt a rush of gratitude that Miguel had been so patient and hadn't pushed her into talking about it before.

He moved past her and picked up the carrots and threw them into the frying pan of hot oil.

"Why don't you get the glasses down and serve us some wine and you can tell me all about it over dinner," he said.

Later that night, back in her single bed at home, Laura thought about the word "surprise." It had almost lost its meaning to her. Her life had for so long been about absolute certainties or complete shocks. There were no mere surprises. But the empty chair that greeted her that morning had come as a surprise. Her father alone in the yard thinking back to a time when his daughter was a girl and he teased her with nicknames, that was a surprise. The laughter she had heard the night before when he was watching TV with Chrissie. All small surprises, but each great in their own way.

It was good to have some sense of surprise back in her life, and Miguel was the biggest surprise of all. He could create masterpieces out of everyday moments, like taking her back in time with a trip to the local cinema, like waiting for her to open up to him despite his intrinsic, maddening curiosity, like dancing with her in the moonlight in the centre of a roundabout full of statues. Laura glowed, thinking of all the memories they had created in such a short time. She was coming to realise a life without random little surprises was not a life. A life is made in those moments. It is in the new glimpses you catch of the people you love. It is in those seconds when you see them as new. And she now needed to test if she had the courage to surprise herself, and of that, she was completely unsure.

CHAPTER TWENTYNINE

"Sorry, sorry, can you just move please, madam." Miguel pinned her to the counter with the full weight of his body. She giggled, trying in vain to break free as he rolled his eyes in mock frustration. "She just won't get out of the way."

One of the kitchen hands laughed as he passed them with a pile of dirty pots. Miguel released her from his grip and shifted himself to his original position, leaning up against the counter, his eyes once more facing intently upward. Laura glanced up at the screen and then at all the people working around them. There seemed to be an order and a rhythm underlying the sporadic shouts, the ferocious massacre of vegetables and the whoosh of raw meat hitting boiling oil. Individually, everyone created their own beat or melody as they focussed on their isolated tasks, but, standing in the middle of it all listening to it as a whole, all the activity seemed to Laura to come together in unintentional unison, like the experimental jazz Miguel was so fond of. She turned to make this observation to him, but then stopped herself, struck by how tense he looked. It was as if he had been mummified alive, so constrained was every muscle in his body.

"Aaaargh!" he groaned loudly. It was as if in the mummification process only Miguel's mouth had been left unbandaged, so that all the trapped energy in his constricted body could only find a release through pained, wailing noises. Everyone else in the kitchen paused to look at the screen before returning to their work. The guy stir-frying vegetables caught Laura's eye. She shrugged and he smiled back, clearly amused by Miguel's outbursts.

"Sorry, it's just they get so close and then nothing. It's frustrating," he said, lifting a hand to wipe the sweat from his forehead with a napkin, his eyes still fixed on the TV.

"But if it's so frustrating why do you …"

He turned placing his hands on her lips, silencing her with a smile. "Three minutes to halftime and then I'm all yours. Let's just focus on the game for now."

"No problem. I'm enjoying just watching you watch," she said, and it was true. Watching him watch football was like studying his most raw and unguarded self. It was almost like seeing him in his natural habitat. Although she had never imagined that the kitchen of a Chinese takeaway could serve as anyone's most natural space, let alone Miguel's. But that was the thing with him; he was who he was no matter where he was, or who was watching. She still didn't quite understand how they had ended up here.

The small Chinese community in the town, which was made up of just a handful of families, was notoriously closed. They barely interacted, other than to take orders over the phone, but Miguel had managed to get them to invite him backstage. Somehow he had become friends with Bing, the head chef, and he'd found out that they had Chinese cable TV in the kitchen, which showed Latin American football, so he convinced Bing to let them in to watch his precious Santa Fe play Millonarios in the Bogotá derby. And now here she was, at nearly one in the morning, surrounded by cooks, perched against the sink, sipping beer and eating prawn crackers, watching a Colombian scream at a small television high up on the wall in the corner of the room, as Chinese commentary blared out over the hustle and bustle of the kitchen. She was two miles from her house and felt like she was a world away from home, and she couldn't have been happier.

Laura's thoughts shifted back to the game as Miguel launched himself forward in the direction of the screen.

"Eeeeee Noooooo," he let out another guttural roar and then collapsed back against the counter next to her. The players started walking off the pitch and it cut to what looked to be an advertisement for washing powder.

"Halftime then?"

"Are you enjoying it?" he asked.

"Yes."

"Really?"

"Maybe, it's strange. I've never seen you so tense. You do know it's only a …"

"Don't say it's only a game."

Laura took a sip of her beer.

"You have to get invested," Miguel went on, "there's no point just being a spectator."

"Isn't that exactly what you're doing?" Clearly, she thought, it's a binary choice; you're either a player or a spectator.

"No! Well yes, but you have to care as if it were you out there fighting for the goal yourself. For those ninety minutes, you have to believe that your destiny, your happiness is inextricably bound up with that of the team. Otherwise, what's the point?"

"Aren't you just setting yourself up for a huge disappointment if you care that much? What if they lose?"

"But what if they win? Imagine the joy, Laura, imagine the joy."

Laura smiled at him, but she still didn't get it. It seemed like a big risk to take with your emotions, why risk such crushing disappointment week after week just for the chance of some fleeting happiness? Her scepticism obviously shone through.

"It's okay, you'll understand when I take you to the stadium this summer. You'll feel the passion, see what it means to really be involved."

"This summer?"

"Yes, I have it all planned."

"You do?"

"I have to leave by end of March, so we'll have three months until your school year is up, but we can talk on the phone, every day if you want, and then in June when school breaks up you can come stay with me in Colombia for the summer."

Laura shifted and turned to reach for a prawn cracker from the bowl on the counter behind her.

"Where would I stay?" she said, examining the greasy cracker in her hand.

"With me, of course, I've already spoken to my grandmother and she's delighted for you to stay. Her place is much bigger than my dad's, and she likes the company, so I'm going to stay with her when I go back to Colombia for a few months anyway."

"You've already spoken to your grandmother? Without speaking to me?"

"Well, yes, is there a problem?"

Of course there was a problem. What was he thinking, going ahead making plans like that without her? She couldn't spend the whole summer in Colombia.

"Is there?" he prompted.

"No, it's just I hadn't really thought about the summer."

"Not at all?"

She shrugged and snapped the prawn cracker in two, feeling the edges disintegrate into her fingertips. It was sort of true that she hadn't thought about it. The question had charged into her mind on several occasions, and each time she'd marched it straight back out again. Telling the future to piss off was the only way she could enjoy the here and now. She put the cracker in her mouth, letting it melt into a sour mush on her tongue.

"Well, don't worry, luckily I've thought about it and I've got it all under control. You'll come for the summer and if you like it, fantastic—and I'll make sure you do—then you can start looking for teaching jobs there. There's an American high school, they teach all their classes in English, so maybe you could teach literature there, and even if you couldn't, I'm sure you could teach English in companies or in an English academy or something. And if you don't like it, well, we'll figure something out. I mean, it won't be easy for me to work here, but … well, you should come for the summer and see."

He was staring straight into her eyes, waiting for a response. But he hasn't asked a question, Laura thought, he's just talked and talked and now he expects me to speak and there's was nothing for me to say. She couldn't go to Colombia for the whole summer. At most, she could leave her father alone for a week, and even then, just contemplating it felt neglectful and wrong. Moving there was simply out of the question.

Everyone around them was still busy cooking and cleaning, still seemingly engrossed in their work, but Laura felt their ears tweak, she felt them incorporate her uneven breaths into their performance, like a discordant backbeat foreshadowing the argument that was sure to follow if she told him the truth.

"That sounds nice," she said, carefully choosing her words so it sounded like she was agreeing with him without actually committing to do anything. He smiled, seemingly satisfied with her response.

She looked up at the TV. They were showing Miguel's team's missed opportunities at goal from the first half.

"So you're team's not doing so well, huh?"

"They should've scored at least five times by now. It's annoying, it's as if they don't believe they can win."

"Do you think they'll win?"

"It depends what they're doing right now. The break

can be critical. As they say, it's a game of two halves, and anything could happen now."

Laura turned towards the screen again, resting on the counter with her body just lightly touching Miguel's. The players started to wander back onto the pitch and she felt Miguel's body become rigid again.

The whistle went, and the players started to move, the red team had the ball and was passing it at lightning speed between them towards the goal. Miguel stepped forward and stood on his tiptoes.

"Sí, sí, sí …" he called through gritted teeth. Bing wandered over and stood next to him. And then suddenly Miguel erupted, "Yes!" he shouted, jumping up and down in the air, nearly knocking Bing over. Laura looked up at the TV; the red team were celebrating a goal. It had all happened so quickly she hadn't had time to really see it go in.

Miguel turned to Bing and hugged him. Then he turned and flung his arms around Laura, picking her up at the waist and whizzing her around, oblivious to all the people who were watching them.

Laura laughed and smiled back at him. She could see why he went to such lengths to watch his beloved team. This kind of happiness was addictive. But all addictive things have to be given up sooner or later, she thought as he set her down. She pushed the thought to the back of her mind. She didn't want to think about giving Miguel up, not yet. And standing there, enveloped with Miguel's joy, it didn't occur to her that Miguel might give up on her.

She felt so secure in his arms that she'd almost forgotten that, in the time between sunset and sunrise, someone you love can disappear from your life completely.

CHAPTER THIRTY

"Patrick O'Donnell is the most Irish of painters. His work has a poetic quality, weaving the smallest details of the landscape together with long brushstrokes that melt into one another. He had a long love affair with the West Coast of Ireland and the powerful ocean that defines it, capturing the roaring waves, the gentle coastal towns of white houses with thatched roofs and the regal lighthouses that stand like goddesses protecting sailors from the Atlantic's capricious twists and turns. Come to admire his life's work in a retrospective in Donegal and take the chance to buy some of his final works."

Laura turned the leaflet over in her hand to examine it again. She had never seen the picture before. It was painted from the perspective of the ocean, looking back to the jaw-dropping white cliffs. At the bottom of the picture, waves crashed violently on the rocks. Perched high on the cliff top was a small cottage billowing black smoke up to the heavy sky. Miguel was right, there was no getting away from the similarities. She recognised the brush strokes, the way one might recognise someone's voice singing a new and unfamiliar song. She turned the page back over to look again at the name. Patrick O'Donnell. It was an answer and a question bound up in one.

Miguel placed two cappuccinos on the table and sat down opposite her. They were in the café that stood on the corner between Back Street and Main Street. It used to be a bank, and there were still some signs of its previous prominence in the high ceilings and marble floors, although its present carnation was a modest café selling tea and coffee, cream cakes and sweaty sausage rolls.

"So …?"

"It's definitely the same style. It could be the same painter. I'm not saying it is, but …"

"But it could be."

"Yes," she conceded.

He looked pleased with himself. It was the look she'd seen on him when he knew the name of a bit-part actor in a film or found the perfect word in English to describe something.

"How'd you find out about this?"

"Just by chance. I went to the tourist office to get some ideas for stuff to do nearby and the leaflet just caught my eye. And there's more."

"More?"

"Well, when I saw this leaflet, I decided to call up to see if they were holding any events as part of the exhibition. The woman at the gallery asked where I was from, so I told her Colombia, and then she started shrieking and saying how great it was that Mr. O'Donnell had such a global reach and she asked if I wanted to attend the opening night. She said the O'Donnell family would be there and anybody who is anybody in Donegal."

"Well, that's probably not too many people."

"So, do you want to be my date for the evening? We can rub shoulders with Donegal's finest and maybe have a chat with the painter?"

"And then what? Say we do go and he's there. What do I say to him? Do I ask him if he painted our picture?"

"Yes, exactly, and then if he did, ask him if he knew your mother."

"C'mon, that's a bit of a leap."

"Maybe, but why not ask?"

"I dunno," she looked around the café to the groups of Saturday afternoon shoppers; they were mainly women and teenagers. All the men were probably in the pub. "I really don't think he'll have anything to tell me."

"So what's the harm in asking?" He reached across the table and squeezed her hand. She pulled it away.

"None."

"Well?"

"Well what?"

"Then what's the problem?"

"There is no problem," she said.

"Great, then we'll go and we'll take a photo of your painting and we'll ask him did he paint it and how did the poem get on there."

"Fine, if it's so important to you we'll go and ask the question. It's not a big deal."

"Who said it was?"

Laura leaned back in her seat and stared past Miguel's ear out the window—she couldn't bring herself to meet his eye.

Over the next two weeks, Laura met the artist hundreds of times and each time it played out slightly differently. Sometimes he would recognise Diane in her immediately and break off his conversation to make his way through the party to welcome them, drawing her close in a big open-armed welcome. Other times he nodded politely and indifferently as she told him about the painting belonging to her parents, with the poem inscribed in the sea. And when she was done, he'd quickly move on. Never though, could she bring herself to imagine what he might tell her about her mother, for she feared that if, by some miracle, he did have something to say, it couldn't be good.

Miguel arrived at ten to pick her up in Mr. Quigley's car, which he'd borrowed to take them to Donegal. He insisted that they leave early so that they could stop for a nice lunch and a drink along the way before the opening, which started at three.

In the car, he sang along to a series of upbeat songs on a CD he'd put together especially for the journey. Whilst he could whisper a lullaby or a love song with feeling, so that if he missed a few notes here and there it was still beautiful, all semblance of musical talent disappeared as soon as he put on rock music. Despite the racket he made, though, he looked joyous when he sang, strumming the wheel with his fingers, his eyes sometimes closing momentarily for emotional effect at a particularly high note, making him look comically serious.

"Are you laughing at me?" he said, catching her giggling.

"No, of course not. Just enjoying the performance, but can you please keep your eyes on the road."

"You are laughing at me! Well I don't care!" He went back to his singing, even louder than before.

"I'm sorry, I have to say this, for someone who has such a passion for music you have no qualms about happily murdering any song."

"Well I don't care. I sing for my pleasure!"

"That's funny, that's what my mother used to say."

"Really?"

"Yeah. She said that she sang for her own pleasure, which my father often retorted was certainly so, her singing was most definitely not pleasurable for anyone listening."

"Very cruel of him."

"But he was right! She was another terrible singer. Atrocious, in fact."

"Another terrible singer? Really, who was the other one? I hope you're not putting me in the same category!"

"I wouldn't put you two in the same category. She at least could sing one song well."

"Hey!" he playfully punched her in the arm.

"At parties. it never took her too long to be persuaded to join in the inevitable sing-along, and she had this party piece that she sang beautifully." Laura could almost hear her mother's voice filled with longing, calling out the melody.

"What was it?"

"'*She moved through the Fair.*' It's an old folk song—it tells the tale of the ghost of a young bride whispering to her lover, making plans for their wedding and a future that she'll never see. Every other song she sang off key, carelessly belting out the wrong lyrics, but this haunting song she knew note and word perfect." Laura could almost hear her mother's quivering rendition of the song. Even though she sometimes struggled to remember the exact tone of her mother's voice, she could always conjure up the sound of her singing this song.

"I think it's better to know just one song perfectly than a thousand others imperfectly," Miguel said.

Laura smiled over at him. "And I take it that you haven't found the song you can sing perfectly just yet?"

"What'd you mean? It's this one," Miguel turned up the volume and resumed his attempt at singing. "It's a beautiful day—far out and la la. It's a beautiful day, woo hoo." Laura nodded her head along to the beat—straining to hear the original under Miguel. When the song finished, they were plunged into silence—both of them slightly breathless from all the exertion.

"So what other memories do you have of your mother?" Miguel asked.

Laura thought for a moment—there were so many, but she wanted to find a happy one—she didn't want to ruin the atmosphere. "I remember hot chocolate and biscuits in front of a freshly lit fire after school. We'd sit together on the sofa and watch Fred and Ginger, as you know. And my mother would sing along with the old show tunes. Well, singing is the nice word for it."

"It sounds like there was a lot of music in your house

growing up."

"There was. You're right."

Another memory came into her mind—of Christmas Eve when she was small, maybe seven or so. The loud music from the party downstairs had woken her, and she started to worry that all the noise might scare Father Christmas away, so she'd gotten herself up and crawled downstairs, still groggy from sleep. Peeking into the living room, she had seen her mother alone; there was no party, she was dancing by herself in the middle of the room and her father was nowhere to be seen. Laura knew it was her mother, but still she felt afraid. She was dancing recklessly, singing without thinking, arms stretched out. And she was crying, but it looked like she hadn't noticed, she didn't even bother to wipe the tears soaking her face.

Laura could still recall the exact lyrics of the song. It was by one of her mother's favourite singers, Dolly Parton. It went: "*D.I.V.O.R.C.E … I love you both and this will be HE double L for me.*"

Laura had snuck back to bed and cried herself to sleep. The next morning her father was back and everything seemed normal—and Laura sometimes wondered if she had dreamt it all or if it was a true memory.

"So what other music do you remember your parents playing when you were young?" Miguel asked.

"Nothing in particular. You have to turn left at the next junction."

The next turn took them straight into Donegal Town Square.

The square was packed with cars—so Miguel had to circle around it a few times searching for a free spot. Each time they drove past the gallery, Laura tried to catch a glimpse of the people inside through the heavy glass doors. She was trying to see if she recognised the artist, even though she had no idea what he looked like. She wished she'd looked him up on the Internet, but she had avoided it for some reason that she couldn't now explain. In any event, she would meet him soon enough.

Laura clutched her bag in her left hand; in it was a photo of the painting to show the artist—and with her other hand she reached over and stroked the hairs at the back of Miguel's neck. "Thank you for bringing me here."

On the way back, there was no joking, no singing and no sharing of memories. There was just the low buzz of anger under the silence. She had fled the exhibition in a white rage. Miguel only caught up with her at the car, their coats in his hands.

"Please can you open the door," she said, looking straight past him so she wouldn't have to meet his eye.

"It's not my fault."

"Open the door."

"But …"

"Miguel. Please!"

He walked round to the driver's side and unlocked the car. She immediately got in and locked her door behind her. It was an unconscious reaction. She wanted to lock herself away in a protected place so she could forget about this whole wasted day. He got in the driver's side and sat for a few minutes looking straight ahead. Laura could detect a low rumble of anger in his breathing. She stared out the window on her side, willing him not to speak with her silence.

"I wish I'd never brought you here." He started the car and it pulled away.

She slumped down in her seat, relieved that they were moving. She wanted to close her eyes and forget, but every time she closed them the whole afternoon would start playing again, like a stilted play with wooden actors. The artist's wife at centre stage, standing rigid and proud, with that awful smile etched on her stony face.

CHAPTER THIRTYONE

The afternoon starts with promise. They arrive and a pleasant girl ticks their names off a list, welcomes them and takes their coats. They make their way into the exhibition room; everywhere around them the paintings echo the sea, repeating its song in the brushstrokes Laura knows so well. They wander through the crowd, holding hands, examining the faces around them, looking for the focal point of the room's attention. Eventually, they stop by a painting of the shore at sunset, a tugboat in the horizon, commenting on the way the artist has perfectly captured the fading light and the movement of the retreating waves.

Laura notices a well-dressed woman, probably in her late fifties, and a man who looks in his twenties approaching them.

"Our Latin American collector!" the woman oozes over Miguel. "Kathy told me you'd arrived, and I just had to come to say hello."

"Mrs. O'Donnell?" Miguel clearly guesses, extending his hand out to greet her "It's nice to meet you, and …" he turns to her companion.

"Hi, I'm Patrick O'Donnell."

Laura glances at Miguel.

"Patrick Junior," the man says, obviously having noted their look.

"Okay, I see, and I suppose the good man is busy with his public," Miguel says, "we're looking forward to meeting him."

Now Mrs. O'Donnell and her son share a look. "I'm afraid my husband passed away some years ago. I would've thought you'd know that."

Laura realises she will not be meeting the artist today, or ever. She leaves it to Miguel to carry forward the conversation, saying he didn't know and how sorry he is to hear that. She stays at Miguel's side, moving her head from one speaker to the next as Miguel continues to make small talk with their hosts. She barely hears what they are saying and says nothing herself. Then the artist's wife is waving to some new arrivals, and she and Patrick Junior move on to greet them.

"You didn't know, did you?" she whispers as soon as they are gone.

"Of course not."

"I suppose if we'd searched for him on the Internet we might have found this out. I should've done that. Why didn't I do that?"

"Don't be so hard on yourself. You wouldn't necessarily have found out that way. I checked, but there are literally thousands of Patrick O'Donnells out there. This exhibition didn't even come up when I searched against his name, plus art and lighthouses. If Mrs. Devine hadn't given me that leaflet, then I wouldn't have even known it was going on. Their advertising is hardly twenty-first century."

"I thought you said that you picked up the leaflet in the tourist office?"

"Oh, ummm, actually, I don't even know why I told you that. I knew how sensitive you are about that painting and …"

"I'm not sensitive about the painting."

"Can you keep your voice down?"

Laura didn't think she'd been loud.

"I just thought that you might've got angry if you thought I'd been searching for the artist who did your painting with Mrs. Devine, it just seemed easier to make you think I came across him by chance."

"With Mrs. Devine? The art teacher from my school? What did you tell her?"

"Nothing."

"I don't believe that."

"I just told her I'd seen a painting I liked and I needed some help tracking down the artist. I didn't mention you."

"So you did research him, so you knew he was dead and you didn't tell me?"

"I didn't know he was ..."

"You just let me come here, thinking I'd be meeting him."

"Let's go outside."

Laura feels Miguel's warm hand reach out for hers but she brushes him off. "I don't want to go outside."

"I would've told you before we came here if I'd known. I promise."

He reaches for her again and she steps back to avoid him, lifting a glass of champagne from a floating tray as it passes. It is not a celebratory glass; the bubbles feel like pin pricks on her throat.

"Do you want to leave?"

"No. It's fine." She tries to muster a smile and keep a steady hand as she drinks. Looking past him, she is suddenly aware again of the crowd in the room.

"Do you want to talk to the son, or to the wife?"

"And say what?" She whispers.

"Ask them if the artist wrote poetry. Ask them if he painted poems into his pictures. Ask them if they know your painting, ask them if they know your town, maybe the artist spent time there."

"That's a lot of questions."

"Well?"

Laura draws in a deep breath—she is making too big a deal of this. It is just a stupid painting.

"C'mon." Miguel pushes. "You're here now and you'll never see them again anyway. What does it matter if they think we're asking too many questions. I'm used to people thinking that about me."

"Fine." She decides she might as well humour him.

They move through the exhibition pretending to admire the works on show, monitoring the movements of the artist's wife and son, hoping to find an opening. They get lucky—the artist's wife soon breaks off from her conversation and comes straight to them. Swaggering over, she places a hand on Miguel's shoulder.

"Do you have a favourite?"

"Actually yes, I love the lighthouse series."

"My husband loved the sea. He was happiest when he was by the sea."

"Did he write about it too?" Laura jumps in.

"No, my husband expressed himself in pictures. I think he probably thought in pictures and even reasoned in pictures." Her voice sounds like plastic breaking in half.

"It's just, we've seen a painting done by your husband with a few lines of a poem written on the corner of the picture, but perhaps you're not familiar with that one."

"Manuel, was it?"

"Miguel."

"Miguel, I saw every picture that my husband painted. He never wrote on his pictures. What a strange idea. Someone must have defaced his work after they bought it. It seems barbaric, doesn't it?"

"You saw *every* picture he painted?" Laura tries to sound neutral, friendly even.

The artist's wife looks at Laura—her eyes snapping

open and closed in the briefest of blinks. Then she returns her attention to Miguel.

"My husband and I were childhood sweethearts, inseparable from a young age. We shared everything."

"It must have been very hard for you when he died."

"Yes, but we are here to celebrate his life's work! I think after ten years, it's about time he had an exhibition again. Today would have been his birthday, so I thought it would be a fitting day to open the exhibition, and it will close on the anniversary of his disappearance, giving us a chance to say goodbye to him properly. He went off for the weekend with just his paints and a few clothes, he said he was going to walk and hitchhike along the coast. He was such a free spirit, he loved being out on the open road, talking to the local people, asking them about their favourite views of the coastline."

"Is he buried here in Donegal?" Miguel asks. "We'd like to pay our respects."

"No. The coastguard worked tirelessly for days, but they never found him. My only comfort is that he died doing what he loved, and the sea that he painted so passionately in his life became his final resting place."

"I'm so sorry for your loss," says Miguel.

Laura is disgusted with herself for the hatred she feels for this woman. Embarrassed, she starts to fiddle with the programme in her hand and then her eyes close in on one detail, they fixate on the closing date of the exhibition. It is three days after her mother's anniversary. The exhibition closes on the tenth anniversary of the painter's disappearance, the wife had said, he disappeared three days after her mother died. Can that mean anything? Or is it just an odd coincidence? Laura looks up at Miguel. He is still chatting to the wife.

"Did your husband spend time in Tyrone?" Laura bursts in.

"Where?"

"Tyrone."

"My husband and I never really spent much time across the border. Oh, I'm sure it's better now, but for a long time it was such a nasty place. I'm sorry, if you can excuse me." Laura watches the artist's wife walk away from them.

"I'm sorry Laura, this was a waste of time. You're right, maybe we'll never figure out how that poem got on the painting. It was worth a shot, no?"

"You're right, we'll never know from *her*, anyway, everything she says is such rubbish. Oh I saw *every* painting my husband painted, we were inseparable, but I have no idea where he was going on the day he died?"

"Laura, please keep your voice down."

"Like saying he never crossed the border from Donegal into Tryone, when they're just next to each other. Really, that's just stupid. What point is she trying to make with that anyway?"

"Laura, please." Miguel presses his finger to his lips to shush her.

"Why?"

"People are staring," Miguel's voice is just above a whisper.

"So?"

"Calm down, will you?"

"Don't tell me to calm down."

"Laura, c'mon," he takes a step closer to her so she jerks back—and bang into the path of a passing waitress. Champagne glasses crash to the floor, sending tiny shards in all directions. Laura looks up toward the army of eyes that have turned toward her. The wife's appalled face emerges from the background, and Laura's only thought is of escape, so she starts to run for the door.

CHAPTER THIRTYTWO

The silence in the car was excruciating. Every time Miguel glanced over at her, opening his mouth to speak, she'd look out the window in the opposite direction and he'd think better of it. The steeliness in her eyes was unnerving. The rational form of arguing that he was so skilled at as a lawyer was useless to him now and, unlike most children who learn by watching their parents tear one another apart before putting each other back together again, he had never even seen two people in love properly fight.

When they reached the outskirts of the town, Miguel flicked the indicator to turn into her estate. He only had a few minutes left to try to put this right.

"Laura, I'm leaving in just over two weeks. Please let's not argue. We should make the most of the time we have left together. It will be a while, at least, before we can see each other again." He chose his words carefully. He tried to sound conciliatory without sounding like he was begging her. Really it should be her making the effort. After all, he hadn't done anything to justify her aggressive reaction.

"I just wish you didn't feel the need to meddle," she

glowered. She had clearly misunderstood what he had been trying to do.

"Listen. You need answers, whether you admit it or not, and the questions you need answers to … well, I didn't know where to start with those. So I thought I would start with a question that I maybe *could* answer."

She finally turned round to look at him. "You're always asking questions, looking for answers, searching out the whole truth and nothing but the truth. Does it ever occur to you that people don't want to drag up the past? That they're better off not knowing? That all you're doing is interfering?"

"And you honestly believe that?" He looked over at her, quickly, trying to read her face, and then back at the road.

"Yes! I don't see what good has come of today. It was a total waste of time."

Miguel pulled up outside her house and turned off the ignition. He turned towards her, trying to stay calm. "Okay, fair enough we didn't achieve anything today, but I don't understand why you …"

"The point is, you come along with your great ideas about facing the past, and you turn people's lives upside down. You strip the scars off wounds that healed long ago and you think it's all okay because of some warped notion of how noble and important the truth is, and you don't even know the damage you've done."

"I suppose it's better to go through life with your head in the sand, is it? Is that why you refuse to talk to the one person who might actually be able to give you some answers?" Miguel felt the volume of his voice rise uncontrollably to match hers.

"What's that supposed to mean?"

"Your father, Laura. You two don't live together, you just co-exist. Tell me, have you ever really sat down and talked to each other in all these years? Like really talked about what your mother did? And why?"

"You know nothing about my family!" she screamed.

"I know you pretend to hate this place and that you're only here for your father, but the fact is you don't want to leave, you're afraid. You love having him as an excuse. You just pretend to be trapped here so you don't have to get out and live your own life, so you don't have to make mistakes and get hurt and take risks."

"Oh God, enough of the psycho-babble! You've no idea what you're talking about. You come here and you run around meeting victims of the troubles, recording their stories, and for what? It's sick, it's like you enjoy other people's misery."

Miguel struggled to retain his composure. "That's completely unfair. C'mon, we only have a few weeks left before I go, we shouldn't be fighting, we should be making plans."

"Stop pushing me, Miguel! Stop acting like it's all so bloody simple. Do you really think I'm just going to abandon my daddy and run off to Colombia with you?"

He reached over to take her hand but she yanked it away.

"No. I don't have the energy to go over this with you again." She jumped out of the car and slammed the door behind her. Miguel watched, shell-shocked, as she ran to the front door and in, not once looking back.

For the rest of the evening, he waited for her call. He went over and over in his head what he'd say the next time they spoke. He'd have to be a bit cold—he wanted to make sure she knew she couldn't just walk over him like that, but he'd still accept her apology, there was no point dragging out the fight to make a point when they had so little time left. He waited all the following day, too, and finally, at eleven p.m. on Monday night, his phone rang.

"Hello," he said.

"Miguel?" The sound of her voice was like a fine whisky, filling him with warmth and happiness.

"¡Hola!" he said, a large smile washing over his face.

"It's about Natalia," his grandmother said. "She's here in Bogotá and she needs you."

CHAPTER THIRTYTHREE

Laura opened her eyes and looked at the clock on her nightstand. 11:37 glowed back at her. Through the drawn curtains she could see it was light outside, so that meant it must be morning. She tried to remember what day it was. Was it Tuesday already?

On Sunday night after the argument, she'd come in and gone straight to bed. She'd been in bed since then staring at the clock, staring at the ceiling or the wall, sometimes curled up, hugging herself, sometimes dead flat on her back. Mostly she slept, and when her body refused to sleep she just stared and concentrated on thinking about nothing. She thought if she stared at the magnolia ceiling spread out above her, punctuated only by a few cracks and a wandering spider, and concentrated hard enough then, she'd force her mind to stop racing and she could figure out what she needed to do.

After the exhibition she'd been fuming, but her rage subsided quickly and she realized what a brat she'd been. Even now, embarrassment burned through her just thinking about the scene she'd made at the gallery. She knew the right thing to do was to call Miguel to apologise, but she couldn't until she figured out what the next step was. They'd make up, and then what? He was leaving so soon and she had to face the reality of letting him go.

Laura rolled over in her small single bed to face the wall. Eventually, she'd get up, put on clothes and return to work. She'd face him and they'd say goodbye. But not today. She still felt the fear swilling around inside, like muddy clothes splashing dark water against a washing machine door. So she closed her eyes and waited for sleep.

A few hours later, there was a slight tapping on her bedroom door. She didn't respond. Then she heard the door ease open and her father clear his throat.

"Laura love."

She lay perfectly still, facing the wall, her back to him, feigning sleep.

"Laura," he said, this time more forcefully.

She stretched her arms out and moved slowly, hoping to give the impression that she was just waking. She turned to face him. He was standing with her door slightly ajar, one foot in her bedroom. He never usually came in to her room. "Are you sure you shouldn't go see the doctor? I could call a taxi to get you to the surgery."

"No Daddy, it's okay. I'm just feeling run down, that's all. I just need to rest."

"Right." He remained in the doorway, one hand resting on the handle, looking like he was trying to remember something important. Laura pulled the duvet up tight around her. His kindness was compounding the guilt she already felt about calling in sick from work. She never took time off.

"I might just try and get some sleep now," she said.

"Right, it's just," he opened his mouth in an O. Laura waited, wondering if he was going to insist on the doctor, but he didn't go on and instead turned and walked away, closing the door behind him.

She exhaled slowly and turned to lie on her back. There was a spider journeying along the crack in the ceiling.

Maybe he thinks it will lead him somewhere, she thought. She considered doing it a favour by reaching up and squashing it, but she didn't, she just lay there watching it walk towards nothing.

All afternoon Laura drifted in and out of sleep until she woke from a fuzzy dream-state needing the toilet. She struggled out of bed. Her muscles were weary from the inactivity of the past few days. On the landing, the floorboards creaked underneath her; the house seemed eerily empty. She couldn't even hear the hum of the television.

She went past the bathroom without going in, and instead found herself walking down the stairs. With each step, the unusual silence became more prominent. The living room was empty. She quickly passed through into the kitchen, but it, too, was empty and still. She turned and ran back up the stairs, taking them two at a time, calling her father's name. She called a second and third time, and still he didn't appear.

She flung his bedroom door open, only to find more emptiness. She pounded down the stairs again, this time flinging open the front door. Nothing. She raced back through the living room and into the kitchen. Pulling up short, she let out a small gasp. From her vantage point in the middle of the kitchen she could see through the window her father outside, beyond their gate, and he wasn't alone.

The world slowed as she saw her father reach his hand up to cup Chrissie's chin and move in to kiss her. Laura stood frozen, watching them. Her mind was completely blank. They moved apart, said a few words, and came together for another kiss. Chrissie turned and walked towards home and her father opened their back gate. Laura turned, ready to rush out of the room, but then stopped and turned again, unsure of herself. Should she confront him? No, that'd be too uncomfortable, best to pretend she'd seen nothing. She went to move just as her father came smiling through the back door. Their eyes met and his smile melted. It was too late. There was no going back now. He knew she'd seen them. It must've been written all over her face.

"I should've told you earlier," he immediately started, moving towards her. Laura instinctively took a step back. He stopped a few feet away from her. "I didn't want you to find out like this."

"Then why'd you keep it from me? How long has this been going on? How long have you been lying to me?" She heard her own voice wavering and fought to control it. She didn't want to sound hysterical.

"Why don't you sit down and we can talk about this."

Laura was still rooted to the spot where she'd been standing when she saw them. Her chest felt tight, and she was acutely aware of her own breathing.

"Please," he said.

Laura looked him up and down. He was wearing outdoor shoes and a jacket.

"How long has this been going on?" Laura whispered.

He leaned back against the kitchen counter. "Well a couple of months ago, I …"

"A couple of months?"

"Hear me out. It was more like six weeks ago, I asked Chrissie in one day for a chat. She'd been round so much seeing you, and she's got that great energy about her. She's a good woman."

"I didn't say she wasn't."

"Okay, I know it's a lot for you to take in."

"A lot for me to take in? You haven't even told me anything yet. Are you just suddenly cured now?"

"That's what I'm trying to explain. Please sit down."

Laura took a seat at the kitchen table. The room was flooded with late afternoon sunlight illuminating the walls and cabinets. Whilst she'd been festering in her bed these past few days, spring had arrived.

He took a seat opposite. "I asked Chrissie in because I wanted to talk to her about my, my … I wouldn't say it's a condition—the situation I'd created."

"Situation?"

"I wasn't sick, you know."

"Could've fooled me." Laura immediately regretted this.

"Me holed up in this place for years. You stuck looking after me. It was wrong, and I was wrong to have let it happen."

"I don't mind looking after you."

"I know that, but it doesn't make it right, and I couldn't let you do it anymore, so I asked Chrissie for her help and well things just …" he trailed off.

"I think I can guess what happened next."

They sat looking at each other in silence.

"I'm just shocked is all," Laura said eventually.

"It just happened. She started coming round just for a chat, y'know to help me a bit, and I found I could really open up to her. For someone who could talk for Ireland, she's actually a pretty good listener."

"And when did you manage to venture out there?" Laura motioned with her head towards the back door.

"Well I spent a long time just standing in the backyard, not able to go any further. And then eventually, I just bit the bullet and went for it. I wanted to tell you sooner, but I was afraid of getting your hopes up and then disappointing you. I wanted to make sure I could really do this. It's easy to build a cage for yourself, but not so simple to break out of it. Thankfully, Chrissie has been prodding and pushing me and I've been taking it step by step. Today is a big day, though. She wants us to go down the town for a wee pint."

"Really?" Laura was thunderstruck. It hadn't quite hit her until now just how much everything had suddenly changed.

"We'll see. That's Chrissie's idea, anyway. If I'm honest,

I'm terrified."

Laura smiled at him. He didn't deserve her anger.

"Do you want to join us?"

"No, I shouldn't."

"Right, I suppose after being off sick from work a night out drinking's the last thing you want."

"Umm hhmmph," Laura looked down at the table.

"Maybe you could have Miguel round. I know you've not had him round much, and you've probably had your reasons, but I don't mind, honestly, this is your house, too."

"I know it is."

"Well?"

"I just feel like a night in by myself."

"Everything okay with you two?"

Laura blinked. "Yes, we're fine," she lied. Nothing about the situation was fine. Miguel was leaving in a fortnight. For weeks he'd been on her case to go out to Colombia in June to spend the long summer holidays with him. He said it'd be a good way for her to see if she could live there. Up until half an hour ago, even the long holiday had seemed like an utter fantasy; but now, the world was a different place.

It felt odd. She expected to feel more of a release. All the freedom she had craved had just been delivered up to her, and she didn't know how to react. She suddenly felt like being alone again. "Listen, I'm going to head back to bed now." At the doorway, she paused and turned around. "I am happy for you. You do know that."

"That means everything to me."

"I just think I need some more sleep."

"Okay. I'll be going out in an hour or so, I won't wake you to say goodbye."

Laura turned and wandered through the quiet living room and up the stairs. It struck her as she went that today she'd probably be alone in her own home for the first time ever. She finally had some space to think about herself for once, and there was a lot she needed to think about.

CHAPTER THIRTYFOUR

Laura padded downstairs shortly after dark. Her father had gone out an hour ago. She'd half expected to hear him come rushing back in a few minutes later, unable to go through with it. It still didn't feel quite real that he was out, and not just out, but out with Chrissie. Laura saw them kissing again in her mind, so easy and close. They didn't seem like a natural fit. Next to her motionless father, Chrissie was almost overbearingly alive.

She wandered from the kitchen to the living room and back again, flicking on the television and quickly turning it off, opening and closing the fridge. She went back upstairs and lay down on her bed. She turned on the clock radio.

The punchy, upbeat horns of Stevie Wonder's 'Sir Duke' immediately filled her little room. The image of Miguel dancing to this song came to her. With nothing on but his blue boxers, he had half marched, half danced around his bedroom, singing along in his own hysterical way. She'd laughed at him and he'd jumped upon her, tickling her in revenge, and she'd screamed and giggled until eventually he lay down beside her, both of them breathless and exhilarated.

"This is a fun song," she'd said.

"I love how he's honouring the people who've inspired him. If you listen you'll hear the names of loads of jazz greats, people like Ella, and Louis and Glenn Miller."

"Ella and Louis? So you know them personally, do you?"

"Very funny," he had attacked her again with tickles under her arm and on her belly and she shrieked with laughter.

"Okay, Okay! I'm sorry!"

"This song's amazing, it's so upbeat and fun. I think it's a great tribute. Music is so special. I love how it has the ability to change your mood, how a song can become part of the fabric of your life, bringing you back happy memories every time you hear it. I'd have loved to have been a musician."

Laura had turned on her side to face him in bed. "That's so strange, I can't imagine you as anything other than a lawyer. You're so passionate about it. I couldn't picture you dedicating your life to something so, so … fluffy as music."

"But sometimes I worry about depriving the world of my talent."

"Oh honey, don't worry about that. The world's *very* grateful you chose to be a lawyer instead."

"You!" He'd reached for her and started tickling her again.

In her bedroom now, just a few months later, listening alone to Sir Duke bursting from her clock radio, Laura couldn't help but smile. Life with Miguel was just like the song: positive and fun. Why was she running away from that?

CHAPTER THIRTYFIVE

Laura listened again to the messages Miguel had left her. They started off angry and controlled. "I'm not sure what happened yesterday. Call me when you're ready." And became more urgent: "I must speak to you. Call me as soon as you get this." She hadn't, of course. She hadn't responded to any of them.

"Laura, this is ridiculous. I need to speak to you this morning." That was his last message, left really early this morning. Laura listened to the automated message that followed: "*to return the call, press three.*" Her finger hovered over the number. Her entire vocabulary raced through her mind as she searched for the words she'd use. No, a phone call wouldn't be enough. After the way she behaved, she had to go to see him, immediately. She snapped shut her phone and grabbed her coat.

She strode through the streets, looping out by the bypass and back in again to town. The air was cool, but it definitely felt like the year had turned a corner. The sky wasn't so black for early evening, and the wind no longer bit against her cheeks. She felt like a child running home after a rough day in the playground, desperate for some comfort.

She hurried past the statues of the musicians and dancers glowing silver in the moonlight and felt a surge of excitement run through her, remembering their first kiss.

She almost raced up his street, eager now to see him. There was a chance he'd be out meeting someone for Survivor's Stories, but he couldn't be much longer. She'd wait in the Chinese below if she had to; she just had to see him tonight. She rounded the corner into the little alleyway alongside the Chinese and suddenly she was there, in his backyard. She looked up towards his flat. The lights were on. He must be home.

Laura put one foot on the bottom of the stairs, ready to run up them when she suddenly pulled up short. She still had no idea what she was going to say to him. He'd probably want to delve into her behaviour on Sunday and analyse it for clues. She almost turned away, but she caught herself. With a newfound courage, she gave herself to the moment. She bounded up the steps two at a time, and suddenly she was standing in front of his blue door. She raised her hand and knocked it softly. Nothing. She raised her hand again and gave it two loud raps.

She heard him walk towards the door at the other side. Her heart pounded. Her face was stretched into a ridiculously large smile.

The door opened slowly and there in front of her was Mr. Quigley. The muscles in her face fell. Great, she thought, they must be having a meeting about Survivor's Stories. Their mini-reunion was going to be witnessed by the school's biggest gossip.

"Oh, hello. I'm here to see Miguel."

"Miguel?"

"Yes," Laura said peeking past his shoulders.

"Oh Laura, he's gone back. Did you not know?"

"Back where?"

"To Colombia."

Laura felt her throat constrict. "What?"

"Oh, you didn't know? I thought you'd have been the

first person he told. He uh …" Laura waited for him to go on, "he was quite agitated about it all. He mentioned something about someone called Natalia? He said she was back in Colombia and he needed to go to her, immediately."

"Natalia?" Her voiced cracked out the word, and she was suddenly aware that she was standing at the top of a flight of stairs and might collapse down them at any moment. She reached for the banister to steady herself.

"Do you know her? I thought she must be important for him to rush off like that."

"Yes I think she's a close family friend." Laura looked past him into Miguel's flat as she spoke. She couldn't bear to meet his eyes.

Apart from her name, Miguel hadn't told Laura anything about the beautiful girl who'd been smiling out from the photo on his windowsill all these months. She'd been too afraid to ask any more. But now, Laura realised, she'd known the answer all along anyway—Natalia was the woman that he'd drop everything for, including her.

CHAPTER THIRTYSIX

Peter placed a withered cardboard box on the kitchen table next to Laura's bowl of cereal.

"I never found any answers in here, but then maybe you have different questions," he said. Laura looked up from her breakfast. "I don't know if I'm doing the right thing, but I suppose you deserve to know her, in her own words."

"What do you mean?"

Her father had already started to back away, his suitcase in hand. Even though it had been nearly a month now, it still felt strange seeing him in a coat.

"I'll phone you when we get there."

Laura looked at the tattered box in front of her.

"Just read it," he said.

Read what? Laura thought. She lifted up the lid of the box and peeked in, not quite sure what to expect. Inside, there were lots of notebooks.

"You'll be okay?" he asked, already halfway out the back door.

"I'll be fine. Don't worry about me, Daddy, " she pulled one of the notebooks out of the box. "But what's …"

"Right, see you in two weeks then."

Laura heard the door close and with that, he was gone. She flicked open the notebook to the first page. Inside the handwriting was slanted and tight, with lots of curls on letters like "e" and "l." It was tidy, but childlike and strangely familiar.

'Dear Diary, Daddy got me this today. In case you hadn't noticed, today is my thirteenth birthday. Daddy says he's seen me scribbling in my jotters and the nuns say I'm good at creative writing so he thinks I should keep a diary. Maybe someday something special will happen to me and people will want to read about my life. I hope so.'

Any of the first-year girls Laura taught could have written it. She scanned the pages: "*my sister Kitty,*" "*my big brother Brian.*" She gasped and dropped the notebook. It fell spread-eagled onto the lino floor at her feet. She quickly bent down and picked it up again, unable to quite believe what she had in her hand. These were her mother's diaries. She placed it back on the table and took a step back, watching it intently from a safe distance, as if waiting for it to talk, or jump, or fly.

The book lay there, waiting for her to come and read its secrets. Were all those books her mother's diaries? They must be. There must be years of her mother's life stored in that box, Laura thought. She suddenly realised this was her chance to find out once and for all what happened in the final weeks and days and maybe even hours of her mother's life. She'd finally get to understand why. Laura reached in, her hands shaking, and pulled out a handful of the notebooks and started checking the dates on the first page of each, looking for the year of her mother's death. She rifled through them, dropping on the floor those that were too early in time. She couldn't move fast enough. She slammed down the last book of the first pile and reached into the box for another handful.

Suddenly she stopped. "This is wrong," she muttered. Why was she rushing through, flinging her mother's life to one side in search of her gruesome death? She lifted the notebooks from the floor and counted them, and then looked into the box. There were well over twenty in total. She pulled out all the books and started to arrange them in date order across the table. She tried not to read the entries on the first pages, only the dates. It was important to read her mother's story in the order it was lived. When she found the notebook from the year of her mother's death, she snapped it shut and placed it at the far end of the table.

When she finally had them in order, she picked up the first ten notebooks and carried them into the living room. She rested them on the floor next to her, and curled up on the sofa with the first one on her lap, and started to read her teenage mother describe her life. She read about her first drink and her first kiss, both on the same night with a boy named Tom Flynn, when she should have been at Saturday evening mass. Both of them, she wrote, left a funny taste in her mouth.

Her mother often wrote about leaving home, counting down the days until she was fifteen and would be old enough to get a job. She wrote about how lucky Kitty was that she was already married and out of the house, even if it was only down the street.

At the start of the third notebook, Laura read of her mother's joy at finding a job in the local nylon factory, cutting the gusset in tights, so she could finally leave school. She read her mother's detailed description, trying to imagine what it was like.

'*Every hour, the men who work the floor bring me a sack of nylon legs. I have to work them over this flat apparatus that sort of sticks up at a right angle from my worktable. When I get the leg nicely in position, I have to press down on a pedal with my foot and a blade comes out of the table and cuts through the slit in the apparatus, making a small incision at the top inch of the leg. This is then sewn up later by the ladies on the sewing machines. I was told off six times today by my supervisor for laddering the tights, and the witch has told me to cut my nails. It's not the most exciting job in the world, but it gives me money and money means freedom. I can save up and get out of this place.'*

Laura never remembered her mother being much of a saver. In fact, her mother's almost tragic compulsion to spend was the one thing she clearly remembered her parents arguing about. She felt her stomach flip. Could it have been debt and money problems? Could that have been what drove her to do what she did? Laura forced the thought out of her mind and read on.

Her mother's enthusiasm for the job soon waned. In quite a few entries, Diane complained about having to stand all day. *"God, my legs are killing me. Some of the women have been working in the factory for over twenty years! They've all got weak knees now, so they have to stand on pieces of cardboard that they've scavenged from the packing department, hoping the cardboard would be softer on them than the concrete floor. I will not be there in twenty years time, I can tell you."*

Laura did a quick calculation; by the time of her death, her mother had been working in the factory for about nineteen years. Laura felt her own legs tingle underneath her. She stood up and shook them out. It was nearly eight p.m. She'd spent half the evening reading and hadn't even thought about dinner. She decided to make herself some soup to keep her going.

Alone at the kitchen table, she slurped up the soup with her right hand as her left hand rested on the notebook, keeping it stretched open so she could continue reading as she ate. Laura skim read the next few entries until she came across an entry that started excitedly. *'Diary, Diary, Diary, I met the big boss today. The owner!'* She read on, wondering what all the fuss was about.

'*I was up in the office area having a fight with the woman from payroll. They'd docked my wages two days last week because I didn't clock in those mornings. I told her I'd just forgotten (really Diary, between me and you, I was twenty minutes late so I didn't bother clocking in so they wouldn't know how late I was). Anyway, last time I'll do that. The aul' doll wouldn't budge. She says they've no evidence of me arriving at work, so they couldn't be expected to pay me for days I wasn't there! I pointed out that I'd clocked out on those days, so I must've been there. And you know what she says? "We pay people to come to work, not to leave it." I was so angry I started to cry, even though I didn't want to.*

And then I heard a voice behind me. His accent was local but softer. Much more refined than anyone I know.

He asked the witch from payroll what the hell she was doing making me cry. She tried to explain herself by quoting company policy, saying she was just teaching me the rules. His rules, she said. As if she was imposing his personal law on me. I suddenly realized that this was Mr. Stewart—the big boss—and I thought I might be in real trouble. It dawned on me then how important this silly job cutting slits in tights is to me. I felt so insignificant next to him.

He asked me who I was, and what was going on, so I told him I was new and wasn't used to this whole clocking in and out thing. And he actually paid attention to me! It was great, he told her to pay me the days I was owed. And when she tried to protest, he said, "I don't need another lesson in my own policy!"

So now I've met the big boss! To be honest, he's probably shorter, rounder and generally a lot less handsome than I imagined him, but still, there's something about him, and it's not just that he was kind to me, it was the way he spoke to her, the way she flustered around him. He has a power, a power that just draws you in.'

Laura read these final words again. She then scanned through the following entries. In nearly all them she found at least a few lines about Mr. Stewart: that he wore a red tie one day, that someone said he had three cars, that his wife spent a fortune on a new sofa. It was like her mother was scraping together pieces of insignificant information to try and make an important whole and then, a few weeks later, there was another long entry about Mr. Stewart.

'*Today was such a fantastic day at work. I'm no longer on the floor! Mr. Stewart has seen that I'm destined for better things! It all started when Lizzy from personnel came down the stairs on to the shop floor this morning. Everyone kept their heads down, suddenly paying attention to what they were doing for once. Apparently Lizzy only comes onto the floor when someone is really in trouble. So I started to worry when she stopped at my table, even though I thought that business about the clocking-in cards had been sorted. But instead of tearing into me right then and there, she just asked me to follow her up to the offices. My mother looked furious as I passed by her. She was obviously thinking I was in some kind of trouble again. When we got upstairs, she told me Mr. Stewart wanted to see me in his room. I went and stood at the door to his office, not sure if I should go in. And then he looked up and smiled at me and told me to come on in.*

So now for the big news … he wants me to join the staff! The staff works in the office with telephones and coffee and nice clothes and get to keep their fingernails long and painted. No more shop floor standing on bits of cardboard and dusty bags of tights for me. From now on I can wear my hair loose, and I can even wear earrings!'

Laura read on to her mother's first day in the office a week later.

'*Mr. Stewart explained that I'll run errands, answer the phone and generally help out the rest of the staff. He says if I do well he could think about promoting me over time. Give me a bit more responsibility and money.*

When he took me into his office to talk about my duties, he came and sat really close to me whilst he spoke. When he was done talking he sort of patted my knee with his hand and said, "I'll make sure to keep a close eye on you and anyone bothers you, you come to me." And then he sort of squeezed my leg and took his hand away. I just thanked him for giving me the opportunity and left. I suppose it was nothing. I don't want to be one of those silly girls that get flustered if a man comes within ten feet. I wanted to show him I can handle men just fine. I actually felt kind of powerful— having Mr. Stewart so close and not flinching in the slightest.'

Laura could sense what was coming. She didn't want to continue reading but she knew she couldn't stop herself. A few entries later ,the advance she was expecting appeared.

"Tonight Mr. Stewart asked me to stay behind to do some extra filing in his office. When the rest of the staff had gone, he called me in. He started saying that he thought there was something special between us, and didn't I feel it, too? He said he wanted to act on his feelings but he was worried that I was too young. I told him I'm no child. He was pleased with this, and he asked me to come closer, so I did."

Laura only glanced over the rest of her mother's description of their first time together, up against the wall behind the filing cabinets, the words *"Mr. Stewart's saggy skin"* leapt from the page.

She pushed her soup away from her. She was horrified, thinking her mother could have been so easily manipulated, she had always believed her mother was stronger than that. Laura reminded herself that it was the diary of a teenage girl she was reading and she should instead be angry with her mother's lecherous boss.

She went back into the living room and grabbed the next book from the pile that she'd left on the floor. There was just more of the same in this one until around early June, when the tone changed. The first entry in July stated:

'Mr. Stewart called me into his office at the end of day today, just as the other girls were leaving. But instead of grabbing me as soon as the door was closed, like he usually does, he told me to take a seat opposite him. He asked me when I last had my period. He just came out and said it, just like that, as if he was asking me what time the supermarket deliveries were being collected!

I told him that I didn't think it appropriate for us to discuss that. And he sort of got angry with me. He told me not to act so shy, that he'd noticed I'd been practically green all week. I told him the smells from the dye house were getting to me. He just said, 'Exactly' and asked me about my period again. I said I didn't know, that I'd not paid attention, and he rolled his eyes. Then he said he would get the factory doctor to look at me tomorrow and he told me to go home.

As I was walking out the door he said, "I really hope you're not pregnant, girl. That would be very inconvenient. I hope you've been careful.'

Diary, could I really be pregnant? My mother will kill me, but then if I'm having Mr. Stewart's baby, she can't be angry with me. He is her boss after all, and then I won't have to work. I'll be taken care of, he'll look after me."

Laura suspected Mr. Stewart's idea of taking care of her was not the same as what her mother had hoped for, and as she read further that became very clear. Mr. Stewart told her mother he'd pay for her to go to Liverpool. He knew a woman who could make the arrangements and she would be "*as good as new*" in no time.

Diane was going to pretend she was going to visit her best friend's sister, but her mother refused to let her go. On the day she was supposed to leave, Diane wrote: *'I didn't take the boat to Liverpool like he'd arranged. There was no way I could get away from my mother, so I had to go to work like normal. He barely looked at me all day, and the only thing he said was 'I assume your personal situation has resolved itself and there's no need for you to go away after all.'''*

Laura wasn't surprised to read that a few days later Mr. Stewart decided he no longer needed an office junior and sent Diane back down to the factory floor to work on the sewing machines. He told her it was the best job on the floor as she wouldn't have to stand all day and she could make more money because the women on the sewing machines were paid per hundred pairs of tights sewn, so if she was fast and accurate she could do well. He told her all this in front of Lizzy from personnel, who escorted her back down to the floor just the same way she had plucked her from it several months before.

Laura turned over to the next entry, disgusted, and her eye was immediately drawn to the centre of the page— where her father's name appeared for the first time.

CHAPTER THIRTYSEVEN

Laura had always known that her parents met in the factory, but she'd never really known the details. She read her mother describe how Peter Kennedy with his '*dark gypsy eyes, thick black hair that glistened, and pale skin*' was in charge of bringing bags of legs to her and the other women in her section every hour for them to sew together.

People always commented when she was young how much Laura looked like her father. She was the opposite of her mother, who was blonde with golden skin. Except they always said she had her mother's eyes, which were a blue-grey colour like steel, or flint from the Irish shore.

Apart from the physical description, though, Laura barely recognized the man in the diary.

'*He seems like the sensitive type. He plays in a brass band and is always talking about classical music. Says Elgar is his favourite. Like I would know who that is. Although he's not all serious, sometimes he says something and if it's joke then it's hilarious, but it's so easy to miss it, his sense of humour is so subtle. I've started watching out for his jokes. I need some diversion these days. I'm so scared thinking what'll happen when I start showing.*'

Laura never knew her father had played in a brass band, or liked Elgar. She had a vague recollection of him listening to classical music in the car when she was young, but usually it was the three of them and her mother controlled the radio so they almost always listened to the country station. After her mother's death, he gave up listening to all types of music completely.

She read on, desperate now to see how things would develop between her parents.

'*I asked Peter Kennedy today if he was going to the dance this Saturday night. He said he probably won't bother, he says boys either go to dances to meet girls, or they go to dances with their girlfriends, but as his girlfriend is going away this Friday for three weeks, visiting her aunt in Galway, he doesn't see the point. He's been going with Chrissie McElwee for about six months. I told him Chrissie wouldn't mind if he took a friend along, someone to dance with him so she wouldn't have to worry about him dancing with strange girls.*'

Why had her father or Chrissie not told her they'd been together when they were young? It was strange to see Chrissie's name thrown so casually on the page, like she were merely an extra walking through one scene in Diane's life. And to think Chrissie now had dinner almost every night with Diane's husband and daughter, in Diane's own kitchen.

Within six weeks of that first dance, Diane and Peter were married. Diane wrote that when she told Peter about the baby he didn't ask any questions about how far along she was, or how she knew so soon that she was pregnant. He was only twenty then. Maybe he didn't know enough to ask such questions, Laura thought. She had never realised that her parents' courtship was so short, nor had she known before that her mother had been on a timetable. She felt a heaviness in her chest when she read what her mother had written on her wedding day:

'So I am Mrs. Kennedy now. He told me that he was sorry it was such a rush, that that is not how he wanted to marry me. He said one day, when our boy or girl is five years old, he will give me the big wedding I always wanted. Like he knows what I have always wanted, like he could ever see into my heart and see what it is longing for.'

Laura turned the page and looked at the date of the next entry. It was a month later.

'So much has happened since I last wrote. As if by some twisted joke, I lost the baby three days after our wedding. I woke up half way through the night with pains in my lower back, and as I got out of bed I noticed a huge circle of blood standing out against the sheets in the moonlight, Peter snoring next to it as white as the sheets except for that crazy black hair of his. When I went to the bathroom, I opened up and huge drops of congealed blood, like the size of tennis balls, fell from me into the toilet bowl. I knew then that the baby was gone, I knew it from the relief I felt, but when I woke P to tell him, he couldn't take it in. He wanted to rush around trying to prevent what had already happened. He called the hospital and put me in the car, praying that we could get there fast enough, when I knew we were already too late.

The next day at home, I watched the sheets go up in flames in our living room. The stain was too deep to erase, what's done is done, so I just sat still and alone on the floor and watched it burn in front of me. My life up in flames.'

Laura stared at the fireplace in front of her and the mat just in front of it. That was probably the exact spot where her mother had watched the sheets burn all those years ago. She thought about the older half brother or sister that she never got a chance to know. She wondered what life would have been like if she'd had someone to look up to, someone to care for her when her mother died.

Laura lifted up the page to turn it over and paused. If her mother hadn't died, would she have ever shared these stories with her? Laura couldn't imagine her mother telling her about Mr. Stewart, or that she'd tricked her father into marriage. She went to close the book, suddenly unsure if she should even be reading the diaries at all, but then she changed her mind. Her mother had chosen to die, Laura reasoned, she'd chosen to leave these books behind, so some part of her must have known they'd be read eventually.

After the miscarriage, Diane didn't go back to work. From the tone of the diary entries, it was obvious that she felt bitter and regretful. Although some days she did write about the joy of marriage, the freedom it gave her not to work, to write, not to bother with looking for a husband.

Laura enjoyed some of the funny domestic stories her mother wrote in this period. Those were the ones that sounded most like the woman she remembered, like the day she tried to use the deep fat fryer for the first time.

'Today I nearly killed P, and I do not mean figuratively—many times I've killed him in my imagination already. Is that a terrible thing for a young newlywed to say, Diary? I suppose it is, but I always make sure to bring him back to life again. Today, though, I almost killed him with my cooking. Poor man. I made him some chicken for dinner. I'm trying to lose a bit of weight, as I've been piling it on since I left my mother's house and have to cook for myself, which means more and more takeaway food – so tonight I thought I would cook for P and just have an apple myself (I'm now starving, Diary, but having seen what I've done to P, I'm too afraid to eat my own food!). I decided to make him some chicken and chips. I turned on the deep fat fryer that Aunt May got us for our wedding and chopped some potatoes into chips. By the time P came home the oil was nice and hot and so I just threw in the potatoes and grabbed a chicken leg from the freezer and cooked it all together.

I thought I had done a great job—the chicken skin was lovely and crisp. He ate through it all, he did look a bit worried when he reached the middle, but he just said "oh it has gone a bit cold" he didn't say that it was still practically frozen! Instead he smiled at me politely and swallowed it.

I didn't realise there was anything wrong until an hour or two later when I heard the groan of his stomach from the other side of the living room, above the nine o'clock news. He ran up to the bathroom and I heard him explode into the toilet bowl. Being married is not romantic at all.

Poor thing still looked green when he emerged from the bathroom. Although he wasn't too sick to make a joke about me wanting his life insurance money. It made me think, what would I do without him? I'm so used to him now, so used to this little life we've created together. And, well, I'd never find another husband, not with my cooking.'

Each Sunday, Diane described the drive they'd taken that day after lunch. She wrote that she was happiest during these Sunday drives with Peter, listening to the radio and contemplating the world shooting past outside. They drove to the lakes near Enniskillen, up along the coast through the seaside towns of BallyCastle and Cushendun, stopping to buy rock or dulse. They also crossed the border into Donegal or down as far as Sligo to see what Diane described as the '*grand, flat-topped Benbulben mountain.*' Laura had been to all these places many times with her parents, and she could almost imagine herself there with them in the car, or walking along the sea front taking in the views.

It reminded Laura of the trips she'd taken with Miguel discovering Ireland together in Mr. Quigley's car. Even though it had only been a month since she'd slammed the car door and stormed away from Miguel after their fight outside the gallery, their time together now seemed like a distant dream. She had long since come to the conclusion that Natalia was a girlfriend that he'd left back home and everything he'd said about inviting her to Colombia had been lies. He'd known the situation with her father all along; he'd known he was safe, that he'd never have to deliver on any of his promises, which was why he'd been so liberal with them. The evidence was there, beyond reasonable doubt, the way he'd turned Natalia's photo so that it caught the light, the way he never spoke of her, the fact that he'd rushed back to be with her. Laura chided herself for letting her mind drift to Miguel and tried to find her place again on the page. It was best just to forget about him. People had hidden things from her all her life; it had been foolish to think Miguel was any different.

She sat up all night reading, sometimes in the kitchen, sometimes in the living room. She felt like she was living it all again, right here in the rooms where the events she was reading about took place, the rooms where her mother had felt these emotions and released them on to the page for eternity.

Finally, Laura came to the year she was conceived. Her parents had been married for over five years by then.

'P said we should think about having a family. That is so typical of him, it's not a baby he wants but a whole family, just like that and all of a sudden. I told him not here, not yet. I thought we were going to go away. I thought we were saving for Australia.

He said to me that being a parent will be the most important thing he ever does. And I thought, yes, but what about me? What about bringing myself up—am I now the person I am going to be? Is this it?'

Laura put the notebook down next to her. She was sitting on the floor in the living room, surrounded by used teacups. It was morning now. She was drained. Spots floated in front of her eyes and she felt cold. She looked at the date of the entry she'd just read. It must have been about three months later that her mother found out she was pregnant with her. Laura longed to lie down under her duvet and sleep. She needed to rest first before she could read on. She would need strength for what was to follow.

CHAPTER THIRTYEIGHT

'Diary, I'm pregnant again. P is delighted. It's very strange. If you'd asked me six weeks ago if I'd wanted this, I'd have told you no. But I feel a warmth inside of me now. Already I can feel a connection with the baby.'

Laura sank back into her pillow and let out a long, slow breath. She felt some of the tension in her neck melt. She'd tried to sleep, but she'd been plagued by stressful dreams of someone breaking into the house downstairs, so she'd gone down and brought up some more notebooks to continue reading in bed.

She read quickly through the following months until finally, five days after her birth, she found herself first mentioned in the diary.

'The baby and I are home now. P is madly in love with her. He watches over her cot when she's asleep. I tell him to come away, but he seems to love sitting there in awed silence, just marvelling at her. She looks just like him; when you see her in his arms there's no doubt that she's his daughter.'

Laura devoured the following entries, even though they were fairly mundane, just listing out how many hours sleep Diane had managed to get, or who had come to visit, and what gifts they'd brought. One passage struck Laura more than the others:

'*I was out walking today with the baby, just coming up the Back Street and turning down Main Street when they stopped me, the army. There were two of them. One of them did the talking in his arrogant English accent—sounded like he was from London. He said he was stopping me under some section of some act—like that was supposed to mean anything to me—and he didn't need to say anything, the other one had his rifle trained on me the whole time—I wasn't going to kick up a fuss about my rights with that in my face. He said he wanted to search the buggy. I told him go ahead. He opened up the baby bag and stuck his hand straight in. "What's in 'ere?" he asked. I took great joy in telling him it was nappies—dirty nappies—he threw it down and away from him as if I'd told him it was full of poisonous snakes.*

Did he think I'd be carrying round a tonne of Semtex in the buggy with my baby in it? They think we're the stupid ones, but they're the ones running around the Main Street in full camouflage gear, crouching down outside the supermarket as if they're in the jungle—when the biggest danger is whether they'll get run over by a shopping trolley.'

Laura couldn't imagine a young mother now having such an experience. Things had changed so much in her lifetime.

She stayed in bed for the rest of the day, reading on through the early years of her life. Her mother wrote briefly, but joyfully, about the main events, Laura's first word, '*Daddy, even though I've been saying mummy to her 'til I'm blue in the face,*' Laura's first steps, and her first teeth. Finally she came across a reference to a camping trip they'd taken when she was seven, and she found that events started to dovetail with her own experience.

It was the first of only three holidays she could remember them taking as a family. Laura remembered her father coming home one Thursday night after work with a big tent he'd bought from a travelling salesman who visited the factory. The next day they drove for two hours north and west through the sweeping Donegal countryside until they reached a small family-run campsite set up on a hill overlooking the Atlantic Ocean. Laura distinctly remembered being surprised by the number of French and German speakers staying at the campsite. She wasn't used to hearing foreigners around her back then because in those days practically no tourists came to the North.

She could still picture her father battling gallantly with the various steel tubes that made up the tent's complicated skeleton whilst she and her mother sat together in the car with the radio on and the doors open, watching.

Eventually, a young German student had come over and offered to help. He laid the various pieces on the ground, studied them briefly and then had the tent up in ten minutes. Laura could remember her and her mother giggling at this behind her father's back. After that, they'd walked into town and her father had treated them to fish and chips for dinner, which they ate out of crumpled newspaper as they walked the coastal path back to the campsite, the moon and the turning lighthouse lighting their way. Laura remembered the feeling of contentment settling into the tent, snuggled into her sleeping bag at her parents' feet.

A few hours later, she woke up absolutely terrified as a furious gale beat the sides of the tent. Her father said that it was normal and that the wind just seemed louder because they weren't used to sleeping outdoors. But just as the words were out of his mouth, the central beam holding up the tent gave way, and the pegs holding it to the ground succumbed to the wind's force. Laura screamed as the tent folded in around them and started to slide down the hillside. Her father somehow managed to open up the zip and push Laura and her mother out and then he crawled out himself, dragging one sleeping bag with him. Even now, nearly twenty years later, she could still picture the tent flying away from them down the cliff top. They spent the rest of the night cuddled in the car, with the front seats reclined all the way and the shade of the sunroof pulled back so they could see the stars. It had seemed like such a great adventure.

Of it, her mother simply wrote: '*We tried camping this weekend. P's idea, of course. Absolute disaster.*'

Laura read on, looking for other events that she could recall with absolute clarity, keen to see those events from her mother's point of view. She came across a reference to the Hiring Fair. Laura remembered the huge fight she'd had with her mother because she wouldn't let her go, and she couldn't understand why.

The Hiring Fair was a festival arranged by the local council to celebrate 100 years since the first Hiring Fair held in the town in the late 1800s. Laura had learned about it in school. Twice a year, farmers from the surrounding countryside would come to the town to hire young boys and girls, sometimes as young as nine years old, to work as farmhands. She'd seen photos from the Hiring Fairs, back when the town had some prominence—before it had been blown to bits in the troubles. There was going to be a big parade through the town during the day, with marching bands and floats, and people dressed like the old days, and in the evening a local singer was giving a free concert in the square. Laura remembered fighting with her mother because she wouldn't let her go. She hadn't thought about that in years. It was just a day out that she'd missed and forgotten. It was strange now reading just how violently her mother had been opposed to the festival.

'*I will not have him take our daughter down to celebrate the Hiring Fair. I'm shocked that the town Council thinks it's an appropriate thing to celebrate. Although with all the gerrymandering the Council is run by prods anyway. It's always the same, prods lording it over us Catholics—so no wonder they think it's something to remember. They're probably having a good chuckle now at all the Catholics down the town, drinking beer and celebrating the old system of fiefdom. For that's what it was, and I can't believe P can't see that. Weren't all those hired Catholics and those doing the hiring the Protestants? And it wasn't just finding people honest work for a good wage—as P seems to think. Those young Catholic boys and girls were bought and sold every six months like slaves.*

I remember my granny telling me about her experience of being hired. She was only a wee slip of a thing when her mother sent her to be hired—but what choice did she have? Catholics were starving all over. When she was hired, the farmer went off trotting on his horse and she had to run along behind him for miles to get to the farm. Like a dog running at the heels of the master's horse. When she got there, they made her sleep in a pen in the corner of the kitchen, and she was up working every day from six in the morning until bedtime—milking the cows, cleaning the farmhouse, peeling potatoes, churning cheese. Without a single day off, just two hours off every other Sunday so she could go to mass. And even though she'd been sent off to be hired because the family were starving, she was still hungry all the time. They fed her their leftovers on a paper bag so she wouldn't eat off their nice china, which was just for them. At the end of the six months, she was marched into the town and she had to hand over her pittance of a wage to her mother and then she would be put up for sale again for another six months. She used to tell me it could have been worse, she laughed that she was a scrawny wee thing that was only good for hard labour—nobody wanted her for anything else—not like the pretty girls. She told me I was lucky that I wasn't born then.'

Laura had never heard her mother tell this story, nor had she ever really been fully aware of the opinions her mother held about Protestants. Although, thinking about it, there had always been a bitterness in her voice when she spoke about them. Laura wondered what religion Mr. Stewart had been.

She continued to devour the words in front of her, every scrap of new information made her mother seem alive again, even if only momentarily. Laura stayed in bed the whole day reading, until finally she realised that she only had one notebook left. It was still downstairs, on the corner of the kitchen table where she'd left it, waiting patiently to tell her its secrets.

CHAPTER THIRTYNINE

Laura turned the red notebook over in her hands and felt the smooth hardback cover. She glanced again into the box on the kitchen table, although she already knew it was empty. Over the past thirty-six hours, she'd slowly robbed it of all its secrets. Well, nearly all of them, there was still one book remaining. She opened it gingerly, the year of her mother's death was scratched in the familiar script across the inside cover. She quickly shut it again.

She took the book and wandered into the middle of the living room. She looked at the sofa and then over to her father's chair. She stood still, not sure where to place herself. Exhausted, her legs almost gave way beneath her and she crumpled down onto the rug. This was where she used to sit when she was a child. Her father would sit on his chair and her mother would stretch out on the sofa, and Laura would sit on the rug in between them. She tightened her dressing gown around her. It was time.

She opened the book and flicked over the first few blank pages until she came to the first entry. It was the third of January. It had a list of New Year resolutions: '*take a yoga class, eat more healthily, look for a new job.*' Laura couldn't recall her mother ever signing up for a yoga class, although it was one of her New Year's resolutions for about four years in a row.

Laura read quickly through the first few months of that year. Diane simply continued to record her petty arguments with Peter and her general low-level dissatisfaction at their life. Laura's eyes stung from lack of sleep and shadows, like ghosts, crouched at the edges of her vision.

Her mother often wrote lists: lists of books she was going to read when she had the time, lists of improvements she wanted to make to the house, lists of trips she wanted to take. Laura wondered how many of those things her mother had managed to accomplish in her short life.

She came across yet another list, dated March third. It was headed '*Cultural Activities to Attend*'

'*French Classes at the Tech*

The Flann O'Brian play by the River Way Theatre Group

The Lighthouse exhibition in Donegal Town.'

Laura felt her pulse start to quicken. She raced through the following pages, her eyes moving quickly from left to right and jumping back again. April fourth brought her speed-reading to a halt. She read the entry once to herself and then again in a loud whisper, as if she needed to hear aloud it to understand it.

'*P is the most wonderful, exciting man I've ever met. When I'm not with him, I feel like half a person, thin and delicate as tissue paper. He has shown me that life can be extraordinary. That I can reach up and face the sun like a flower in bloom. We can do things that make a difference in the world. How can someone make such an impact in such a short space of time?*'

Laura wondered what her father had done to inspire such praise, and what could her mother have meant by the last line? By then they had been married for over twenty years. She read on, and paused again at another similar entry written a few days later: '*P understands what I feel when I look out at the ocean. He has a passion for life that inspires me. He inspires me to take action, to change things, to do something new, to do something spectacular.'*

Laura turned the page. There was only a short entry on one side and the other side was empty. No, she thought, that can't be it. She flicked frantically forward. The rest of the book was empty. She'd already come to the final entry. She turned back to it. It was dated a week before her mother's death. Her eyes bulged with tears and she fought to see the words shaking in her hands. It was a mere two lines: *'Diary, I know it's the right thing to do, but I'm afraid of what comes after. When we do this, it will change everything.'*

Slowly, methodically, Laura turned over every remaining page in the book, searching for the ending. But that was it; the rest was blank, the story was over.

CHAPTER FORTY

"Hello?" Laura's voice croaked and she realised she hadn't spoken a single word in two days.

"It's me love, I'm just phoning to see if you were alright." The familiar sound of her father's voice seemed to reach out from the phone and wrap a caring arm around her.

"I'm okay."

There was silence at the other end. Laura didn't want to talk about the diaries, but she seemed incapable of starting a conversation about anything else. She was relieved when her father spoke first. "Things are fine here. We've not had the best weather, but we've been making the …"

"Daddy, I read the diaries." Laura listened to her father's faint breath. "Did, did *you* read them? I mean after she died?"

"Every day for a month when you were at school … over and over again."

"Why didn't you show them to me then?"

"Laura, you were barely fifteen."

"And?"

"And …"

She waited. She was standing with the house phone in her hand at the bottom of the stairs, staring at the lighthouse painting.

"You were so young, so fragile. I had no idea what to say to you. And those damned notebooks didn't give me the words I needed."

Laura felt her eyes sting and she blinked, trying to stop the water in them from falling down her face. She was glad he couldn't see her.

"I scoured those books and couldn't find anything, love."

She hated how apologetic he sounded.

"Me too," she whispered, "will we never find out why?"

"It'd almost be easier if I could tell you that something terrible had happened to make her snap. Or that she was clinically depressed, or something, anything. But y'know, truth be told, she was the happiest I'd seen her in those last few months. Do you remember I took her away for the weekend to Donegal for St. Patrick's Day that year? You stayed at some friend's house. You should've seen her, so full of life. She even got up and sang 'She moved through the Fair' at a session in the pub. And then two months later, she's gone. If I could only have seen it coming sooner."

"You couldn't have known." They both fell silent again. Laura could hear her father's short breaths. She wondered if he was crying.

"Did you … did you and Mommy go to an exhibition about lighthouses? When you were visiting Donegal?

"No. Why do you ask? Was it on one of her lists?"

"Yes, it's just," Laura paused, what did it matter if they'd gone to the exhibition? Joining the dots wouldn't write the story. She'd still just be left with an incomplete outline. "How's Chrissie?" she asked instead.

"She's grand. I suppose you saw about us, when we were teenagers …"

"Yes. I can't believe you two were together all those years ago."

"And here we are decades older, and we're courting again. But Laura," he stopped.

"Yes?"

"You know I don't regret my choices."

"Choices?"

"You know, marrying your mother."

"But she didn't give you a choice. She lied to you."

"I didn't need the diary to tell me that. I knew from the moment she told me she was pregnant that I wasn't the father. I let her go on thinking she'd fooled me because I loved her. To be the father of Diane Devenny's baby, even if it wasn't mine —well, that was good enough for me."

He was a good man. She felt she needed to say something to him, something that would bridge the gulf between them. It had been ten years in the making, and she couldn't find words big enough.

"Love, I need to go now. Are you sure you're okay?"

"Yes, I'm fine. Enjoy the rest of your break. Send Chrissie my love."

Laura put the phone down and closed her eyes. She searched for a memory of her mother and father together. She wanted to examine her memories in light of what she knew now, because there had been so much that she imagined, so much that she convinced herself of and so much that she pretended to know.

We love people in fragments, she thought, in gestures and moments that ebb and flow with the tide of a shared life. And when they are gone, we go on loving them, but the rhythm of the tide is broken, it no longer swells and fades as we dance closer to each other and then break away. It becomes like a shattered mirror. The tiny pieces held precariously together, reflecting back to us the fragments of our love for them in the lines of a poem, a long-gone smile from a photo, the echo of a favourite song sung at the end of a party. When the people we love are gone, this is all we have left, although we still chase the tide, like children at sunset rushing in to catch the retreating waves.

Laura was exhausted from the effort, from trying to grasp for something that no longer existed and she suddenly felt the urge to forget it all, to banish all the images that had flowed from the diaries. Instead, she just wanted to cut to black.

CHAPTER FORTYONE

Miguel stood just a few meters away from the open grave. Two gravediggers at the opposite end shovelled soil onto the coffin. They worked quickly, like they were trying to cover her up as soon as possible. This is just another day at work for them, he thought.

Most of the mourners had moved away from the graveside, each of them stopping for one last time to pay their respects to her family before they got into their cars. A few people nodded to him as they walked past him, but no one stopped. Miguel knew that he didn't occupy any special place in the group of mourners. On her death, his importance to her was even less certain than it had been when she was alive.

He looked down again at the grave. The coffin was almost completely covered now. He felt his shoulders start to shake again and his face contort as he fought back a fresh wave of tears. He'd never see her smile again. They'd never just be together again, relaxing and joking around, being their best selves. He'd never pick up the phone and hear her sweet, delightful voice. The past month he'd had to live without all of that, but he'd never accepted for a second that it might be permanent.

He had dropped everything and jumped on a plane as soon he heard what happened. He thought if he could just speak to her, and hold her hand, that he'd be able to get through to her. But she was impenetrable. By the time he got back to her, the girl he'd loved had already disappeared.

Miguel pulled out a handkerchief from his pocket and wiped away the tears and blew his nose. He took deep breaths, trying to regain his composure. He could feel he was being watched. He raised his head and looked around. Her father was coming towards him. Miguel barely recognized him in his black suit.

"We're going now. Will you come back to the house? We're having a lunch."

"Yes, sir. Of course I'll come."

"I know it sounds strange. But I want it to be a happy occasion okay?"

Miguel nodded. He felt the urge to tell him what an amazing woman his daughter had been. But he knew he wouldn't be able to get the words out without breaking down again.

"I want to celebrate the life that she lived. And so many of her best times were with you."

Miguel swallowed hard, trying to push down the great stone of sadness that was rising up in his throat. Her father reached up and placed his hand on Miguel's shoulder and Miguel suddenly became aware of how much he was shaking.

"I remember you two running around together, no more than knee high, into everything, you were. Remember the time you and her snuck a golf club out of your father's bag and took it out to the club car park to play? One of you sent a golf ball flying into the club captain's car and smashed the windscreen, and neither of you would tell us which one of you had done it. Like fingernails and flesh you two were."

What was the equivalent expression in English? Miguel thought, "as thick and thieves." That was probably more fitting. He smiled, remembering Natalia dragging the golf club, which was almost as big as her, out the door as he distracted their fathers.

"I'd almost forgotten about that," her father went on, "but then I overheard you talking to her about it in the hospital one night."

"I thought if I …" Miguel felt the stone rise up again and he couldn't go on.

"We all did." Her father looked like he was on the verge of breaking down, too. He suddenly pulled Miguel close to him into a strong embrace. "Thank you," he whispered into Miguel's ear and released him.

"I didn't do anything."

"You came. As soon as we told you about the accident, you were on a plane from Ireland."

"I wish I'd got here sooner. By the time I arrived, she'd already slipped into the coma. I never got to say goodbye."

"You did. I don't know if she could hear us exactly, but I feel certain she felt the love around her."

Over her father's shoulders, Miguel could see Natalia's mother, clinging on to Olivia, Natalia's little girl. Olivia reminded him so much of Natalia, the same large brown eyes and little bow lips. Next to them, Natalia's husband, Pedro, stood staring off into space, his eyes completely empty. All the years of jealousy and resentment that Miguel had felt towards him now transformed into a well of sympathy.

"Just give me a minute," Miguel said.

"Take your time." Her father turned and walked back to join his wife by the car.

Miguel moved closer to the grave, which was now full up with a mound of soil on the top. He crouched down and patted the earth in front of him.

"Nati, I was honoured to have you as my best friend. It was right that we stayed friends. That's who we were. I'll miss you so much. You were always able to get through to me, even when I was being stupid and stubborn. I really need you here now. I've done something stupid and I need you to send me a sign to tell me how to fix it."

CHAPTER FORTYTWO

His grandmother was sitting at the kitchen table when he got home, having her evening coffee and cheese before bed. She would never let anyone tell her caffeine and cheese late at night was bad for you, she didn't follow conventional wisdom. She didn't need to, Miguel thought, her own brand of wisdom was far superior. When she saw him, she stood up and fixed him with one of her wide smiles. Even after the day he'd had, he knew not to expect a hug; she wasn't the tactile type. But it didn't matter; her smiles were enough to engulf the recipient in love.

"Shall I re-heat you some meat and beans? Maybe some rice, too? Do you want a fried egg with that?" She was already moving around the kitchen, getting things ready.

"No, it's okay. I'm not hungry."

She stopped, still with the fridge door open, and looked at him. "Just a small plate?"

There was no such thing as a small plate of food in her house. "I had something at Natalia's," he lied.

"You sure?"

"Yes. Sit down, finish your coffee." Miguel slumped down on one of the chairs, and she came to join him, taking her seat again at the head of the table.

"How are you?" She asked.

"I'm okay."

"You look exhausted. Do you want some hot milk?"

"No, it's fine."

They sat for a few minutes in silence, her sipping her coffee, him staring intently at the line running in between the tiles on the wall in front of him. All day, Miguel had felt as if he were his own shadow, following the real Miguel around, hearing and seeing all the same things as him, but incapable of knowing his feelings. Now, sitting here, in the familiar surroundings of his grandmother's yellow kitchen, he finally started to feel like he was part of his own body again, and he suddenly became aware of the jumbled set of emotions that were trapped inside, desperate for a release. He shifted in his chair and reached his hands up to his hair, it was still damp from the rain earlier.

"I still can't believe it," he whispered.

"It'll take time to sink in," his grandmother said.

"It's been weeks now. I've sat by her bed for weeks. I was there at the hospital when the doctor told us that she'd gone. I watched them close the coffin this morning, I stood there and saw the lid come down over her face. God, I even helped carry it! I mean, what more do I need? Why do I feel like I can just pick up the phone and call her?" He stopped and took a deep breath; he could feel his insides swell. His grandmother waited for him to go on. "Even though I felt that crushing weight on my shoulder. In my mind, the coffin was empty. In my mind, she wasn't in there. In my mind, it's impossible for her to be dead."

"Well that's a good thing. In your head and heart, she lives on. People never die who leave people behind who love them."

Miguel looked at his grandmother's soft, serene face. From anyone else, this might have sounded glib, but from her, it was entirely sincere. This woman knew about loss.

She'd lost her husband when she was barely into her forties. But, as she'd told Miguel on many occasions, she'd had no time for sorrow because she had six children between the ages of eight and twenty to take care of. She kept a close and loving family that she protected like a wolf. But she couldn't protect them from everything. Her oldest son died in a motorbike accident just three days before his twenty-fifth birthday. And then three years later, Miguel's mother had died. On her seventieth birthday, to Miguel's horror, his grandmother had said that she felt really hopeful, really content that, now that she was in her seventies, the next death in the family would be her own.

"How were her parents?" she went on.

"Her father tried his best to be strong, but you could see it in his face; it's like his heart has been ripped right out."

"No parent should have to bury a child. It's just not right," she said.

Miguel thought about Olivia, Natalia's small daughter, standing at the graveside in her little black coat, her tiny hand in Pedro's, her lips trembling. And no child should have to bury a parent, he thought.

He picked up the white ceramic pepper pot from the middle of the table and started to examine it. It felt cold and smooth against his skin. He blinked, and in the fleeting darkness, an image of Natalia, pale and expressionless, suddenly flickered in front of his eyes. To counter it, he searched for a colourful memory of her. Something where she was moving, something where he could hear her voice, but all his mind offered up was a series of black and white stills of her lifeless body in a hospital bed. He slammed the pepper pot down on the middle of the table and stood up.

"I'm off to bed. It's been a long day."

"There's nothing wrong with being angry," his grandmother said.

"I'm not angry," he retorted. His grandmother stared up at him, her face still and expressionless. Over the years, he'd noticed that she was a master of not reacting, of simply waiting. He'd seen her do it so many times, when he was a bundle of emotions, she'd just smooth out her face and wait, letting him know that he could feel what he liked, that she would be right there, no matter what.

"I'm not angry," he repeated. He paced along the length of the kitchen and back again to the table. "I suppose when anyone dies, it's hard to take in. But this seems especially senseless, she was so young and …"

"And?"

"I don't know, I suppose it's also the way she died," he said.

"What do you mean, 'the way she died'?"

"I mean the accident. She didn't die in the accident, obviously, but that's what killed her. That's what put her in the bloody coma that she never escaped from." Miguel reached for the back of one of the chairs for support. "In all these weeks of sitting by her bedside, with her father, and mother and Pedro, no one has been able to explain why she left their country house so late, and what she was doing driving around at that time of night by herself."

"What did they tell you?" His grandmother asked.

"That she'd decided to drive back into the city because she wanted to get up early the next morning."

"To do what?"

"Who knows? They mentioned something about her wanting to go to an art class. But something about that doesn't sit well with me. She could've just driven in that morning; it's not that far out of the city. I suppose I'm just being paranoid. I mean, why would her whole family lie?"

Miguel sat himself down again, this time next to his grandmother, and reached for a morsel of cheese from her plate. He looked over at her, but she was no longer looking at him, she was staring straight ahead at the wall. She held her cup in both hands, lifted just halfway to her mouth.

"Did it ever occur to you that they didn't know what she was up to?" she asked quietly, still not looking him in the eye.

"Then why tell everyone she was heading back into the city for a class?" Miguel asked.

"Maybe they wanted to protect her."

"I don't understand, why would they need to protect her? It was a single vehicle accident, no one else was hurt, and it left her comatose. What could be worse than that? What could she have needed protecting from?"

His grandmother stood up and took her plate and cup to the sink. She stood with her back to him, rinsing them for much longer than was necessary. Miguel knew her. He knew there was something she was fighting with.

"Abuelita, what is it?" He asked.

She turned to face him. "Maybe they want to protect her memory. The image people have of her as the good daughter, the loving wife. You know people say never speak ill of the dead, well, it's because they only want to hold on to the good things."

"But she was a good wife and mother."

"I know she was. It's just well, you hear things, don't you?"

"What things?" Miguel twisted his whole body to face her. She was drying her cup, twisting the drying cloth back and forth inside.

"I heard she wasn't that happy in Brazil, and, well, it's just talk."

"Go on," Miguel said.

"I heard that she'd started drinking a bit, well, a lot, and when she came home for the holidays her mother pulled her up on it, and then there was some kind of argument about her drinking and, apparently, it could just be gossip, that she ran out drunk and got into the car before anyone could stop her."

Miguel's stomach muscles tightened. Natalia hated being told what to do. She always had a bit of a short temper. Nothing serious, but she was the kind to storm off in a huff. It never lasted long, she'd always come back half an hour later and apologise.

"Where did you hear this?"

"Consuelo said she heard it from Paula, you know, who works for Natalia's grandmother."

Of course, Consuelo was his grandmother's maid, and in this neighbourhood all the maids knew each other. They all met at the market and gossiped about the families they worked for. Bogotá was a village with a population of over seven million.

"I shouldn't have said anything. It's just gossip. I don't suppose we'll ever know what really happened. But that's not important now."

"What do you mean, it's not important?" Miguel said.

"So they said that she left the house happy that night, so they tell people she was on her way back to go to a class. It's just a white lie. If it helps them to keep her memory intact, then there's no harm done. Olivia can grow up thinking her mother and father were happy together, and it was just a cruel accident that killed her mother. Isn't that a better memory for a young girl to be given? Isn't that better than what the truth might be?"

Miguel felt a lump shoot up and down his oesophagus like a truck tearing up a dirt road, leaving a messy track of thick bile. How many times had he spoken to Natalia in the past six months, he thought. Once, maybe? It was last Christmas eve, when he got back to his flat after midnight mass with Laura. High on the excitement of this new relationship and with a belly full of mulled wine, he had spent the entire conversation talking about Laura. "You sound like you're really happy there," she'd said, "You should hold on to that." Miguel remembered saying something about how he was worried about what was going to happen at the end of his trip, and she'd said, "Do everything you can to keep her, don't be afraid to tell her how you really feel. Don't be afraid to fight for the relationship. You'll always regret it if you don't."

Miguel struggled to recall the rest of the conversation. Had he even asked Natalia how she was doing? He couldn't remember. He supposed he'd said the words, he must've. 'How are you?' is such a staple of everyday conversation, but he hadn't really bothered to make any effort to find out how she really was. Would it have made a difference, he thought, if he'd asked, would she have told him the truth? Their whole lives, had they ever really told each other the truth?

"I think I need to lie down," he said. He stood up and kissed his grandmother on both cheeks.

"I shouldn't have said anything." She looked at him, concerned.

"It's not that, I'm just exhausted." He forced himself to smile.

"Will you be okay?"

He nodded and started making his way down the hallway to his bedroom. He needed to lie down; he needed a quiet, dark space to think about Natalia. He wanted to talk to her again, even if only in his own imagination, and this time he'd really listen to whatever she was telling him. He wanted to believe that she could still communicate with him, wherever she now was.

"Oh, I forgot," his grandmother called from the kitchen just as he'd reached his bedroom door, "a package arrived for you today. I left it on your bed. It's from Northern Ireland."

CHAPTER FORTYTHREE

Miguel lifted the thick brown envelope off his bed and looked at the round "Royal Mail Belfast" postmark that all letters from Northern Ireland bore. Could it be something from Laura? With both hands trembling, he ripped it open, tearing the envelope in two. A white envelope fell out and on to the bed. It was addressed to his old flat above the Chinese. Why would she have posted him something there? He picked it up and examined it more closely, then he dropped down on to the side of the bed, his shoulders collapsing into his chest as his excitement left him.

Of course it wasn't from her. She wouldn't have posted something to his old flat, particularly knowing that Mr. Quigley would be picking up the post. In fact, why did he think she would want to contact him at all, after the way he'd just disappeared following their fight after the exhibition? It was ridiculous to have even considered it, as if life would arrange itself so neatly that Laura would just reappear in his life on the same day he said goodbye to Natalia.

So many times this past month he hadn't given Laura a second thought—in those hellish hours in the hospital, he could only focus on Natalia—watching her, scrutinising her body for any sign of thought or emotion, willing her face to break into a smile—and then he'd step blinking from the hospital into the cold Bogotá night and Laura would rush into his thoughts. It was as if Natalia was his force field—his amulet protecting him from the pain of remembering Laura by a far deeper, more immediate pain—like stabbing yourself in the eye to distract yourself from a dull stomachache.

Images of Laura now flooded his mind. Her curled up opposite him on the sofa, engrossed in a book, standing at the edge of the Giant's Causeway looking so vulnerable and scared, her wide smile, her look of rage when she stormed out of the car the last time they saw each other. No, the letter definitely wouldn't be from her.

But if it wasn't from Laura, then who was it from? Miguel picked up the white envelope and sliced open the edge with his finger. Inside there was a DVD in a clear plastic case and a short note written in blue ink on paper pulled from a school jotter. "*Here's the DVD you asked for. Hope it helps with the investigation. If you need anything else please call me. Regards, Aideen McHugh.*"

Miguel stared at the note, trying to decipher its relevance to him. The answer was stored deep in the archives of his brain, and it took a minute for him to realise that it was from the young bride—she'd promised to send him the DVD her uncle had made of the wedding, and he'd asked her to send it to the flat instead of the office. Why had he been so interested in it? He must have wanted to see if there was any footage of the red car, but he wasn't quite sure why. It definitely wasn't to try to get a view of the terrorists; those cowards would have been long gone by the time of the wedding. The red car containing the bomb had been there since early that morning. There was some CCTV footage of it turning into the Main Street at around eight o'clock, although it wasn't good enough to get a clear picture of the driver inside, and either by luck, or more likely design, he had parked it in a CCTV black-spot, so there was no footage of him getting out of the car and walking away.

Miguel's head felt heavy and empty at the same time, both from sheer exhaustion. The DVD could wait. He wanted to lie straight down on top of the sheets and fall asleep, but he forced himself up onto his leaden legs and into the bathroom to clean his teeth. He looked at himself closely in the mirror: his eyes were dark and sunken, and his skin bleached. The weeks sitting by Natalia's bedside had taken their toll. He'd spent all day, every day at the hospital. Sometimes sitting right by her side, other times just standing listlessly in the corridor, waiting, drinking bitter machine coffee. He had refused to pray. He had too much hope for that. Even up until the very end, he had believed he could pull her from the abyss. When Pedro and Natalia's parents went home in the evenings, Miguel had stayed, cherishing those hours where he could speak to her alone, reliving so many of their shared memories, each day trying different combinations of favourite moments as if he were a code breaker trying to unlock the vault within which she was trapped.

Just three nights ago, he'd spent an hour telling her how much she'd influenced him at major turning points in his life, trying to make her see how much he needed her, in the vain hope that he might convince her to cling on. It had been Natalia who had convinced him to apply for law school. "It's a perfect choice for you," she'd told him all those years ago, "you have that keen eye for detail. You're always able to remember the smallest things from the past that I've either forgotten or never even noticed in the first place."

Little did she know that that was because he had spent a good part of his life studying her. He could write a fifty-thousand-word dissertation on her various smiles alone.

"And you're relentless," she'd once said, "anytime we're having a debate about something, you always hold your position; you never give up. To be a lawyer, that's important, you have to be tenacious."

"Do you remember telling me that?" he'd asked her one night when he was alone with her in the hospital, holding onto her inert hand. "That I was relentless? But truth is, I only ever took on challenges that I knew I could win. When it came to you, I never believed I could, so I didn't try. I wasn't relentless, I was the opposite; I was painfully passive."

Now, alone in his bathroom, his eyes started to fill again with tears, remembering how, in response, she'd simply lain there motionless. He wished for an alternative reality where she had opened her eyes and questioned him, maybe asking what he meant by painfully passive, or, if she'd understood, asking why he'd been such a coward for so many years, why he hadn't seized the moment before. But she hadn't moved. She probably hadn't even heard him. He dropped his toothbrush into the glass and rubbed both eyes with the palms of his hands, pushing the tears back to their source.

He rinsed his teeth with a stinging mouthwash and wandered back into the bedroom. With his mind in this state, sleep wouldn't just come and take him; he'd have a fight against his own consciousness. He sat back down at the edge of the bed in front of the television and picked up the DVD. It wouldn't hurt to watch it quickly, he supposed, just to give himself something completely different to focus on. He was pretty sure there'd be nothing of interest on there, so he might as well check now and get it out of the way.

He put the DVD in the machine and turned the volume down so he wouldn't disturb his grandmother. It started with a view of the church spire against the blue sky, panning down to the huge wooden doors, and then turning round to catch some wedding guests walking up the church steps. The men were all in uniform black suits contrasting with the women dressed in the whole range of pastels, with wide-brimmed matching hats. Some of them, as soon as they saw the camera, ducked down in a vain attempt to avoid being filmed so that only their foreheads or the feathers on their hats were visible scurrying across the bottom of the screen. Others simply smiled and waved and hurried on past, and a few people stopped and, looking straight into the camera, gave the bride and groom a message of good luck. Miguel fast-forwarded, watching more and more guests jauntily stream up the steps and past the camera.

Then the direction of the camera changed slightly; the cameraman must have shifted position, and the familiar red car came into view in the background. Miguel pressed play and the film resumed at normal speed. People continued to rush past, trying to get into the church before the bride arrived. But Miguel barely looked at them; his eyes were glued to the red car.

A bus pulled up in front of the church, momentarily blocking the view of the red car, and a man got off carrying a rucksack and a small wooden case. The picture wasn't very clear, but he looked to be in his late forties or early fifties. In the bottom right-hand corner of the screen, the limo carrying the bride pulled into the Main Street, just as the bus was pulling away. The man crossed the road and dropped the rucksack and wooden case next to the red car. What was in the wooden case? Miguel wondered.

The man leaned with his back against the driver's door, and stared straight ahead in the direction of the bus stop. In the bottom right-hand corner of the screen the bride was getting out of the limo, helped by three bridesmaids in mint green and her father. Miguel remembered what the bride had told him; she was just seconds inside the church when the bomb went off. His eyes darted to the red car again; the man was still waiting there. His unusual wooden case still at his feet. Miguel stood up. He felt the need to rush to the man's rescue, to tell him to move—quick. But he couldn't do that—what he was about to witness had already happened long ago.

The bride was already at the top of the steps now and the camera zoomed in to her smiling face, leaving the red car and the man waiting next to it out of the picture. Miguel rewound to take another look at the wooden case, then he let the film play on as the camera again moved in to the close-up of the smiling bride and then followed her to the door of the church.

A man's voice from behind the camera said, "Here, hold this will ye. I want to get a photo before she goes in."

A woman replied, "I don't know how to work this thing."

"Just throw it over your shoulder for two minutes" came the man's voice again and suddenly the image on screen started to whirl around, first the pavement, then the sky, until finally it came to rest, at a slanted angle, on the street scene in front of the church. The other side of the road, where the red car was parked, was no longer visible. However, the limo and the bus stop next to the church steps were both still on screen.

A bus pulled into view and people started filing out. Even though the picture was quite blurry, Miguel thought he recognised Bob Smith and his wife, except the Bob Smith Miguel had met a few months back was a middle-aged man in a wheelchair, and the Bob Smith on screen was a tall, young man holding on tight to his wife's hand. They were followed off the bus by a slender, blonde-haired woman carrying a small suitcase. Miguel pressed pause and looked at her. It was too blurry to make out her features. Her long blonde hair was piled up on her head, she wore jeans and a white blazer and a green and white polka dot scarf around her neck. Miguel stared at her, trying to place her in the collage of victims and witnesses he'd met at the Tribunal. Her name wouldn't come to him. He pressed play, desperate to see what would happen next.

"Give me that," the man's voice said off screen, and

suddenly the image was spinning again – pavement, sky, street, church, coming to settle on the bride as she stepped through the church doors. The camera followed her into the church and focussed on the silhouette of the bride, arm in arm with her father, as they took their first tentative steps down the aisle.

Miguel started to count as they walked: one, two, three and boom. An almighty bang shook the church and the camera fell to the floor. A few seconds later, the screen went black.

Miguel grabbed the remote and pressed rewind, searching for the last image of the man standing by the red car. He found it and pressed pause. He looked so relaxed, leaning back against the car, his arms folded across his chest, his bag by his feet together with that small wooden box. This was their John Doe, or Joe Bloggs as they called him at the Tribunal, Miguel was sure of it. But who was he? Why had he got off the bus and just stood there waiting across the road? He must have been waiting for someone. And what was in that wooden box?

Miguel looked at it again, and then he realised. Why hadn't he figured it out before? It was so obvious what it was for and what it contained.

CHAPTER FORTYFOUR

Laura stumbled forward. The satchel stuffed with jotters weighed down her right shoulder, beating the top of her thigh as she walked. She'd decided to take them home to mark them at the kitchen table. It was Chrissie's afternoon off, so her father would probably be out with her walking Harry along the river. She moved slowly; there was nothing to rush for these days.

Halfway down the hill, she heard her phone ringing from deep within her bag. She fished around trying to find it underneath the mass of jotters. It had stopped ringing by the time she hauled it out. She looked at the missed call onscreen—it started "+ 57", the country code for Colombia.

She moved over to the side of the footpath to escape the steady stream of pupils racing past her down the hill. There wasn't a more public place in the world than the road down from school at this time, overrun with curious teenagers. Above their chatter, she could hear her pulse ringing deep and heavy. She stared suspiciously at the phone in her hand as if it were possessed by some voodoo. Suddenly it started to chirp again, demanding her attention—and there it was, the same number. She hesitated—this was the call she'd planned for, rehearsed over and over again and never expected to receive. She watched her finger press green to answer, as if someone else were moving her like a puppet, and suddenly the phone was at her ear and she was saying hello.

"Laura, it's Miguel."

"Hi," she held her breath tight in her throat and waited for him to speak.

"I have some news," he sounded excited. Laura's stomach lurched, it must be about Natalia. Was he calling to say they were back together, or worse, getting married? Why was he even bothering? He hadn't cared enough to tell her anything when he disappeared last month, not even a single email of explanation, why did he suddenly feel the need to come clean now?

"Go on," she tried to keep her voice flat, and deceptively emotionless.

"I think I've figured out the connection between your mother and Patrick O'Donnell."

"What?" she asked, startled. When she'd thought about the possibility of speaking to Miguel again, she'd imagined many conversations—in some he was repentant, begging her to let him come see her, in others he made small talk, gingerly tiptoeing round the pain he caused her with casual chatter—sometimes she cried, other times she shouted, other times she played along and hid behind trivialities too, and sometimes it was simple and fun, just like it had been before. However, in none of those scenarios had he called to talk about her mother.

"I think they knew each other. I have this DVD and looking at it, it's not clear, you can't make out the faces, but I think he was waiting for her when he died."

"What are you talking about? What DVD?"

"It's a long story, but I got hold of a DVD which shows the street just before the bomb went off."

Laura forced a smile as some of her year-ten pupils sauntered past, staring straight at her, not even bothering to pretend they weren't listening. She looked behind her up the hill, a mass of navy uniforms and clattering heads was still swarming towards her.

"Listen, I'm not really sure what you're talking about." Conscious that she was completely surrounded, she tried to sound business-like and impassive. "Anyway, I'm surprised you found the time to call." She paused, and then despite herself she added, "I thought you'd be busy with Natalia." There it was, she'd flung it out there without thinking and she'd get her answer now, whether she was ready for it or not.

"Natalia?"

"Don't sound so surprised. Mr. Quigley told me that's why you'd gone back."

"Of course he did. Laura, as soon as I heard the news, I had to leave."

Was that it? No apology? Just a bare statement of fact, that he simply had to leave? "What news?" She pressed.

"About Natalia's accident."

"Is she okay?" Laura didn't know if she sounded concerned or simply curious, not that she cared either way. What did it matter to her if his precious Natalia had hurt herself? She listened as he exhaled slowly—a slight quiver in his breath.

"She's at peace now … We buried her yesterday." His voice was no louder than a murmur.

"What happened?" In spite of everything, this time she really was concerned.

"She was in a car accident. That's why I came back here; she was in a coma and I thought I could help. But it was useless, I talked and talked and she just kept slipping further and further away from us. We all tried so hard, me, her parents, her husband."

Her husband? Natalia had a husband? Laura thought back to the photo of Natalia that took pride of place on Miguel's windowsill. "Just an old friend," he'd said. Had be been telling the truth, after all?

"I'm so sorry to hear that."

"Laura, I should've contacted you before now. I owed you more than that. I thought about calling you, a lot—I don't know why I didn't."

"Not even an email."

"I know, I just got so caught up with things here at the hospital. I should've told you I was leaving, I was still angry after what happened at the exhibition. The last time we saw each other you weren't exactly very nice, and then I just got swept up with things here..."

"Don't blame me. I know I overacted after that stupid exhibition—like this Patrick O'Donnell was somehow important—but that was no excuse for you just to disappear like that."

"I know, but that's why I'm calling. I think you were right, I think there is a link between Patrick O'Donnell and your mother."

"Miguel, I've given up on that theory. I've given up on them all. I don't want to spend my life asking questions anymore."

"But I have this wedding DVD, and I'm sure you can see Patrick O'Donnell arrive. He's just standing there, with a wooden box of paints at his feet, waiting—like it's clear he's expecting someone, and then this woman gets off the bus wearing a green and white polka dot scarf, just like the one you have, didn't you say that was your mom's scarf? And you don't see them together because the cameraman follows the bride into the church—but they must have been meeting up when he was killed."

"Miguel, I'm not following you."

"I think your mother and Patrick O' Donnell were meeting up, and she saw him die, and that's what led her to do what she did. Maybe because she was so traumatised, she couldn't live with the image of him being blown up right in front of her, or because she felt guilty because he wouldn't have been there if he hadn't been meeting her, and it just got too much for her."

He finally took a pause. Laura started pacing back up the hill again towards school, just so she'd be moving. As she walked, the idea he'd been rushing to express started to come together in the silence that followed—when his theory was fully formed in her mind she examined it and the flaws became immediately apparent.

"That's impossible," she said quietly, "he disappeared three days after my mother's death. That's what his wife said. They were closing the exhibition on the anniversary of his disappearance, and it was three days after my mother's anniversary. That's what got me so upset that day, it seemed like such a cruel coincidence. I had been stupid enough to believe there might be some link between him and my mother—that he might help me understand, but he was gone, too. It was a crazy notion anyway, as I now realise she's the only one that can tell me what was going on in her mind and she's gone. I'm never going to know, and I just have to accept that. So what you're saying doesn't make sense. Patrick O'Donnell didn't disappear until a week after the bomb, so it couldn't be him on the DVD. The timeline is all wrong."

Laura was now back up at the school gates; she headed away from the main building and towards the temporary classrooms, looking for a quiet corner to speak.

"But what if his wife lied?" Miguel asked.

Laura thought this was an absurd suggestion. "Why would she do that?"

"To protect his memory. Maybe she knew he'd gone there that day to leave her and so instead of reporting him missing and having to face all the questions about what he was doing that day and who he was with, she decided to wait and report him missing a few days later. Telling people he kissed her goodbye and then got lost at sea doing the thing he loved is a far better story to have to tell for the rest of your life than telling people your husband was killed in a terrorist bomb going to meet his mistress."

"Miguel, you have no basis for that. Where do you get these conspiracies? Wouldn't she have searched for him at the hospital?"

"Maybe she did. There was a man's body that was never identified, the police put out a description of him—well what they could from what was left of him—maybe she saw that."

"This is all just speculation." Laura could feel her head start to throb. She didn't want to be talking about this—not now.

"I really think you should look at the DVD."

Laura heard a twig crack on the grass behind her. She spun around and came face to face with Mr. Quigley. She'd forgotten that he patrolled the school grounds at this time looking for smokers. Although it was only the real dummies who smoked on the premises. Her face turned red with shame, as if she were doing something wrong. As a teacher, she was perfectly entitled to loiter by the classrooms chatting on the phone, but there was something about the way Mr. Quigley talked down at her, so benevolently, that made her feel like she was still a pupil rather than a colleague.

"Listen, can I call you back sometime?"

"Okay Laura, I get it, you're not interested. I'm sorry I bothered you."

"No, it's not that. It's just," she wanted to say, "I can't talk right now," but Mr. Quigley was almost next to her, pretending to inspect some damp on one of the walls, and a phrase like that would just pique his interest further.

"I'll call you back tonight. I promise."

"But will you?"

"Yes, I promise. We'll speak tonight."

"Okay," Miguel said, sounding unconvinced.

"Bye."

She put her phone away, with full intentions of walking home and going up to her bedroom and calling Miguel straight back. But on the way home, she changed her mind. They'd just end up talking at cross-purposes again. He'd just push and push his theory, and she wasn't interested in hearing it. She was exhausted by theories. This conversation had to stop. So she broke her promise to him and decided not to call back. It was bold and terrifying, but what she was doing felt like the right thing to do. She just prayed she wouldn't end up regretting it.

CHAPTER FORTYFIVE

She picks up her suitcase and tiptoes towards the stairs. It is just after five in the morning and the daylight is beginning to seep into the hallway from the cracks underneath the closed bedroom doors, mixing with the darkness and turning everything a silver-navy hue. Even though her heart is racing, she moves down each step slowly, trying to make as little noise as possible. She doesn't want to disturb them. She hasn't told them that she's leaving—she doesn't know what to tell them—she has no idea what today holds for her. Maybe these tentative steps will take her to a glorious new life, or maybe she is about to make a crushing mistake.

She gingerly removes her jacket and green and white polka dot scarf from the hook on the wall next to the lighthouse painting, pausing to take in the passionate brushstrokes that she knows so well. She strains her ears, listening for any sign of movement upstairs. Nothing. They are both still fast asleep. Then she eases open the front door and carries her case to the end of the garden so the noise of the wheels on the path won't wake them. Her journey has begun.

Hours later, she is standing in front of an official in a dark green uniform answering his questions. Why did she come here? She tries to find an answer to his question. "To see someone," is the best she can do. "A boyfriend?" he asks. She pauses, unclear how to respond, but it doesn't matter, as the official is now waving her on. He has enough people to deal with today. Her heart beats loud in her chest as she walks away from him.

Soon she is in a car being driven through unfamiliar roads towards a destination that she knows only by the address on the scrap of paper clasped tightly in her hand. She has no idea what awaits her when she gets there. She stares out at the city passing by. It is completely unlike anywhere she has ever been, but he was right, it seems big and vast, but not terrifying like people expect. It has a mountain of deep darkest green hugging protectively one side of it, and the crowded streets seem almost like a playground. They pass women crushing fruits on street corners, and when they come to the traffic lights, children juggling tennis balls and balancing on homemade stilts perform for the entertainment of the waiting cars.

Finally, after over an hour of weaving through dense traffic, the car pulls up outside a large red brick apartment building, overlooking a long narrow park. The sun is falling in the sky and the park is filled with people taking advantage of the last hour of daylight.

"You will wait, won't you?" she asks the driver.

"Yes. I wait here. We go to hotel when you are ready."

Laura places her hand on the door handle and takes a deep breath. Up until this point, it has all been strangely easy. Within twenty-four hours of booking the flights online, she was on the plane. Years of living rent-free with her father and squirreling away her salary meant she could afford the exorbitant cost of booking so last minute. It had to be that way. If she had planned in advance, she would have had too much time to change her mind. She then made a booking at the Hilton downtown and asked them to send her an English-speaking driver to pick her up at the airport. In the email she told the hotel to explain to him that she wanted to make a stop along the way. Then, after her father and Chrissie had gone to bed, she had packed a bag and lay on top of her duvet, wide-eyed with nerves, until four a.m. when it was time to get up and sneak out.

She keeps her hand on the door handle but doesn't open it. She contemplates telling the driver that there has been a change of plans, that he must take her straight to the hotel, that she has made a mistake. That would be better, she doesn't even know if he is home right now, or if he is, whether he wants to see her. She looks up towards the mirror in the middle of the windscreen and catches the driver staring back at her reflection, waiting for her to move. She can't meet his eyes, she knows how she must look to him, unsure of herself and nervous, drained of any colour after so many hours travelling. She averts her eyes, looking past his impatient stare straight ahead out the front window to the park—a man in his sixties, tanned and slim, jogs past, two teenagers stand under a tree kissing, with a large labrador lying bored at their feet, three middle-aged women move slowly in time together, possibly practicing Tai Chi or something similar, and a dark-haired man sits alone reading a book on a bench in the far corner of the park. He has thick curls, broad shoulders, and slim, wiry arms, and for the first time in days, maybe even weeks, her face relaxes into an unforced smile.

Miguel stares at the words on the page. He's not really reading, just holding the book in front of him, almost as a shield. He wanted to sit on a park bench and be engulfed by nothingness, but he didn't want to attract the kind of chatterbox stranger that preys on people alone and unoccupied on park benches, assaulting them with small talk, so he brought the first book that came to hand with him. It's not actually a book, but a play, 'Philadelphia, Here I Come," and he is struggling to understand why Gar Private is so different from Gar Public.

He feels that special self-pity that only the strongest hangover can induce. He met some old friends last night, people who'd known Natalia, too, and for the first time in months he'd got very, very drunk. At the time, it had seemed like a good way to fight back against the loneliness, clinking his glass with people he'd known for years, even laughing at their jokes, and talking, lots of talking, about Natalia, about his experiences in Northern Ireland, about his plans to look for a teaching job at the University de los Andes, maybe even do a Ph.D. Now, feeling toxic and tired, the loneliness is back—stronger than before—and mocking him for thinking it could be that simple.

He puts the book to one side and looks around him. He is clearly out of place; apparently only healthy and contented people frequent this park. An old man jogs past glowing with vitality, a few middle-aged women move slowly in time together, devotees of some Eastern form of dance or meditation—or maybe it is for self-defence—in his befuddled state, he can't quite recall.

And then he sees her, standing directly opposite him at the edge of the park, tall, willowy, her dark hair around her pale face and those beautiful eyes. Even from this distance, they look like precious stones, refracting the remaining sunlight, drawing him in. She lifts a hand to wave, and for the first time in weeks he feels his face relax into an unforced smile, and joy flows back into his being.

ACKNOWLEDGMENTS

It takes a village to make a writer. Thanks to the staff at Brixton library, London, where much of this book was written in a quiet corner on the second floor; to Colm Toibin whose book Bad Blood: A Walk Along the Irish Border made me see different perspectives of my homeland and provided the inspiration for some of the viewpoints held by characters in this book; to Maurice Harron whose stunning sculptures "*Let the Dance Begin*" on the Stabane/Lifford border provided the inspiration for the statues in this book, and are well worth a visit; to Jacqui Lofthouse and Kate Lyall Grant who read early drafts and offered much needed editorial advice and constructive criticism; to Valerie Valentine for her careful copy-editing (in both English and Spanish); to Scarlett Rugers for taking my vision for the cover and making it so much better than I had imagined; to my parents for all their support with absolutely everything; to my big sis for her constant interest and encouragement, who'd have thought you'd end up being one of my best friends; to Erin who took my writing seriously even when I didn't, your enthusiasm helped me persevere; to Juan, the best husband imaginable, who keeps his promise to make me laugh every day, thanks for all the joy you bring to my life, without you there would be no book.

ABOUT THE AUTHOR

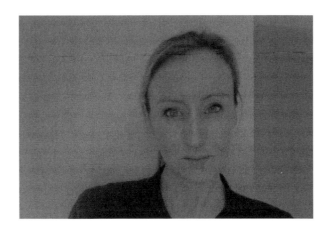

Caroline Doherty de Novoa was born in County Tyrone, Northern Ireland. Over the years she has called Bogotá, Manchester, Madrid, Oxford and London home. She has worked as both a lawyer and a teacher; she is now a writer and an entrepreneur. Her home is wherever she and her husband Juan are together.

11197260R00157

Printed in Great Britain
by Amazon